Joanna [illegible] Friends' School, Hobar[illegible] University, and RMIT [illegible] er mysteries set in the [illegible] a and the wine and high country of North Eastern Victoria. She also writes online about murder mysteries, why they are so enduring, and why they are not trivial.

The Elsinore Vanish

Joanna Baker

First published by Soren Press in 2019
This edition published in 2019 by Soren Press

The Elsinore Vanish

EPUB: 9781925786675
POD: 9781925786682

Cover design by Red Tally Studios

Publishing services provided by Critical Mass
www.critmassconsulting.com

Prologue

Later, Clare would wonder if she should have seen it coming — from Tim's mood, maybe, or all the talk about secrets. Maybe, if only she'd seen what was happening, noticed something in the room, done something different, she could have saved him.

But that's the thing about hindsight. You get it afterwards.

'It's all lies, anyway. Look around you. Show me one person who isn't full of bull ...' Tim stopped.

He was making an effort not to swear, Clare realised, which was kind of sweet. It was because she was younger. She made a mental note to say something that would show him she was fifteen, not twelve.

'Oh yeah. I could tell you a thing or two about this lot.' Tim waved an arm towards the front of the room — the band on the little stage, the dancing figures. In the soft yellow light the clothes looked richly coloured, like an oil painting.

But that's not what Tim saw. Suddenly he sprang out of his chair and started shouting at the dancers. '*Let me set it down here.*' He was waving both arms now and nearly made himself fall over. '*One may smile and smile and be a villain.*'

That was weird. It was almost as if he was shouting at a particular person, but Clare couldn't tell who.

They were at the Remember November Charity Cabaret at the Beechworth Town Hall, sitting at a table at the side of the room, squashed in under some of the heavy wooden honour boards. It was a variety night, organised to raise money for the Neighbourhood Centre, and Clare had come with Anna Langton and her family. Tim Williams had just finished Year Twelve with Jacob Langton and he'd been staying with them during term, so he was dragged along too. And Tim's mother and her boyfriend had come to fill up the table.

The night was exactly what you would have expected from the name — a lot of locals reciting poetry or singing or dancing or doing little plays. In one corner of the stage there was a jazz band from Milawa, playing music between acts so that people could dance. Anna's grandfather was up there, on drums and cymbals. At first, Anna and Clare had groaned and mocked the music and they had made sure their dancing contained a lot of irony, but gradually they'd started getting into it. And really, thought Clare, it didn't matter how stupid this was. This night was like everything that happened in Beechworth — you knew everyone here and if there was any lameness, well at least you were all in it together. The people here were aunties and parents and grandparents. You really didn't have to worry about how you were coming across.

And the old hall was actually a nice place. It had high curved ceilings, painted pillars and a wooden floor that felt soft and hollow.

Now, around ten thirty, Anna was up on the dance floor with Choof Fuller from the brewery, looking pleased with herself — and why shouldn't she because she was gorgeous. But that meant Clare was a bit of a social liability. Everyone else had gone to talk to people at other tables, but Tim had stayed to keep her company. It was kind of him and it was a lot better than sitting by herself. But she wished he'd quieten down a bit.

Now he was expanding on his big theme. 'I mean look at Perry in that red number.' He was sneering at the woman from the quilting shop, who was holding some balloons, swinging them around by their metallic ribbons. 'What's that all about? Is she pretending to be twenty-one? Or is it ... kind of ...' He wiggled his head and put on a high woman's voice. '... I'm a fun-loving, sensual person.'

'Don't be like that,' said Clare. Mrs Perry wasn't pretending anything.

She didn't know what to make of it. You got the impression Tim wasn't usually this nasty. He had a soft face, a bit pink in this light and crowded by too-long bushy hair. It was a nice face. It was just a pity it wasn't more — well, attractive. But it did show exactly what he was like — clever and funny and kind, and not at all up himself.

The music dropped back a bit. Tim knew she was looking at him and that made him uncomfortable, so he started raving on again. 'And how about the no alcohol thing? It's such bullshit.'

He had brought a silver flask to the cabaret and when they'd arrived he had plonked it on the table in full view of everyone. It was some kind of big gesture. At nine o'clock he'd stood in full view at the front of the dance floor, waved it in the air and then sculled. Fortunately — or unfortunately if he was hoping to make a scene — no one much had noticed. His mother's boyfriend, Calvin, had gone over quietly, said something, and taken the flask.

Now, an hour later, Tim was still complaining about it. 'They know we're going to go out and get written off after this.'

'They just don't want to see it.'

'Exactly.' Tim leant towards her, his lips wet and loose. 'It's all about honesty.'

'Honesty is very important in life.' She edged away, hoping he wouldn't notice. 'If you can fake that you can do anything.'

But he wasn't listening. He turned and looked behind him. Clare followed his gaze. Across the room, between some bush poets in Akubras and the Latin dancers in satin and sequins, was the door to the shire offices. Calvin had taken the flask out there somewhere.

'They'll be thinking about honesty tonight, though,' Tim muttered. 'I'm going to give them a fright. Just you wait and see.' He almost chanted the last words, as if he'd had this thought many times before.

At this point, Anna's grandfather did a riff on his cymbal and the band leader announced they were going to play the Macarena.

'Oh-h-h.' Tim groaned in pain and dropped his forehead to the table. Then he leapt instantly back again and started dancing in his chair. 'Oh Mrs Perry. You - sex-y - thing.'

Clare wondered what was wrong. He was funny, though, flicking his hands like a bad Bollywood dancer and doing a kind of chook movement with his head. And the whole I-want-to-be-a-rebel-but-I-haven't-quite-managed-it thing made him kind of vulnerable. You wanted to tell him everything was OK.

Now he'd got himself worked up. He pushed to his feet and started shouting at the dance floor.

'I know you! Nothing escapes me!' A few people turned and looked, but most didn't seem to hear. 'You're all the same. Frauds. Fakes. What about little Johnny Lingham there? Dancing like a virgin. Mummy and Daddy are so proud. What about getting suspended, Johnno? What about wearing a nose stud to year eleven presentation and telling Carberry to fuck off!'

So much for trying not to swear.

Clare put a hand on his arm. 'Sometimes it's polite to be fake.' She pulled him back down. 'At least everyone's pretending they can't hear you.'

He thought about this and then threw his arms out again. 'Wouldn't you like to escape it all, Clare? Wouldn't you like to just … disappear?'

She looked at him blankly.

He pushed his chair back. 'Let's go and have a dance.' The worried look came back. 'I mean I'm not trying to crack onto you or anything.'

She laughed. You just couldn't help it. 'It's OK.'

'Yeah. It's OK. Let's just …' He shook his hands in a flicking movement, shaking off all the serious stuff. 'Let's just dance.'

He was a nice dancer too. Not great. Nice. He didn't seem to care what anyone thought. He did a lot of jumping and arm-flinging, in a kind of mock-hip style, half Beyoncé, half Mr Bean.

It was one of those sayings, wasn't it? Dance like no one's looking.

Around eleven, it was Tim's turn on the stage.

Clare had danced with Mick Caro and then Anna's grandfather, Angus, who had got down from the stage just to do it. And then she'd talked to Anna and a couple of other Beechworth Secondary girls at the back of the room and they'd watched the ageing saxophonist do a solo and commented on his tragic Loki hair.

Now most people were sitting down. On stage were the two girls from Acton Olives, who could actually sing. The tables were littered with curling streamers and half-eaten chocolates and coffee cups. Everyone was back at the Langton's table — Clare, Anna and Jacob Langton, Mr and Mrs Langton, Tim's mother and her boyfriend, Calvin.

Jacob and Tim stood up and went onto the stage. Clare watched Jacob, tall and easy-moving. Straight jaw. Perfect. You just couldn't take your eyes off him. He pulled out a table covered with small objects and put it on the right, near the band. Then he dragged forward a narrow cupboard. He opened it to show it was empty and closed it again. The band did an introductory tune.

Tim had put on a black jacket and a bow tie. He went to the front of the stage. 'Hello. I'm Tim.' Something about the simple way he spoke made the room fall silent. 'And I can make things disappear.'

He paused again. Then he went to stand behind the table and picked up a red scarf. 'Of course, my mother has known this all my life. She would say I only have to touch things and they vanish. Books for example.' He picked up a book, and swirled his scarf over it. The scarf was a rich red. It moved with a heavy swirling motion, but at the same time it seemed weightless. When it stopped moving, the book had vanished.

Now Tim began picking up things from the table and naming them. 'Mugs … Grandma's glasses … car keys … money …' With each word he swirled the scarf over the object and make it disappear. 'Food.' At this he picked up a baguette and took a bite. The audience laughed.

'Mum's boyfriends.' This time he had a small plastic man, dressed in gold. He threw it into the air. 'Be careful, Calvin.'

The little doll spun upwards, its shiny plastic suit flashing in the stage light. Tim swung his scarf at it. The scarf seemed to move slowly through the air but it caught up with the falling doll. He gave the scarf a flick and pulled it back. Nothing fell to the table. The doll had vanished.

He was completely amazing, Clare thought. He must have spent his whole life practising this.

After the round of applause, Tim strode to the middle of the stage and spun slowly around, allowing the scarf to swirl behind him. He was confident now, his movements balanced, his voice rich and strong. 'Those things have all gone to the mirror world. The shadow world.' He allowed the scarf to drift in the air in front of him. 'But don't worry. Sometimes, things come back again.'

At this, Jacob opened the small cupboard to show that all the objects that had disappeared were now in there.

After more applause, Tim began talking again. 'Amusing to be tricked, isn't it? But I have to warn you. Not all magic is nice.'

The band started playing some low, creepy music.

Tim said, 'I can make other things disappear.' He looked around the audience. 'Reputations.'

The room fell silent.

'Because that's the thing about me. I'm a watcher. I am observant. I know secrets. I see lies.' Tim moved back to the table. 'So if you're wearing a mask …'

There was something else lying on the table and now he tipped it up. It was a stand holding three masks, painted papier maché things, oval, smiling faces, their eyes blank.

'Well, you all know how this works …' Tim threw up the masks in rapid succession, flicking his scarf each time, making them vanish. Immediately, Jacob opened the cupboard. Now it held only the three masks.

During the applause, Tim went to the table and sat back on it. 'I really did think of tearing off a few masks tonight. I really did. But then I realised — you don't want that. I thought, probably, what you would all *prefer* … is if I disappeared.'

The silence was deeper now. Someone moved a chair.

'And I can do that.' He stood up and flicked the scarf in front of him. 'But disappearing is scary. It's lonely and it's hard and it actually really hurts, so before I do it, I'm going to need some courage.' He swirled the scarf. 'I brought some courage tonight, in a little silver flask. But unfortunately …' He looked at the back of the room. '… my courage has left me. My courage has gone to the land of lost things. I will need someone to go and get it back.' He turned to Jacob. 'Jacob, will you go and find my courage for me?'

Jacob smiled a wide smile full of perfect teeth and Clare's throat gave a little squeeze.

Tim went to the side of the stage. He dragged out a tall post on a wheeled stand and let a black curtain fall from it, hiding Jacob. He lifted the curtain to show Jacob standing there, let it fall back, then walked up and down a few times. Angus did a drum roll. Tim flicked his scarf lazily, walked around, flicked the scarf again, and lifted the curtain.

Jacob wasn't there. And there was nowhere to hide on the empty stage.

This time Tim ignored the applause. He tipped his head back and called to the ceiling. 'All right, Jake. My courage — do you see it anywhere? Can you bring it back with you?'

He closed the curtain and stood in front of it. Angus started running a chain over one of the cymbals, making a high hissing sound that felt like someone was sprinkling sand on your skin. With a big flourish, Tim pulled the curtain aside. Jacob wasn't there.

Tim laughed weakly. 'Sorry… Whoops. OK.' Angus repeated the cymbal sound, and Tim lifted the curtain again. No Jacob.

Tim started to look uncertain. The trick was going wrong. He said, 'Band, could you play some coming-back music, please?' The band began to play, a cheery, lively piece of music. Tim turned to the audience. 'It's not actually that easy getting back from the shadow world. Do you think we can give him a bit of support?' He brought his hands together and the audience began clapping.

Angus did a long drum roll. Tim started pacing up and down, clapping his hands above his head. The music got louder and faster. People were clapping and stamping their feet. There were whistles. Someone in the audience called 'Ja-a-acob ...'

Tim lifted the curtain then stood beside the it, looking sad and embarrassed, as if he would like to disappear too. He looked around the room.

And at that point Jacob reappeared.

He threw open the double doors at the main entrance, and for a moment he stood there, broad shouldered, fair haired, smiling his wide perfect smile. He raised a hand to show that he had the silver flask. Then, with the music thumping and spinning and the audience clapping, he ran up to the stage. He waved the flask around to make sure everyone saw it, yelling something triumphant and defiant, enjoying the applause, and with a bow he presented it to Tim. Tim made a silent roar. He mouthed the word 'Courage' and held the flask up, glittering and flashing in the golden light. Then, in one sweeping movement, he threw back his head and drained it.

Afterwards, no one could say exactly what had happened. The band was playing. People were clapping. Some had stood up, others couldn't really see. Tim pushed the flask out in front of him, upside down to show it was empty. One drop of liquid fell from its silver lip. With his free hand he punched the air above his head.

But halfway through, the gesture seemed to go weak. His face went blank, as if he'd forgotten what he was doing. The hand spread and clutched a few times at the empty air. His skin darkened, his chest heaved and his mouth came open in a strangled gasp. Calvin started running towards the stage from the back of the room. Tim's right arm made a big panicky sweep as if it was trying to fight something. The bottle slipped and went flying out over the audience.

For a minute, the silver flask seemed to have escaped gravity. It flew free, making a graceful arc and catching bits of light, flashing green and then pink and then shining silver. But soon it curved down and all the colour, all the fire, went out of it.

And as it fell, Tim fell too.

Chapter 1

The edge of a leaf isn't sharp. Close up — the leaves right next to you — they're sharp, with definite edges. But further away or in the shadows, they get blurred. Even against a blue sky, an edge isn't sharp. You think it is. You tell yourself you see a hard line, but as you stare at it, it slips. The sharpness isn't real. It's in your mind.

I've learned to concentrate on things like this — surfaces, edges, light. It's been a bad year.

But today I wasn't going to be allowed to concentrate for long. Today I was in a garden, a large Open Garden in Beechworth. Not exactly thrilling for our Year 10 spring holidays. There were about a million other people here. I'd come off to one side and found a bench facing a lake and I was hoping to sit quietly and look at leaves and things, but there were people everywhere.

Someone walked across in front of me. I kept staring at the trees and at first it looked like he was going to keep going, up a path. But he stopped. He stood very still, staring at me until I had to look at him. I was sitting in dappled shade but he was in a patch of sunlight, almost as if he was on a stage.

He was just a kid, about twelve, plump and soft-looking, in a white t-shirt and blue boardies. He had bright dyed orange-red hair. He didn't say anything, but as soon as I moved my eyes to him he pulled something out of a pocket and held it up for me to look at.

It was a doll, a plastic man in a black suit and bow tie, the kind you see on a wedding cake. It was not the sort of thing a kid owns and for a minute I thought he was asking me if I'd dropped it. I was starting to shake my head but before I could say anything he threw it into the air.

He threw it really high and straight up. You couldn't help watching it. The little man flickered as he moved through leaf shadows and then, at the top of his flight, he seemed to stop in mid-air, spinning against the sky. Just as he started to come down the kid produced from nowhere a piece of cloth, a scarf or a hanky or something, deep purple and satin. He held one edge and swirled it up over the falling doll. It rippled in soft folds. When it fell down, the doll had disappeared.

I looked at the kid's face. Under the wild hair it was round and pale and had no expression at all. Maybe there was a hat somewhere for me to put a coin in. I couldn't see one. I tried to think of something to say but before I could he walked away.

As soon as he'd gone I saw another guy and this one drove the kid right out of my mind.

There was no real reason why this second person should have worried me. He was about eighteen or nineteen and he wasn't rough or anything. He was actually extremely neat, with smooth fair hair and ironed jeans and a polo shirt with creases down the sleeves. But he was huge. Not just tall, broad in the shoulders and muscly in the arms and neck, with a stomach that stretched the shirt tight. And he was staring at me, too.

What was it with this place and all the starey people? I looked away, trying to pretend I hadn't noticed, but I could feel his eyes on me. My face went stiff and kind of numb. He was making a point. I just wasn't sure what the point was.

After a few minutes, which were probably only seconds, he turned and walked away, leaving me sweating and feeling like an idiot. And at that moment I heard a voice behind me. It said, '*poison*'.

Or maybe not. Somewhere I could hear people talking but I couldn't make out any actual words. Maybe someone had been talking about how to get rid of weeds and that one word had just stood out.

More likely the word had been in my head. It had been supplied by my own sick brain. And that meant I was losing it again.

Not good. Irrational anxiety. Hearing things. I was supposed to be over all that. It wasn't the fault of the big neat guy. He was just being a dick for some reason. He wasn't to know that I was a borderline psycho case.

My thoughts were interrupted by a whack on a shoulder and another voice, high and nasal. 'There you are. What are you doing?'

This time it was nothing mysterious. It was just Chess and for once, what with the word 'poison' and everything, it was a relief to see her.

She came around in front of me, holding a white mug. 'They've got this terrific refreshments table. The yummiest sandwiches.'

'Chess, I …'

But Chess was never one to listen to other people's problems. She doesn't even understand her own, operating on the principle that all those inner things — dreams, sadness, fears — are a nuisance, and if you can stay busy enough and ignore them, then they won't really exist.

'I got you a coffee.'

She was standing close to my knees. She had on a pale too-loose T-shirt and light brown cords. I sighed.

Enter Me Into the Hall of Geekdom. I should say something. She had asked me to help her with her clothes. But when she got into the car this morning it had been too late for her to change. And there was nothing to do about it now. I decided not to waste my breath.

'Thanks.' I started to reach for the mug but she held it close in front of her.

'It was a dollar fifty.'

She watched while I rummaged for the coins and only held out the mug when I produced the money. That made it all wrong. Instead of being two friends sharing coffee, it was now something between people who don't trust each other, like a drug deal on a street corner. It wasn't that Chess meant it to be like that — she would've gladly bought me a coffee if I'd asked her — it's just that she doesn't realise when she's being weird.

I've known Chess a long time. Her mother is dead and her father's an alcoholic — long story — but she's been half living with us since we were eight. The weirdness happens a lot. Chess behaves differently from other people and she gets things wrong — the little things that no one ever talks about, like where to stand and what to do with your arms and legs. Her rhythms are all out of whack.

I said, 'Thanks,' again, to show her — to show myself really — that I wasn't letting it bother me.

While I sipped at the coffee, she said, 'Aren't you coming to look around?'

'Yeah. Maybe. I was just ...'

I waved vaguely towards the trees, but I didn't want to talk about leaves or blurred edges.

Chess's expression hardened. 'You're not going to go all gloomy again are you?'

This time I had to say something. 'There! That's one.'

'One what?'

'One of those words you use. "Gloomy". That's one. Like "terrific" and "yummy".' I stopped but she was inspecting me harder than ever, so there was nothing to do but keep talking. 'You wanted me to explain why that kid said you were a ... you know ...' I lowered my voice and tried to look apologetic, '... a freak. Well, that's one of the words you use that other people don't use.'

'Gloomy?'

I shrugged.

'What's wrong with it?'

'Nothing. Nothing at all.' I was wishing I'd never started this.

'All right,' she said. 'I'll see you up at the house in a jiffy. We have something important to talk about. And we can have something scrumptious.'

Then she left. I was glad I hadn't mentioned the T-shirt.

It didn't take me long to forget her and calm down again. Chess and I have had hundreds of conversations like that.

The lawn in front of me was rough, edged with soft grey stone. I looked at the creamy trunks of some lemon-scented gums. On the lake something jumped, making the reflections tremble, and then they went still. To calm myself down, I thought about colour. Water isn't blue. It's grey, or brown, or white, depending on what's reflecting in it, and what's underneath ...

Without knowing it was coming, I did a big shiver. I didn't want to think about what was underneath. But it was already too late. Some thoughts just rise up out of nowhere and when you push them down they slip sideways and rise up again, like bubbles.

Last Christmas, with another girl, Chess and I found a dead body. We pulled it out of a pond.

Since then, water has never looked the same.

There'd been another death, too, and Chess and I had exposed a murderer, someone truly, unbelievably evil, who'd been living among us the whole time, hiding their real thoughts under a shiny surface.

It's a shock, an event like that. Most people never have to go through anything like it. But everyone can see that much — that it's a shock.

I handled it badly. Of course no one actually said that, but I did. I went weird. I kept drawing, because I could never stop doing that, but everything came out in thin black lines, in huge grids of angular shapes that took up the whole page. I was trying not to draw what was really in my head — hard white faces streaked with mud, and bodies lying on gravel roads, and two little children screaming.

You get the idea. More than bad. The complete nervous breakdown scenario, only quieter.

Anyway, a lot of stuff was done with counsellors and things and not much of it helped. In the end it was grass that got me back. Not the smoking kind, the garden weed kind. I'd have these days at school where I did almost nothing and spoke to almost no one, and then I'd go into our back yard and stare at the grass — flat smooth blades against the wall, or tight clumps, or thin waving wires with seed heads like clouds of water vapour. I started to draw it. Suddenly it became very important to understand how it all worked — edges and surfaces and textures and colour. Then, gradually, because I'd spent so much time on it — the leaves, the light, the garden — I began to feel it belonged to me, as if I was part of it again.

I drew myself back into the world. I wouldn't tell anyone that, but that's how I think of it.

By July I was working at school — a bit anyway — and I seemed to have friends again, and I started listening to music. By the end of Term 3 I was doing all the normal endearing old behaviours like eating pies that were made for other people and breaking wine glasses with indoor soccer and elbowing the end of cereal spoons, levering missiles of sticky Weet Bix onto the old place on the kitchen wall.

And that was the point at which my parents realised they had their dear old Matt back again, and it was time I went away for a while.

Chapter 2

Going away for a while is a bit of a habit in our family. We take it in turns to be the one who isn't coping and needs a break. As Mum says, it's cheaper than drugs.

I was happy. Our town of Yackandandah is small and historic, with a lot of trees and thick lawns and banks of flowers and vegie patches. It's a great place to live — if you are a chook. When things get heavy it has this way of closing in on you. And everyone had learned to be worried about me, so whenever I left the house I felt as if I was being watched.

We haven't got any spare money, so whenever we need to get away we have to stay with someone. This time Dad came up with an old mate called Mike who was in Beechworth for a few months and invited us for a week of the September holidays.

As I said, very not thrilling. Beechworth is only twenty minutes drive from Yack and it is also tiny and old. At my school, Wangaratta High, we've all been to Beechworth for a bazillion excursions, looking at Ned Kelly museums and gold mining stuff and the Chinese burning towers. But it was marginally more exciting than staying home for the whole two weeks. Mike said he had Foxtel, and the new thing called Netflix and good fast broadband, so I was half-intending just to watch things. Also I'd managed to split and stack firewood for a few people, so I had a bit of money, and there was a fair chance I'd be able to find some other people and enjoy myself.

Chess came too. Not for the same reason as me. Like I said, she had handled the whole murder thing pretty well. But Chess had her own problems — the drop-kick father, who was drinking more than ever and had started disappearing for days at a time, and a dark, decrepit house that the Yackandandah people had found for them to live in, because their own house had burnt down.

I didn't mind her coming. She can be mind-numbingly annoying, but I'm used to that, and when you've been through some really major experiences with someone you kind of feel responsible for them. Also, she lets me use her smart phone. I'm the only person in the world who doesn't have one.

I hadn't even minded when, on our first morning in Beechworth, a Saturday, Chess had insisted we come here, to the Langton House Open Garden. Even Mike thought it was a stupid idea for an outing. He drove us there and went home to do some work.

But Chess seemed happy. So now I intended to get back to the serious business of doing nothing. The gums were making a whispering warm-afternoon sound. I thought soon I might lie down on the bench.

Another voice. 'Aaah the dear little things. *Schoenia filifolia*.'

Old women spouting wanky Latin names. The place was full of them. I sank lower in my seat.

'Full sun and semi-shade ... computerised drip-system ... blood and bone ... well-rotted ... asphyxiated ... cyanide ... terrible death.'

My scalp did a sharp squeeze around my brain. *Death?* I turned around. Through a gap in the bushes I could see two people. But they were just ordinary old biddies — short curly hair, narrow shoulders, elastic-waisted pants. They were touching the plants and talking about them.

I dragged in some air. I must've fallen asleep and had a nightmare. It was because I'd been thinking about the water. Horrible, but it could have been worse. A few months ago I was having full-blown panic attacks and they really are bad. Now when

I get them they're more like slightly-nervous-and-behaving-stupidly attacks, so that's progress.

Chess came up behind me. 'Didn't you hear what I said? I want to show you something.'

'Wait on.' I wanted to tell her about the voices. 'Chess I'm …'

She was walking away. As if I was a little dog who'd just tag along. *Come on Matt. Here, boy!*

But the peace and quiet idea had been a failure. So this time I did follow her, up a path to the lawn below the house.

I stood for a minute looking around. Langton House was long and low, made of some kind of pale stone. There were square pillars right along the front, and behind those you could see dark windows. There was something silent about this house, something closed off and secretive and lonely.

I shook myself. A minute ago I'd been hearing things. Now I had a secretive house.

Chess had sat on a bench in front of a row of roses. She had that flat-faced look she gets when she's thinking so it was safe to sit next to her. I was going to get a minute of peace.

It was nearly three o'clock. The sky had white clouds that looked distant but clear and flat, as if someone had taken photographs of clouds and stuck them there. There were a lot of people walking around or reading their printed sheets. All the colours were clear and simple, as if the whole scene had been done with textas from a pack of six.

Chess finished thinking and reached into her cloth bag. She pulled out a piece of computer paper and stuck it in front of me. 'I want you to have a look at this.'

It was a photo, the sort of thing you find in a school annual. It showed a group of kids in rows with teachers standing around the edges. A private school by the look of the uniforms.

'These are last year's year twelves at Rawdon Grammar,' said Chess. She pointed to some kids in the middle of the third row. 'This is Jacob Langton and Tim Williams. They're best friends.'

'OK …'

In the back row of the photo was the big starey guy from the garden. My breath went tight.

I looked around. Over near the house a little girl sat on the lawn, playing on a phone. Just like kids do. At a tinny table there were two old people rubbing sun-screen into their hands, looking at it and talking about it. Just like old people do.

But something wasn't right.

A woman with a black Lego-man haircut walked past. She glanced up at the house.

Do you ever get the feeling you've stepped into a parallel universe? One minute everything is normal — and then suddenly it isn't? And the worst thing is you can't put your finger on it. You look around and everything is exactly the same, but somehow it's also completely different. You try to work it out. Is it a smell? Or has the light changed? But it's like the air, it's everywhere and at the same time nowhere. You just know that suddenly, for no reason, nothing is quite the same as when you came in.

Across the lawn, near a sundial, a group of people were talking. They looked worried and intense, occasionally glancing over their shoulders as if they were telling secrets.

'What?' Chess was wondering why I wasn't looking at her photo.

'Nothing.'

Since we found the dead person, my lungs get these little jerks, like small hiccups, so that instead of one smooth breath it's like taking three little gasps. They were doing it now.

'So,' said Chess. 'What do you think?'

I dragged my eyes back to the photograph. 'What?'

'These two people? What can you tell me?'

Behind us a high voice said, *'They reckon Clare was all over him.'*

'What about this one?' said Chess, pointing to one of the guys. 'You're good at faces. What can you tell me about him?'

Through the roses came another piece of girly gossip, *'Anna really hated him.'*

There was nothing unusual about any of this. I forced my voice to sound calm. 'Who is he?'

But behind us there was whispering and giggling. It grated on my nerves like static electricity. ' — *someone started screaming* —'

'Jacob Langton,' said Chess. 'He's the person we've come to see.'

That wasn't right. We'd come here for a rest.

'— *just screaming and screaming* —'

My heart was starting to thump. 'Hang on a minute, Chess. You said —'

' — *and his face is swelling up* —'

Without thinking I jumped to a gap in the roses. I shouted at them, 'What the hell is going on??!!'

They were just kids. Ten or eleven. Skinny legs and big feet, tin butterflies in their hair. They squealed in surprise and scuttled backwards, grabbing and pushing at each other with green fingernails. They ran off, shrieking and giggling.

Two women were staring at me. I went back to the seat. 'What the hell is going on?' My voice was squeaky. I was sweating.

'People can't help gossiping.' Chess spoke lightly but she couldn't meet my eyes. 'It's human nature. Everyone's worried. And curious.' Her voice fell so low I almost couldn't hear it. 'Because of the murder.'

'Murder!?'

She nodded.

'A real murder?'

'What do you mean? Of course a real murder. What other kind is there?'

'Here?'

'No of course not here. But this is where the victim lived. With his friend. And the friend is quite traumatised. This boy here.' She tapped the photo. 'We've come to help him.'

I couldn't speak. Someone had been murdered and people were talking about it. It was real. I didn't know if that made things better or worse.

Chess said, 'I thought you would have cottoned on. Didn't you read about it? Last November? The boy who was poisoned at the charity cabaret?'

I frowned. 'Maybe. I was going to Canberra or something — I thought he killed himself.'

'That theory was quickly discredited.'

My voice sounded weak. 'Well, I didn't follow it. And then in December ... you know, we had our own problems. And after that ... people try not to talk about things in front of me.'

'Yes. I see,' said Chess. 'Well to be honest there wasn't much in the press at the time. Sometimes the police don't release much information. But it's pretty clear that the poor boy was poisoned. And the police seem to have made remarkably little progress with the case, even now, ten months later.' Chess waited, to let this sink in. 'No one has ever been charged for Tim Williams's murder. The *Border Mail* did an article a few weeks ago, calling it a failure of the justice system. And the whole town is still upset about it.' Her voice faded to almost nothing. 'That's why we're here.'

My head started floating. I worked through her words in my brain. Then, from somewhere a long way away, my voice said, 'We?'

She took the photo and studied it, as if what she was saying was really a side issue. 'The boy who lives here — Jacob Langton — for some reason a lot of suspicion is falling on him. Unfairly. And the longer it takes to identify the real killer the worse it is for him.' She looked up at me. 'He sent me this photo and invited us here. To see if we can help.'

For the hundredth time I wondered how Chess could pretend to be so cool about things. I knew she felt this as much as I did. I tried to draw in another deep breath, but it was still jerky. 'There was a murder.' I glanced at the house. Way up one end there was a dim yellow light but the rest was dark. All I could see were the edges of curtains.

'Not here. At the Town Hall.'

'But someone has asked you to come here.'

'Jacob Langton. I've been tutoring a few of his friends. Through R.O.U —' She realised I wasn't going to know what she was talking about. 'The net tutoring thing I do. So he heard about us being involved in a murder last year. And he contacted me.'

'Langton. As in the house.'

Chess started looking less worried. 'You didn't notice did you? I was the one who suggested we come to Beechworth to stay with Mike. Of course I didn't mention the Langtons. I said we needed a break, but really we came to see Jacob.'

Slowly my thoughts began to clear. I wasn't crazy. I wasn't having hallucinations left over from my bad year. I'd just been aware of the atmosphere here. The owners of this house had been involved in a murder. They were probably suspects and all the people here knew. Everyone was gossiping about it. They were pretending to look at the garden but half of them had come just to peer at the house.

And I could see something else. Chess had tried to manipulate me. She'd brought me here without telling me why, because she knew if she told me I wouldn't come.

And now she was trying to take it further. 'The Open Garden closes at four. Then we're going up to the house to talk to Jacob.'

Suddenly I was angry. That's the way it is sometimes, with fear and anger. All the emotional energy was still there and now that I wasn't afraid any more it had to go somewhere.

'No way!'

I had shouted. I could feel my cheeks burning and my eyes wet with fury. Chess wasn't worried. She looked at me coldly, calculating how best to deal with me, and this made me worse.

When I'm upset I'm never that creative with words. But I must've been aware of all the people around, because I lowered my voice and what I said was, 'No jolly way.' Then I started repeating myself. 'No way, Chess. Not in a million years. I will not have anything to do with it. No. Way. No jolly, jolly, jolly, JOLLY WAY!!!'

'Tell you what.' Chess looked around. People were staring at us. 'I'll give you the full story. That will help you make up your mind.'

Chapter 3

I let her tell me her story, not because I wanted to hear it, just because there didn't seem to be any other way of dealing with this. My anger was fading but I had to make Chess see sense.

I suppose, in a way, it's strange that I had to make her see anything. To me, it was obvious what we should do — just walk away from here and keep on walking. It wasn't that I didn't care. If someone had been killed in front of the people who lived here, a friend of theirs, that was terrible, and if people were blaming an innocent person, that was worse. And true, Chess and I had caught one murderer. But we hadn't done it because we wanted to, and there was no way we were ready to do it again. I knew that without thinking, by the way my limbs had gone weak and my tongue was dry and my breathing jumped every time I thought about it.

A chestnut tree was throwing shade across the lawn, sharp and black against the green. People were starting to drift back towards their cars.

When things bother Chess she tries to go towards them. She likes to think, analyse things. It provides her with a kind of armour. People say she's Asperger's or something but that's not it. Like I said, she definitely feels things the way I do. She's just determined to push all that down. She uses puzzles and maths and things to distract her. So far that seemed to be working.

Now she made a happy little throat-clearing noise. I stole a glance at her. She was sitting very straight. She looked firmer than she used to, less rubbery.

I'd been noticing this lately. Chess had learned she could deal with things better than most people and now, every time things got tough, she got tougher too. Is there a mythical creature somewhere that goes into a fire — or you shoot rays at it or something — and it absorbs all the energy and comes out glowing and even more dangerous? Doesn't matter, it was probably Stranger Things or some Manga show. But that's what Chess was like. She didn't get stronger in spite of trouble. She got stronger because of it.

Now, with a little kick of her feet, she thrust the photo towards me, tapping it again. 'This is Tim Williams. The boy who died.' She watched it hungrily in the air, as if it was a hundred dollar note.

Just to get it out of my face, I snatched it.

'Jacob told me about it, and of course I've looked up everything I could find online. I even did some Facebook Stalking.'

She said that as if it had capital letters.

'Chess …'

'Last year, Jacob Langton and his friend Tim Williams were in year twelve at Rawdon Grammar in Albury. Tim's parents had moved to Queensland but he wanted to stay at Rawdon, so he was living at the Langtons' during term time. They were both bright and they must have worked very hard, because they had both got into Law at Monash.'

Chess isn't good at telling stories. She puts in too much detail. I tried to concentrate.

'In November they both got back from Schoolies and I think Tim was supposed to be packing up his room to go to Queensland for the holidays. But first there was a charity event in the Beechworth Town Hall. A variety show arranged as a cabaret, with tables and music.'

On the edge of the lawn there was a fat water hen, nibbling at a puddle with a wet gobbling sound. It looked up and gave a honk that sounded like one of those paper party blowers with a hole in it. Chess likes to laugh at mad things if she's in the right mood. Today she didn't even hear it.

'At the cabaret, Tim was in a bitter and rebellious mood. He had been for some time. His parents had split up and he didn't like the new partners. But he wasn't, by all accounts, depressed or suicidal, just a bit unpredictable. It was supposed to be an alcohol-free event, but he had a flask of whisky. Early on he drank from it in full view of the room. It was some misplaced gesture of defiance.'

I made an irritated noise with my lips and slapped the photo hard on the side of my leg.

'The bottle was confiscated by someone and taken out to a storeroom. Later in the evening Jacob went to the storeroom, grabbed the flask, and ran up to the stage where Tim was performing a magic act. He handed it to Tim.

'Unknown to either of them, while it was out of the room, the flask had been laced with potassium cyanide. Tim drained it in front of everyone and then died more or less instantly.'

When her house had burnt down, Chess had ended up with burn marks on her arms, pink and white and crinkly. I don't know if they hurt her, or itched, but whenever things bothered her she rubbed at them without knowing. She started doing it now.

'It is by no means certain that Jacob was the one who put the cyanide into the drink, because anyone at the cabaret could have done it. However, Jacob was the one who handed Tim the flask, and now he finds he is the town's number one suspect.'

'Well, that's no good, obviously. But —'

'Then, when the *Border Mail* article came out, the Rawdon Grammar kids started talking about it, and someone told Jacob about us and our murder.'

'Our murder?'

'Jacob e-mailed me and asked me to come and see him. He needs our help.'

It was time to make her see sense. 'Chess you can't just —'

'Think about this,' said Chess primly. 'Jacob Langton gave his friend a poisoned drink and the friend died right at his feet.'

A little voice in my head said *Poor thing*. I pushed it away with another angry noise.

'It would have been very distressing to witness. Cyanide is one of the fastest acting poisons known to man. Its effect on the body —'

'No!' I took a breath and tried to sound calmer. 'Actually, Chess, no, OK? I don't want to know.'

She ignored me. 'Ingestion of a lethal dose results in a racing pulse, sweating and vomiting and convulsions.' This part of the story was hard for Chess too. Her voice lost its normal rise and fall. The words came out separate and flat, like a computer voice. 'The tongue and throat swell so that you can't —'

'Chess. Jeez! Don't tell me that.' This time I did get up and stood with my back to her, too dizzy to walk.

All around us the light in the garden had become a deep green. The distant sounds of people getting into cars seemed to intensify the silence.

Chess said flatly. 'He would have died gasping for air.'

I doubled over, trying not to hear. 'I don't care, OK?' It wasn't true. My mind was dancing with ugly pictures. I just didn't want to care. I sat down again, shakily. 'This stuff …' *It makes me sick. It reminds me of Debs. It's too soon.* 'You hate it too. Why don't you just admit it?'

We both stared out over the lawn for a while. The roses behind us were giving off a thick sweet scent. Slowly my thoughts settled and my breath steadied.

Finally, I knew what it was I wanted to explain to her. I hadn't thought it through but I was ready to give it a go. 'Look, Chess, you have to see this for what it is. You of all people. Murders …' I had to stop and think at this point, then I got it. 'For most people a murder is just something that happens … out there. Not in their own places. Murders are things in the paper. People gossip about them and it gives them a thrill.

'But we're not like that. We know a murder isn't just an exciting story. It happened to a real person and there was fear and … pain … And that person knew other people, people who liked them — or maybe people who didn't like them but saw them every day — friends and parents — and those people will never be the same again. OK, the people at Langton House, the people who are affected by this guy's death, they probably can't leave it alone until it's sorted. But we're not in that group this time. This one isn't for us.'

At this point my voice started to falter. For a second I had a feeling I'd made a mistake somewhere, but I didn't know what it was. I decided to forget it.

Chess said, 'I think we could hear Jacob's story. At the very least we could tell him about our own experiences. Contribute some common sense.'

Common sense. Teacher word, old fart word, something people trotted out when they're trying to make other people look stupid. I threw my hands around. 'You can't! You can't just …'

Chess looked at me with exaggerated calm. People with common sense didn't get upset in discussions. 'Can't just what?'

'We found a dead body, for Christ's sake!'

'So I'm supposed to carry on like a pork chop, having hysterics every five minutes?'

'Well, you don't have to pretend you don't feel anything.' It was something that had been bothering me for a long time and up until now I'd managed not to attack her about it. But now I didn't seem able to stop. 'We — pulled — Debbie — out — of — a pond. We felt her. You pretend it doesn't bother you.' Chess looked away from me with an irritated toss of the head. I kept on at her. 'You don't fool me. I know you think about it all the time. But you act as if it was just some kind of puzzle that proved how clever you were.'

That made her think. I thought that for the first time she might be wondering why she was like that. She said, 'Maybe I'm just more used to it. I've been through bad things before.'

Well that was true. Chess's history did have some bad stuff in it.

'I explained it to you a long time ago,' said Chess. 'Facts, logically arranged. The truth. Clear thinking. They are what will get you through. Getting emotional never helps.'

'Yeah? Well I, with my fantastic perfect life, where nothing has ever gone wrong — I do still have normal emotions and I hate murder and I'm not touching it.'

Chess flicked a leaf off her leg. 'Jacob stood beside his best friend and watched helplessly while he died.'

I heard it again. *Poor thing*. I took a breath.

'The police haven't managed to find out who's responsible. And Jacob's friends and family were there.

They saw it too. They all did. Naturally, there's now a lot of emotion attached to the whole thing and that only gets in the way. A case like this needs to be looked at coldly. Preferably by an outsider. I am good at thinking logically.'

'A lot of people are good at thinking logically.'

Chess's eyes had gone damp and her cheeks were pinker than normal. 'But I'm the one he's turned to.'

Is anything ever really over? Chess and I had had experiences most people never have to deal with — the kind of thing that takes you apart and rebuilds you, and in the process puts in something that wasn't there before. Something deep inside, which means you'll never be completely the same again.

Now even though I was basically OK again I had new kinds of thoughts. I saw things I never used to see.

I started thinking about Jacob Langton. He had sat on the floor with a dead friend, touched the body, touched him while he died. He'd be having visions, like I did. He'd be haunted by dead faces. Whenever he closed his eyes, pictures would appear in unnatural colours on the back of his eyelids. He'd go whole nights without sleep, tossing and sweating and mangling pillows. He'd get up at three in the morning and watch YouTube clips about kite surfing, with the sound turned down so no one heard.

In the daytime he'd be creeping around, afraid of what might come out at him from his own dark thoughts. And he'd know that no one around him could possibly understand. He'd be thinking he'd left the human race.

Suddenly I realised where my mistake was. You *are* involved. If you've had the same experience as someone it gives you a connection. It means there's a lot you understand about them, that other people wouldn't understand. And that means you might be able to help.

And once you've decided that doing the right thing is important to you, you don't always have choices.

Of course that day in the garden I didn't have words for all this. That came later, when I thought it through. At the time the only words I had in my head were provided by that inner voice that wouldn't go away. *Poor Thing.*

Chess was still trying to persuade me. 'I think Jacob might have something important to tell us. He must think there's something we can do.'

It went off again, *Poor thing, Poor thing. Poor thing.* I didn't like the words it chose. They were the sort of thing little girls say about sick pussy cats, and there was no way I was going to say them out loud. But I couldn't turn the voice off. And when I finally managed to move, all I did was punch my knees with anger at being trapped into something, and the stupid words kept going in my head while my own voice said,

'All right, Chess. We'd better see what he has to say.'

Chapter 4

So that's how it started. Even though my first experience with murder had been a major blow sanity-wise, even though it still seemed an insane idea, we ended up going across the now-empty garden and knocking on the front door of Langton House. Because there'd been a murder and, believe it or not, we wanted to talk about it.

The front door was set back under a heavy porch, between two narrow windows that did not reflect light. It was opened by a sharp little woman in an apron who made it clear by the way she stood that she was very busy and we were interrupting her. I let Chess do the talking which is never a good idea. She'd been so busy persuading me to see Jacob that she hadn't planned what to say at the door.

She spluttered something about the open garden that didn't make any sense then stopped suddenly, leaving a little silence in which we all goggled at each other. Then she started again, managing two words, 'We were ...' and stopped.

The woman shifted her weight from one foot to the other. Finally, when Chess managed to say, 'There's an appointment', she interrupted. 'I'll get Mrs Langton. Wait here.' She hurried away.

The door was left half open, which gave us a view of a triangle of tiled floor. Chess stood obediently still, staring at it. But I heard something.

It was a kind of wail. Female, faint, weak, and wobbly at the end — a bit like one of those spooky cries a peacock makes.

I looked around. A few metres away was the front gate, between stone posts. When we'd arrived there had been cars parked all along the road, but now the bit I could see was empty. The last visitors, two families with little kids, were going out. At the gate, an old guy was folding up a card table and a woman stood beside him, holding a tin box. They had turned to look back down towards the garden.

Along the driveway there were some old pines, the ragged black-trunked kind, and under them, in deep shade, was the little red-haired magician. The big super-neat starey guy was standing next to him with a heavy hand on his shoulder. I had the sense they'd been looking at each other but now they had turned and they were watching me. The kid had one hand pressed into his own neck, as if it had just been hurt. The big guy had the same expression as before. He watched me for about ten seconds (which is actually a really long time if you count it out) then he shoved at the kid's shoulder and went out through the gate. and disappeared.

Exactly at the moment he went out of sight we heard footsteps in the house. Because of the timing it felt a bit like a piece of magic — someone disappears in one place and immediately reappears somewhere else — and for a brainless moment, I half expected to see the same bloke pulling open the door. But of course it wasn't him, it was Mrs Langton, tall, suntanned ... and unfriendly.

I sighed. Here was another busy person who didn't like being interrupted. Mrs Langton had her face set hard and blank. Her big smile looked as if it had been painted onto a wooden mask and that was how she meant it to look.

'Can I help you?' She thought we were people from the open garden, trying to look around the house.

Fortunately, by now Chess had had time to recover and prepare a speech. 'Hello, Mrs Langton. My name is Jessica Febey and I'm a friend of Jacob's.'

It was like some kind of password. Mrs Langton's face melted into human skin. 'Oh-h-h … Jacob … I'm sorry. Well, of course.' She took half a step back from the door, as if she was about to usher us in, then she stopped. 'Jessica, did you say?' A tiny frown appeared as she tried to recognise the name.

'He might not have mentioned me.' Chess's olive-skinned face darkened, which is her way of blushing, and she started sweating on her upper lip. 'I'm actually a friend of a friend. Friends. I was tutoring some of the year twelves in Data Structures. So … not really a friend, so much … a tutor. A computer tutor.' She gasped a bit, startled by her own rhyme.

Luckily Mrs Langton didn't need a sales job. 'How marvellous! Goodness you don't look old enough.' She stepped back and waved us in, now sounding excited. 'Jacob will be delighted. He hates these Open Gardens. So many old fuddy duddies.' Her eyes flicked uncertainly towards me.

Chess was looking normal now, just a bit pale. 'This is Matthew T…' After her stupid-sounding rhyme there was no way she was going to say my surname. (It's Tingle. OK. That's over. Needn't be mentioned again.) 'We're from Yackandandah.' Chess seemed to think that explained something.

Mrs Langton smiled. 'You precious thing.'

She had grey hair cut short and very smooth. She was wearing three-quarter walking tights and hi-tech shoes, and a zippered top with that perfect look that meant it was expensive. She led us through a door on the left into a huge lounge room.

'And what brings you to Beechworth? Do you know people here?'

'Michael Manelli,' said Chess.

'Manelli?'

I knew what was going on here. Women in Yack do it. They try to find out where you fit into things, who your relations and friends are. Then they know how to treat you.

'He's a building contractor. He's here for six months, building the White Hill winery.'

'Oh, yes.' Mrs Langton beamed at us. I was glad Chess could remember details. 'Building contractor' was obviously a good thing. And old people always warm up when you use the word 'winery'.

The room we came into was vast, with a polished floor and creamy walls that no Weet Bix had ever stuck to. There were two groups of armchairs with thick soft covers and bookcases with shiny things on them, and mirrors in big solid frames. Down one side were the floor-to-ceiling windows that looked out past the pillars, towards the lake.

'This is a nice house,' I said.

'Well, thank you, Matthew. How nice of a boy to notice.' Mrs Langton looked happily around the room. 'We have recently redecorated. Adrian is in

Hong Kong but he's very generous about things like that.' That made it sound as if the money all belonged to her husband. I wondered if that was a rich person thing. Last time I looked, the Tingles had a hundred and twenty-three dollars in the bank and fifteen dollars eighty in the jar on the kitchen bench, but it belonged to all of us.

Mrs Langton got us sitting on one of the couches, then stood back and admired Chess. 'What a dear little thing you are. So you tutored some of the Rawdon boys, did you? Databases, did you say? I'm sure Jacob would be able to tell me what that means.' She got that eager, shiny-eyed expression parents get when they're trying to let you know how clever their own kids are, without actually boasting about them. 'What about you, Matthew? Are you a computer whizz, too?'

'No, I'm ...' I was supposed to come up with a two-word description of my personality, but I'm no good at this kind of thing. '... not.'

'Never mind.' Mrs Langton thought she had to make me feel better. 'You'd have to know more about them than I do.'

'Is Jacob here?' said Chess.

Mrs Langton looked a bit startled. 'Jacob and his grandfather are in the study, finalising his subject selections. He starts a law degree next year.' Her head wobbled from side to side as if it was on a spring. 'It's not easy to get into something like that. Of course it wasn't all natural ability. He worked very hard.' I wondered why my parents didn't think I was this fantastic. 'His grandfather is encouraging him. My father. He was a wonderful lawyer in his day. Jakie decided to defer for a year, but he'll love uni I'm sure. When he's back on his feet.'

She stopped suddenly, as if she had heard herself saying things she shouldn't.

I thought I should tell her we knew all about it. 'I'm sorry about that guy.' That sounded wrong. 'I'm sorry about Jacob's friend, the one who died.'

Mrs Langton's face went hard again. She did a slow blink, letting her eyelids swing down over big round eyes, the way a puppet does. 'We've agreed not to discuss it. It doesn't help.' She took a step backwards. 'Now you just make yourselves at home while I go and find him. Two special guests from Yackandandah. We mustn't keep you waiting.'

When she was gone Chess and I looked at each other with small smiles. Mrs Langton was clearly a major airhead and too posh for my liking but she was also kind of nice, and it didn't seem fair for two special guests from Yackandandah to laugh behind her back.

From deep in the house we could hear clattering noises, people working in a kitchen. There was a smell of new fabric and dried flowers and somehow, even though the ceiling was high, there didn't seem to be enough air.

When Mrs Langton came back her voice was unnaturally bright. 'Here they are.'

Chapter 5

Chess and I stood up as a guy of about nineteen came into the room. He was followed by an old man, short and chubby, dressed in a V-neck jumper with a shirt and tie.

Mrs Langton was dressed to go for a walk or a run but she didn't seem in a hurry to start. 'Darling come and join us.' She had spoken with extra warmth, as if Jacob was a much younger kid who might be shy.

And I could see why. He looked nervous. 'Hi,' he said. 'You must be Chess.' His voice was tight, made worse by the fact that he tried to sound cheerful. He looked uncertainly at me.

'This is Matthew,' said his mother.

I pushed at my hair. I don't wear it as long as I used to — not since I stopped worrying about the shape of my ears — but I still shove it back when I'm nervous and there was something about this guy's tension that was catching.

Mrs Langton introduced Jacob's grandfather as Mr Burden and he looked embarrassed and told us to call him Angus.

'You go if you like, Grandpa,' said Jacob, still trying to make his voice light.

'Oh, I …' Angus gave a gentle laugh and blinked a few times.

'You go, Dad,' said Mrs Langton sharply.

Jacob said, 'I need you to print out that foundation subject thing.'

Angus gave Jacob a worried look but he said, 'Oh yes.' He went out and shut the door.

Jacob said, 'Sorry Mum. I should have answered the door. I didn't realise how late it was getting.' He wouldn't meet her eyes. I couldn't see why. Mrs L wasn't annoyed.

'Oh Jakie look at you.' To us she said, 'He gets so tired.' She turned back to him with a little pat on the arm. 'Poor old soldier.' Underneath the silly words she was worried about her son.

To get the attention away from him she started talking quickly about the warm weather and Yackandandah, organising us onto the chairs as she talked. She said something about drinks and went to the door, but I don't think she wanted to leave us alone, because instead of going out she called to someone in the kitchen.

In the moment her back was turned, Jacob leaned across and shoved an envelope into my hands. He made furious gestures, telling me to hide it. There was something hard inside the envelope. I shoved it into a pocket just as Mrs L came back.

Then we were into pleasantries. Chess was sneaking glances at Jacob and was obviously overwhelmed again, which meant she wasn't going to be able to say anything meaningful for quite a while so, while she went through her darkening, sweaty and pale phases, I did the answers. We talked about the weather and the garden and how I hoped the Rawdon guys had done well in their computing exams and yes, Yackandandah was only twenty minutes away and no, we weren't tired. My parents are always bringing new friends home. I can do pleasantries without really thinking.

While that was going on, I had a chance to study Jacob. I'm not sure if you'd call him actually good looking. His hair was just kind of brown and normal and his eyes were no particular colour and he had a fairly wide nose. But he was tall and straight in the shoulders with a strong face. And his skin was smooth. You got the impression that inside that mouth there would be a long row of perfect teeth.

After a while we fell into an uncomfortable silence.

Jacob said, 'So Mum did you pick up on the surnames? This is Matthew Tingle and Jessica Febey. They're the kids that were involved in that murder at Yackandandah last December.'

'Oh no. I had no idea. So you are those poor children.'

I didn't like being this famous. A lot of people had worked hard to keep our names out of the newspapers but it was impossible to stop people talking.

Chess squeaked her rubber soles together.

Mrs Langton said, 'And you invited them to drop in, Jacob?'

'Yes.' Jacob raised his chin defiantly. 'Matt and Chess have been through the same kind of thing we have. I thought it might be good to talk about it.'

Chess was frowning. She didn't think Jacob had asked us here to express feelings. We were here to investigate.

'Yes I see.' Mrs L looked worried. And obviously it would be much worse if she thought we were here to try to find the killer. That was why Jacob was looking so nervous.

Now she turned to me, shaking her head. 'Poor Tim's death was sensationally publicised in the media. And then just last month the jolly paperstirred it all up again. No doubt there was plenty of gossip in the garden today.'

'Yeah.' I gave an apologetic laugh. 'It was actually kind of creepy.'

'People are so ghoulish.'

Jacob tried to lighten the mood. 'One guy appeared in the study window. He'd climbed into a garden bed. Grandpa and I stared at him and he just stood there, sinking into the soil with a hydrangea between his legs.'

We all laughed and I took the opportunity to ask something. 'I was wondering about it actually.' I tried to keep my voice light but I was watching for signs of resistance. 'Why is everyone so interested in this place? I mean this Tim guy, he didn't … It didn't happen here, did it? It was at some charity show.'

'It happened at the Beechworth Town Hall,' said Mrs L.

'So why —'

'The poison was here.' Jacob gave his mother a wary look but she folded her hands in her lap and sat back. 'When we all left for the hall the poison was in the house.'

'Potassium cyanide?' This was the first time Chess had spoken and she hadn't picked up on the need to go carefully. She started swivelling in her chair, looking around the room. 'Where? Why would you keep something like that in your house?'

'It wasn't ours,' said Jacob. He made an awkward swallowing movement as if he was pushing something down. 'It was his own. It was Tim's.'

His voice had broken on the name and now Mrs L did stop him. 'I'm sorry Jacob but is there anything to be gained by going over details? I'm sure Matthew and Jessica have had enough of these tragedies, as have you yourself.'

Silently I cursed Chess for charging in like that. We weren't going to learn anything with Mrs L here. And I wasn't going to be able to look into the envelope he'd given me, either. Then I reminded myself I didn't care. It wasn't my idea to investigate this death and, in a way, I agreed with Mrs L. Jacob's cheeks were hard and his lips were pale. He didn't look as if he could handle anything too heavy.

Mrs L saw me looking at him. 'I must be honest with you. I don't believe in endlessly talking things over.'

'I absolutely agree,' said Chess.

Mrs L put a hand on her son's knee. 'There has to be a time for putting things behind us and getting on with our lives. Jacob has already missed a year of his education.'

Jacob was looking at me. Through the tiredness there was a look of frustration. There was something else he wanted to say.

But all I could do was give him a sympathetic look and try to get on to something more like normal conversation. 'So you deferred uni. Have you been working?'

The question seemed to embarrass him. 'Not really.'

Mrs L said, 'He was offered an administrative position in a local law office but he didn't feel sharp enough, mentally, to accept anything. He did an RSA course and a barista course but … rest has been more important. Rest and exercise.'

Jacob was a bit old to have someone telling his stories for him but he didn't seem to mind. He just looked drained.

No. It was more than that. I knew what I was seeing. After the murders in Yack, I kind of closed up on myself, imploded, collapsed under my own gravity. I stopped doing things, stopped playing music, stopped going anywhere. I could hardly even have a conversation. I felt different from everyone else, as if I was made from different stuff — glass, maybe, or some kind of anti-matter with a cold smooth surface that everything just slipped off. It was as if the whole world had swelled up around me, too bright, too noisy and not quite real. And, by the look of him, Jacob had some version of the same thing.

Outside, the garden was blurring into shadow. The air in the room seemed to soften. I tried to say something helpful. 'I used to sit in my room for hours. With a ukulele.'

The ukulele story made me look an idiot but it was kind of bizarre and I thought he might like it.

'Not a real one. It was just this old thing Dad bought at a market. It had cracked orange varnish and a couple of dented silver stars glued on the front.'

Chess gave a tight sigh and pushed her palms into her knees, locking and then relaxing her elbows.

I said, 'It sounded like someone rattling a bag of aluminium cans. But that meant I could just bang away at the strings without caring or thinking or feeling anything. I just used to sit there going twang twang.'

Jacob had one of those super wide smiles that spread easily, as if his face was being released into its natural shape. And I was right about the teeth. Suddenly I was glad we'd come.

The smile only lasted a second. He said, 'It's like being let into some huge secret. The things I know now that other people don't know. Things you only know if —'

Unfortunately 'know' is one of Chess's favourite words. Suddenly she sat forward, too intense, too eager, and completely missing the point. 'What is it? What do you know?'

Jacob was stunned. 'It's hard to — Something like —' He thought for a minute. 'Life isn't solid. It's like water. You can slip. You can sink.'

I said, 'Yeah.'

'And it's murder. Someone deliberately caused it.' His intensity had gone up a notch. 'So does it help? Is it better when you find out who did it?'

Chess said, 'The truth always helps. Even if it's bad.'

At this point, Mrs L interrupted. 'Oh heavens. You sound just like Jacob's grandfather. Maybe you would like to have a look at his books.' She moved in front of Chess, lifting an arm towards the bookcases. 'They're all about logic. Plato and Aristotle and things like that. Come and see.' Chess had no choice but to follow her over there.

Somewhere a dove was making a lazy bubbling sound.

Jacob said, 'You just think about dying a lot.'

Well this was really plunging into it, but that was OK with me. 'Yeah.'

At this point Angus came back in carrying a book. He took it to the bookshelves and glanced shyly at Chess. He had a bulging forehead, made bigger by the fact that his hair started half way back on his head.

Jacob lowered his voice. 'You think how easy it is to die.'

'Yeah.'

Mrs Langton said something to Angus but she was glancing back at us, trying to hear what we were talking about.

'You wonder why no one else seems to be worried. You wonder how people can all just walk around.'

We were on the south side of the house and the light was becoming grey and cool. Over near the door there was a sideboard where a lamp had been left on, shining down on a lot of photos in gold frames.

'Have you got a photo of him?' I stood up and went over there. Jacob came with me.

They were mostly of the family, Jacob and a fair-haired girl that must be his sister. Actually, most of them were Jacob — standing on a block at the pool with a medal round his neck, and in a soccer team, middle of the front row, and playing hockey, and shaking someone's hand on a stage. You could see what sort of boy he'd been — one of those little blonde-headed gods that win things and come top of the class.

Now Angus was talking to Chess. He was holding a book. I heard him say something about the universe being fundamentally rational.

Chess said, 'Oh I absolutely agree.'

I wanted to ask Jacob about the envelope, but Mrs Langton was edging closer to us, tidying a pile of magazines on a coffee table.

'That's Tim,' said Jacob.

He pointed to a brightly coloured photo. It showed a stage magician, dressed in a black suit and bow tie, standing in front of a rich blue curtain. He was posing for the camera, his arms in the air, one hand holding a silver ball.

I recognised him from the school line up but here he looked like a different person. His hair was smoother and his arms made a graceful arc. He was light and balanced and totally absorbed in what he was doing.

I said, 'There was a little guy in the garden today. He had red hair and he was doing tricks.'

'He was a friend of Tim's.' Jacob made a pained expression. 'He said he was going to walk around and do a few of Tim's favourite tricks. He just wanted to …'

'A tribute.'

'Yeah.'

Over at the bookshelves, Angus was talking about enlightenment and someone called Daycart. Chess had pushed her neck forwards. She was looking at the books as if she'd like to devour them.

In Tim's photo there was a table holding two shiny cylinders. They were about thirty centimetres tall, painted metallic blue with stripes of burnished gold. Next to them there was a green box with a face on it.

'Nice props.' I turned slightly and lowered my voice. 'Jacob, what's in the en–'

'Oh yes,' said Mrs Langton right behind me. Tim loved all his funny props.' She pushed between us. 'The blue things he called the Whispering Chimneys. The box is the Golden Devil Box.'

In the light of the desk lamp the photo seemed to glow as if it was lit from within.

Mrs L said, 'Magic was such a lovely escape for him.'

Jacob liked talking about Tim. 'He said the less real things were, the better.'

'What does that mean?'

He shrugged. 'He said things like that — being sick of reality. It was just a kind of anger. And sadness. He was really getting pretty crazy, doing a lot of bad stuff. You couldn't do anything about it. All he would talk about was how bad things were, and escaping from it all.

Mrs Langton said, 'Poor Tim. He was a very confused young man. Really quite lost.'

'He had this big idea for his final act. He used to practise with the curtains. He was going to make himself disappear.' Jacob gave a sick smile. 'He was going to do the trick and straight away leave town. But instead …' He turned away so I wouldn't see his face.

Mrs L put a hand on his shoulder. 'Now old thing, I think you're getting tired.' She looked meaningfully at me.

I said, 'We should go.'

Mrs L took a step towards the door. Chess and Angus were watching us now. Chess was holding a book. It was called *Elementary Logic*.

Mrs L went into a wind-up speech. 'It was very kind of you to come here and I'm sure it wasn't an easy thing to do. Your visit will have helped Jacob immensely, although, as you can see, he finds it a great strain to talk about Tim. I hope you'll understand.'

'Yes.'

'And what are your plans for your week in Beechworth?'

This was a message that we wouldn't be seeing them again.

'Not much. Resting.'

Angus turned to Chess. 'I will write down my email address for you, in case you have any questions.' He turned away, towards a side table.

'Are you going to eat out at all?' said Jacob.

This was a bit sudden. I thought he'd dropped out of the conversation.

'Mike's going to take us out tonight, actually.'

'Where to?'

'Not sure.'

'You should try Luca's.' He nodded as if this was important to him. 'It's good. Tapas.'

'Thanks,' I said.

'OK. Well, see you.' He turned suddenly and went out.

Mrs L said, 'How were you planning to get home?'

'I'll ring Mike,' said Chess. She pulled out her phone. 'He'll come straight away.'

This would mean we'd be waiting around for another ten minutes. Mrs L quickly said, 'Oh, dear me there's no need for that. I'm going to Stanley for a little walk-run with my friends. I have to drop Margie Cleeves in town first. So I can run you in. Just wait one minute.' She went out a door at the back of the room.

Angus touched me on the arm. 'It was good of you both to come and talk to Jacob.'

I said, 'It's all right.'

'I hope you managed to enjoy the garden as well.'

'Oh yes,' said Chess. 'The sandwiches —'

'You didn't see anything unusual, did you?' Angus suddenly looked sharper. 'Anyone acting strangely?'

I immediately thought of the big guy and the magician kid, but I didn't know if that's what he meant and I didn't want to go into it.

'No,' said Chess.

Angus looked towards the windows. 'There was one very large young man. He looked familiar, but he was completely out of place.' He frowned for a minute and then said, 'But there, now.' He gave a feeble smile. 'After all my talk of being rational. Never mind.'

At that point Mrs Langton came back with the other woman and we went to the car.

But, more than the whole conversation, more than Jacob's obvious stress, that last moment had really got to me. Just for a second Angus hadn't looked like a sweet old guy, or a shy grandad who bored people. He hadn't even looked like someone who is worried about his grandson and is trying to hide it.

He had looked afraid.

Chapter 6

In the car Mrs Langton and Margie did most of the talking. I did my pleasantries thing and Chess stared out the window. I didn't want to risk them seeing the envelope, so I left it in my pocket. It didn't feel important or urgent anyway. Jacob might have wanted to tell me something but he was sad and stressed and his mother obviously wanted him to be left alone. I decided it had been my imagination, thinking the old guy was afraid of something. The meeting had actually been pretty normal. The idea of turning this into an investigation to amuse Chess — well it now seemed a sick joke.

About half way home, Mrs Langton said, 'It was good of you to chat with Dad about his books.' She made a quick half-turn of her head and then went back to watching the road. 'He can be a bit of a bore.'

'Oh no, he's wonderful,' said Chess quickly.

Mrs Langton shook her head. 'Poor old Dad. He loves teaching young people things.'

Margie said, 'Old men need to be reassured that they're still useful.'

They were talking to each other now. Mrs L said, 'Dad would love Jacob to be a barrister. I think he was disappointed that he never became one himself, so he's loving helping his grandson.' She wiggled her head. 'Adrian has a little joke about him. He says he needs to think he's still as good as he never was.' She gave the steering wheel a little squeeze. 'Adrian is such a tease.'

I realised what it was that showed she was wealthy. It was the fact that she didn't have to try to sound sensible. It meant she was used to being looked after.

'But he's a wonderful tutor. And Jacob will be fine, if he gets a chance to recover.'

This was her final message to us. Leave Jacob alone.

We came to one of the main roads and turned downhill, past the old mental hospital and some galleries, to the centre of town. The afternoon was fading into evening. At the bakery there were people at tables on the footpath and a balcony with a jazz band playing, which gave me a little holiday-beginning kind of thrill. In Yack everything is curved, sloping and closed in. The two main streets of Beechworth are straight and wide. The old buildings are made of granite, and bits of the road are paved with it. The town feels gritty but also shiny, as if there is glittering dust hanging in the air.

I got Mrs Langton to drop us in Loch Street, leaving us a block to walk. Chess didn't protest. She knew we needed some space to talk. As soon as the car had gone she sat on a low brick wall and said, 'Let's see what he gave you.'

I pulled out the envelope and held up what was inside. It was a key, very ordinary, with a leather tag with a word burnt into it. 'Elsinore'.

Chess looked disappointed. 'Do you know what that means? I mean apart from Hamlet of course.'

'No idea. And really, it doesn't matter. We can't go ahead with any of this, investigating a murder.' I laughed to show how bizarre the idea was. 'You can see that, can't you?' I shoved it back in a pocket. 'Jacob doesn't look as if he could deal with this. His mother didn't think he could handle much at all. I'll put the key in his letterbox or something.'

I sat beside her. She needed a minute for that to sink in. There were elm trees right along the street. Their roots had pushed the ground up into lumps and there were green papery seed pods everywhere, giving the place a comfortable, homely feel. I took a deep breath. Things were going to be OK. The Langton side track would now blow over and we could go to Mike's and relax.

Chess said, 'I liked Mr Burden. It's so refreshing to find someone who recognises the importance of rational thinking.' She dug in her shoulder bag and pulled out a small black notebook. 'Did you catch those names? Aristotle, of course, and Daycart. But what were the others?' She wrote a few things down. Looking over her shoulder I saw that Daycart was actually spelt 'Descartes'. Typical. She made a brisk little line under the names and looked up. 'And fancy lending me a book.' She patted the bag. 'He doesn't even know me.'

'He probably doesn't often meet people who will actually listen to that stuff.'

I hadn't meant it to sound mean. I thought Chess could do with a few friends. But at any minute she was going to get the book out and start telling me about it and I didn't want that.

I tried to make a joke. 'Maybe he could be your guru. You can sit at his feet and gaze up while he spouts out wisdom about Aristotle.' I tried a guru voice. 'Be logical, Jessica. Feel the enlightenment.' This made me think of something. 'He could be your Yoda.'

'My what?'

'Don't pretend you don't remember. Kids when we were. Watched it we did.

She stood up and started walking.

'That's who it is, though.' I followed her. 'Face his shape is the same as.' Then I caught up and said, 'Wait on.' We stopped.

During the car ride I had realised something. We couldn't rush straight in to see Mike. His wife and kids had stayed in Sydney. He was by himself and that meant we'd have to talk to him. He knew all about our terrible year. He knew we'd come here to forget it. If he realised we'd been talking to people about another murder, he'd be worried. We probably couldn't deny seeing the Langtons, but we'd have to downplay the whole thing. And to do that properly we had to get our stories straight.

I'd learned to go carefully with Chess. If I tried to tell her what we should and shouldn't be doing, she'd get her back up. So I said, 'We should think about Mike.'

'Definitely. There's something I want to point out to you. We need to be very careful what we say to Mike. We'll have to admit we've met the Langtons, but any hint of premeditation should be avoided. And we must definitely not say we were ever contemplating investigating Tim Williams's murder.' She glared at me.

'I agree. They'd send us straight back home.'

'Good. I was hoping I could make you see sense.'

This was a shady part of town and relaxing to be in. The houses were made of those soft-looking pink bricks, or else they were tiny wooden cottages, and a lot of them had corrugated iron rooves with peeling paint.

There was no one around. Mike's house had a wooden verandah out the front and a low picket fence. It was too much like a Yackandandah house for me to actually like it. But it wasn't actually in Yackandandah. At least there was that.

Chess stepped towards the gate. 'Come on. We've got a lot to be getting on with.'

'Whoa.' I grabbed her. I knew this had been too easy. I realised she had never actually agreed to leave this murder alone. 'OK. Wait. No, no. Just a sec.'

Not my best argument but she got it. And she didn't like it. Her chin went up.

I said, 'Look I know we had to go there and see Jacob. We agreed that. But we've done that now.' I stepped around to get in front of her. 'And we did it well. And I know you have a nice new book and you can email Angus about Plato. But that's it.'

Chess made a little shrugging, head-tossing movement.

'That's *it*, Chess. OK? We're not doing the detective thing, collecting evidence, trying to prove stuff.'

As an answer she reached for the gate again.

I knocked the hand away. 'Chess!' Any minute Mike was going to hear us and come out. 'They don't want us!'

Chess went quiet at this. Not being wanted is always something that gets to her. But she didn't stay quiet for long. 'Not correct, actually. Mrs Langton is protective, but Jacob still wants it to happen. '

'I don't think so.' But I remembered Jacob's face, frustrated and pleading.

'Wasn't he telling you to go to Luca's? That had to be a clue of some kind.'

'It was a restaurant recommendation!'

Then Chess said something weird. It came out very quietly, as if she'd just thought of it and wanted to see how the words sounded. 'What was I put on this earth for?' She took a step back and turned to face me, staring at the ground. 'Look at me.'

Well I was quite happy to do that. I got in front of her again, waited till she looked up and then gave her one of her own direct stares, daring her to give me her best argument.

But all she did was repeat herself. 'Look at me.' She moved her hands in a sweeping downwards motion that took in her whole body. Immediately I knew what she was getting at. It was all there for me — the whitish, yellowish skin, the thin round shoulders. And there was a lot else I knew about. Being clever was her only thing. She could have wins over other kids, but Chess was an outsider. It wasn't just her clothes that never fitted properly.

At the side of the road there was a top-knot pigeon, walking around with that stupid head movement they do. Across the street a man went past with a snuffling, wheezing dog.

Chess stomped past me. Her eyes stayed fixed on the ground but she repeated her first question and this time she'd thought about it and knew it meant something. It wasn't really a question. She was making a point.

'What was I put on this earth *for*?'

Well, what do you say to something like that? What was she put on earth for? What were any of us put on earth for? It was way too deep for me, and I basically didn't have an answer.

So I followed her into Mike's. We went down the central corridor to the tiny kitchen-living area at the back. And, as it always happens when you've psyched yourself up for something, the whole don't-mention-the-murder idea turned out to be a complete non-issue. Mike didn't ask us anything about what we'd been doing. He was tidying up his papers from the kitchen table. He grinned and reminded us we were going out and said we should get cleaned up.

Chess had been given the spare room across from Mike's. I had a kind of sleep-out between the laundry and the back door. In compensation, Mike had put a small flat screen TV in there with a DVD player, and he'd hooked it up to his Foxtel connection, so I was happy enough.

Somewhere Mike had found me a narrow bed, the kind with a piece of foam on a trampoline of metal wires. I'd slept in these before. They dip in the middle, so that after about half an hour you end up in a shallow trench and you have to lie in a straight line all night, because if you put an arm or leg out to the side it has to go uphill. There's only one way to deal with beds like this, and there was just enough room to do it. I pulled the mattress onto the floor, squeezing it between the wall and the bed frame. Then I put the DVD player on the bedsprings and balanced the telly carefully on top so that I could see it when I was sitting in my low nest.

I changed my clothes, splashed cold water on my face in the laundry and then I went out, thinking about food. Mike and Chess were standing together in the living room, ready to go. Mike handed me a sweating Coke. 'Pre-dinner drinks.'

'Thanks.'

Mike had thick grey hair, blow-waved back off his face like you see on TV shows from the seventies. He smoothed it back from his forehead. 'It's a bit early for tea, but I'm starving.' He looked at Chess as if they'd agreed to something. 'We're going to Luca's.'

Chapter 7

As well as the big stone buildings, Beechworth has rows of old shops with rickety awnings that I'd like to draw. The footpaths are wide and instead of gutters there are huge stone gullies with little bridges over them. During the day the footpaths are cluttered up with touristy stuff from the shops — baskets and plants in wooden pots and barbecue aprons with cartoons on them — but at night they pack this away and you can just wander along, looking at the painted doors and all the big shadowy windows.

Even this early on a Saturday night there were quite a few people around. I decided it was because of the spring. Those first warm afternoons, the soft feel of the air on your skin and the smells you're not quite aware of — spring makes you feel like getting out and about and forgetting all the serious stuff. I think even Chess had stopped worrying about what she was on earth for.

I leaned out past the awnings and looked up at the darkening sky. Stupid, I know, but when I'm somewhere lit up and busy that always gives me a thrill.

Luca's was near the top of the hill, where the awnings ran out. It was in a square old house attached to the side of a pub. The door was open and there were tables on the street. Inside it was part restaurant, part café and part bar. The walls were yellow and streaky with big splashy paintings on them and the whole place had a warm earthy feel. But there was also plenty of chrome and glass, so it felt clean and modern as well. The bar took up half the width of the place, with tables squashed around it. There was a smell of pizza that activated my big aching hollow hunger.

Behind the bar there was a bald guy, rubbing at a glass with a cloth and staring into space with his eyes out of focus, like someone who has forgotten what they were doing and is trying to fake it until he remembers. He kept that expression while he looked at Chess and me but when he saw Mike he stopped the rubbing action.

'Hello Calvin,' said Mike.

Calvin was around forty. He had on a white T-shirt with a bit of leather around his neck. What hair he did have was cut about a millimetre long, a thin black fuzz. Instead of answering, he put his glass down and leaned his hands on the bench behind the bar. Now that his brain had reconnected with his face he looked mournful, as if all his thoughts were sad ones. Around him, metal and glass things glowed silver-gold. The espresso machine let out a short airy sigh.

'So,' he said, as if it was a whole sentence.

Mike said, 'Wolfhagen's have got the gorgonzola in.'

They went into a discussion about cheese and terrine and something called cotechino. Chess and I were definitely out of the conversation. I started looking around.

There were a few people inside and a lot more outside. Mostly they were older people. Anyone our age would've gone somewhere cheaper.

'Drinks?' said Calvin, and, because it was the first word I'd actually understood, it drew my attention back.

Mike said, 'This is Matt and Chess, my friends from Yackandandah.'

Calvin gave me a long thoughtful look, slid his eyes to Chess and narrowed them, as if he was realising something. Now he didn't look sad, he looked resentful.

Chess said, 'Hello,' but I just nodded.

'So.' Calvin was looking at Chess as if she'd insulted him in some way. 'Out for a bite?' He said the word sharply, with a spitting sound on the t.

'I think I'll go for the Waterwheel shiraz, by the glass,' said Mike. 'And a couple of Cokes.' He looked at Chess. 'OK?'

'Raspberry, please, actually,' said Chess. She had her hands locked in front of her, as if she was praying for it. The effort of talking to Calvin made her take a step backwards. She went straight into a blonde girl who was going between us and the nearest table. The girl charged on without looking at us.

Mike grabbed Chess to stop her falling. 'We'll choose a table.'

'Sweet,' said Calvin.

At the back of Luca's it was dark, with couches and booths and low orange lamps. Mike looked at these for a while but then led us to a table at the front widow. A bit of cool air wafted in from the street.

Mike spent about two seconds reading the menu and then sat back in his chair and looked at me. 'Have you had Tapas before?'

'I've seen it on TV,' I said.

And how stupid did that sound? It's at times like this you're actually glad you're out with old people.

But Mike didn't laugh. 'What if I just order a few things and you can see what you like.'

Mike turned out to be pretty easy to get on with. He's one of those oldish blokes with grown up children who like talking to young people to show they still understand us. Sometimes that can be pretty painful. They say things like, 'How are those Yackandandah girls treating you,' and dig you in the ribs. But Mike wasn't like that. He had a knack of turning almost anything in his life into a funny story — usually featuring himself looking like an idiot — and he liked to say stupid things with a dead-serious expression. He didn't mind listening either, which was also unusual. After he finished ordering, he told us a story about him in year eight, running up to a fence and impressing a girl by leap-frogging onto his testicles.

So you get the idea. No one was feeling as if there was something we were avoiding and by the time the food arrived, we were all relaxed.

There were Turkish bread and dips, and chorizo and prawns and chips and other things. Some of them looked good and some looked awful and one thing looked exactly like dried doggy doos, but I didn't care. I wanted to tip the whole lot onto my plate and shovel it all into my mouth — and then eat the plate.

Instead, we ate politely and chatted for a while and then Mike said, 'How was the afternoon?'

Chess had a cheesy tart of some kind. She bit off half of it and held the rest in both hands staring down at it while she chewed.

'It was good.' I tried to match Mike's careless tone.

'Mmm,' he said. 'Anyone talking about that boy that was poisoned last year?'

He said it with a weak smile. It meant he wasn't probing us for information. He'd just put the topic out there, so we could talk about it if we wanted to.

'Ye-a-h.' To give myself time to think I picked up a bit of chicken. I dipped it in some kind of sauce and watched a shiny drip fall to my plate.

Mike gave an apologetic laugh. 'The hairdresser I went to last week calls it Cyanide House.'

I tapped the chicken on my plate, making little red dots.

'Not very sensitive,' said Mike.

I didn't want him to feel bad. 'Some things, people need to make them into a joke. It helps them deal with it.'

'Yeah. I suppose that's right. ' Mike looked at me closely. 'It isn't a joke, though, is it?'

'No.'

OK so far. And that might have been all there was to it. Unfortunately I'd been ignoring Chess. She was gripping the arms of her chair as if she was being interrogated. When Mike's eyes fell on her she sat up straight. 'We looked around the garden first!'

'First?' Mike frowned. 'Are you saying you went inside?' He saw the answer in her face. 'I didn't think they'd open the house.'

Great. Good one, Chess. Already Mike had read part of the story out of just one word. And good one Matt, for playing with your food instead of changing the subject.

Chess started digging in her tart with a fork, picking out small grey things.

'Funny coincidence, actually,' I said. 'We met … we ran into …' I stressed that phrase, making sure he saw it was a big accident, '… Jacob Langton. The son. And it turned out Chess has been tutoring some of his friends.' I looked at Chess and made a surprised expression which she tried to copy.

'Right.' Mike raised one eyebrow. 'Hope they paid you all right.'

'Oh-h. Huh-huh.' Chess had finished her operation now. She waved the tart around.

'I'm sure they did.' Mike grinned. 'That's something I heard about you — that you were a survivor.'

That was a good word for her. Chess had always had to run her own life. Getting paid properly was something she had totally mastered. She did a lot of tutoring and babysitting and she could organise things like paying bills and getting things repaired.

She wasn't great at witty replies though. 'Huh-huh.'

I looked over her shoulder. Out on the footpath there were people at every table and a family of about ten kids walking past with ice creams. My eye was drawn to three girls standing over to the right.

Not because I liked the look of them. It's just that they were hard to miss. The middle one was the girl Chess had bumped into before. In her long blonde hair she had darker streaks and she had on one of those tight tops that emphasise the curves, bright orange with a high neck and no sleeves. And she behaved in the way of people who want attention, laughing loudly and swinging her arms to show what a good time she was having. One of the other girls was almost as bad, but it was clear she was just copying her friend. She had a black top the same as the orange one. The third girl was paler and quieter and had less make-up.

Calvin came up with the wine. He dropped a blue plastic stick into Chess's raspberry. It had a dolphin on the end. 'Thanks,' said Chess, delightedly. She shoved in the last of the tart, swallowed it in one huge difficult-looking gulp, punched herself in the chest and brushed happily at her shirt. She hadn't looked at Calvin's face, which was just as well. He was looking as if he'd like to throw us out.

'Don't spill the chilli sauce.' He pointed to a small bowl. 'It bubbles the laminex.'

Mike laughed. Then his eyes sharpened. With a sideways look at Calvin he spoke to Chess. 'So how is Jacob Langton? Getting on all right?'

Calvin took his time opening the wine.

'Do you know him?' said Chess, surprised.

'Never met him,' said Mike with another glance at Calvin. 'But we're all concerned.'

'Actually,' I said, 'he seemed stressed and exhausted.'

'Poor Jacob. With the private school and the new cars, and off to Melbourne for the law degree. He's under a lot of pressure to succeed.' Mike gave a rueful smile. 'That's the gossip around the town anyway. And apparently he was never that good a student. Tim Wilson was much brighter.'

Was he trying to say that Jacob resented Tim? I remembered what Chess had said. A lot of people around the town think Jacob was the murderer.

I said, 'Jacob's actually pretty wrecked about Tim's death. His mother's worried about him.'

'His mother?' said Mike. 'From what I hear she's a bit of a dill.' He looked at Calvin.

Calvin nodded. 'Wouldn't know if her Guccis were on fire.'

He pronounced that 'goocheys.' It's a brand of shoe or something — but in that tense moment, I was thinking goocheys were some kind of embarrassing body part, so I didn't ask.

Mike must've been able to see how unimpressed I was. 'Sorry,' he said. 'It's terrible but it's been dragging on for so long. Everyone's starting to say the Langtons were involved.'

Calvin poured Mike's wine. 'It doesn't help that they've got the biggest house in town.' He looked right at me as he said that and the look was full of … that thing that starts with m. I thought again, he didn't want us here.

Malice. That's the word.

Fortunately at that point he left. Mike watched him go. 'Sorry, that wasn't fair. The Langtons have been decent to Tim. And he brought them a lot of trouble, long before he got himself killed.'

'What do you mean?' said Chess.

'Pretty wild kid by all accounts. Did a lot of drinking, stole cars. Smashed a window here in the main street. He never seemed to get charged for anything. I think the grandfather did a fair bit of work behind the scenes.'

'Angus Burden was his mentor,' said Chess, looking impressed.

'The word is that Angus paid a few witnesses off and did some fancy legal work.' Mike shrugged. 'It's only what I've heard.'

My eye was drawn back to the girls outside. They were sitting down now. The quiet one had lightish hair, cut short, sticking out at the ends like a rag doll.

I don't know why I looked at them right then. I just had the feeling they'd had their eyes on me and had quickly looked away.

'I thought Angus seemed nice,' said Chess. 'And very clever.'

'All those Burden lawyers and judges,' said Mike. 'Might come in handy soon.'

Chess said, 'I hope you're not making assumptions about the murder of Tim Williams. That isn't warranted.'

I winced at the prissy tone. Mike put on a mournful face and looked at me, shaking his head in sympathy. 'Don't you hate it when your friends talk like your mother?'

I grinned. 'I hate it when my mother talks like my mother.'

But Mike didn't really mind. He said, 'No, Chess. You're right.'

Chess said, 'No one's in a position to make a judgement about something as serious as murder unless they're in complete possession of the facts.'

'Whoa, Chess,' I interrupted. 'You're slipping into smart arse territory.'

Mike stared at me, a bit shocked.

'It's OK. She wants me to tell her.'

And at least I'd made him forget about the Langtons. I shovelled a giant dollop of hummus onto some pita bread and settled back in my chair. Mike started asking Chess about her tutoring and Chess started some long answer that no one understood.

It wasn't until after dessert that my eyes went back to the girls in the street. And this time I did catch one of them turning her head away quickly as if she'd been looking at me.

Mike saw it too. 'They were checking you out.' He wriggled his eyebrows at me.

'I wish.' I get on well with girls because I'm easy to talk to and I tell them jokes. But I don't get looks from strangers.

Mike was staring openly at the girls now. He caught the eye of one of them and put on a big grin.

'Just ignore them,' said Chess with a little wiggle of her head. 'There's no need for us to be immature.'

She got a jab in the ankle from me but it was too late. Mike was trying to laugh but he was offended and I didn't blame him. He'd only been trying to lighten things up after the last time Chess had insulted him. Chess saw it too. Her face went dark. She pressed her lips together and then opened them.

Apologise, I was thinking. Just apologise.

She said, 'I'm going to the toilet.'

Mike didn't know it but that was a sign she was ashamed of herself. When things are a bit tricky Chess's brain shuts off from what's really happening and comes up with random words. It's one of the things that makes people think she's a bit mental.

Now she stood up and trotted towards the back of the restaurant. Outside, the three girls said something to each other. The one in the black top went off up the street and the other two came inside. They went past our table as if they didn't see us and headed towards the back of the restaurant. They went straight to the door leading to the toilets.

That wasn't good. A lot of girls like to give Chess a hard time and, although these two didn't know her, they had been talking about us and now they had that focussed look about them. They were definitely planning something. I couldn't just leave her to them.

'Me too,' I muttered and left Mike sitting there.

I used to try to avoid getting involved in Chess's problems because they have a way of being painful and humiliating for her and for anyone around her, but I don't do that any more. It was that belonging thing again. And sometimes you have to help, just because no one else can.

Out the back of Luca's there was a narrow corridor, lit up with that harsh, green-white light that makes you look sick and shows up the shabbiness of things. From my left, through a thin fibro wall, came the sounds and smells of a kitchen. The wall on my right was brick, painted dark brown, and the floor was covered in pink Scrabble-size tiles, badly laid in long crooked waves, giving you a feeling of dipping and sliding as you walked.

I rounded a corner and found the two girls leaning against the wall, staring at the floor and not talking. Opposite them were two doors marked Men and Women. The Women door was shut.

Past the girls there was a door to the outside which was open, showing a bit of cement block wall, topped with some bent poles and barbed wire. The girl with short hair gave me a quick glance and then looked back at the floor. The one with the orange top looked at me for longer, as if she thought I might talk to her. But now Chess came out.

Orange top said, 'Come out here a sec.'

Chess said, 'Pardon?'

'We want to show you something.'

She took Chess by the arm, in a friendly way, and it looked as if Chess was about to go with her.

I said, 'Hang on a sec.'

It's important to get these things exactly right. Instead of strong and protective it had come out sounding as if I wanted to go with them. Orange girl flicked her streaked hair back over her shoulder. She looked as if she thought something was funny. The other girl just looked worried.

I got sterner. 'She's not going.'

They weren't fighters. Short hair said, 'We're not doing anything,' and I was pleased to hear she sounded as embarrassed as I was. The other girl dropped Chess's arm but she was still smirking.

Then we all stood there looking at each other, breathing in the sickly smell of cheap air freshener mingled with spices from the kitchen.

Outside, somewhere past the barbed wire, there was a scraping sound, as if someone had bumped into something metal and pushed it along the concrete. There was a low grunt. Nobody moved. The worried girl started to look even more worried.

Orange top said, 'We want to talk to you.'

'No way,' I said. 'Come on.'

I grabbed Chess by the other arm and yanked her away.

Chess wasn't happy. She followed me back into the restaurant but stopped up the back, among the dimly lit booths. 'What are you doing?'

'Keeping you safe. It's what I do.'

She made an angry flapping movement. 'That was Jacob's sister, Anna. I saw her online. And she had something to tell us.'

'Why would she?'

'Jacob told us to come here, didn't he? He must have had a reason.'

'He wouldn't have sent his sister.' I wasn't as sure as I sounded. 'She wasn't here to help us.'

'How do you know?'

'You can just tell.'

Chess made a snorting noise.

'And anyway, there was someone else out there.'

I didn't want to stand here arguing about it. I could see Mike was at the bar again, talking to Calvin. I started walking back towards them. 'They were going to do something to you.'

Chess said, 'You're imagining things.'

'Really? Well, Chess, maybe imagining things is how I stay out of trouble.'

Chapter 8

The next morning I woke to the sound of voices in the kitchen, right outside my door. I pulled my head out from under the pillow and opened one eye. Voices, one excited, one calm, and movement and the clinking of plates and glasses. I sat up and scanned the bed frame for clothes.

Chess was saying, 'He won't do it.'

The other voice was Jacob Langton's. As I dragged on some pants I heard him say, 'You tell him.'

Chess needed help. I went to the door with my socks in my hand. Jacob was standing behind a kitchen chair, clutching the back of it.

'That is my bed right there, you know.' I sounded like a sulky kid. But I had just woken up.

Jacob didn't look as if he'd slept well. His hair was dull and flat and in the cold light of the kitchen his skin was the colour of soap. He looked angry, ready to fight me about something.

And I just wasn't in the mood. 'Morning pikelets. Chess you are an artist.'

Chess put a plate on the table. 'Actually I'm not and it isn't.' She looked pointedly at the clock which showed it was half past twelve.

I got my brain into gear. It was Sunday. Mike had gone out to lunch with the winery people.

Chess said, 'And I know you don't like pikelets. But I'm sure you'll find something suitably sugar-laden in the cupboards if you go looking.'

We'd practised this routine before. Matt and Chess, being pally, having goes at each other. We do it with her father when he's in one of his moods. It was a message to Jacob from both of us that things would go better with a bit of normal behaviour. I got out the orange juice and three glasses. Chess pulled out a chair but no one sat down.

Jacob's shoulders were rigid under his clean blue T-shirt. 'You know what the key is, don't you?'

There was no point stuffing around. Through thick morning lips I said, 'Something to do with Tim. But you can have it back.'

'I need to find out who killed him.'

I started pouring the juice.

He said, 'Chess offered to help.'

'I don't see how we can.'

'You don't know anything about it, yet.'

It's always the same with that first mouthful of juice. It expands on your tongue, clean and cold, and you can feel the sugar seeping into your blood and suddenly your mouth melts into something that will move the way it used to.

'Chess's pikelets,' I said, poking at one with a finger. 'They kind of stay with you all day, know what I mean? And if there are any left over, they're good for sticking posters on the wall.'

Jacob didn't give even a glimmer of a smile. In fact the weak joke seemed to be enough to make him completely crack. 'Will you just let me tell you how it was? Will you just listen? Will you just do that?'

There was a vein bulging in the middle of his forehead. And when someone keeps saying the word 'Just' at you, making it clear that what they're asking is really, really tiny, it's hard to refuse.

'OK.' I tried to sound as if it was no big deal.

'Good.' His hands loosened slightly. 'Thanks.'

The trouble was, he hadn't thought beyond this point.

Eventually Chess said, 'Actually, I'd love to know about … the poison.' She glanced uncertainly at me. 'I do think it's the obvious place to start, logically speaking.' She was wringing her hands together, lacing the fingers through each other and twisting. 'I mean it's such an unusual way to die, isn't it? I would have thought in this day and age most poisonings involve drugs of some kind — party drugs or overdoses or spiked drinks. Cyanide just seems so old fashioned.'

Jacob looked a bit stunned. He wasn't ready to go into details.

'What if we go outside?' I said quietly.

'Yes.' Chess lunged forwards and grabbed my empty glass, grateful to have something to do. She put it on the kitchen bench.

We took the chairs out to a tiny wooden deck looking over a patch of unmown grass, a plum tree and a clothesline. It was a bit stupid being out here, but no one really cared. We were all thinking about what Jacob had to say. And at least there was a breeze.

Jacob still looked lost, and so wrecked — even worse than yesterday. I thought again it couldn't hurt to let him talk. But not about cyanide. I said, 'What if you tell us about Tim?'

'OK.' He leaned forwards, put his elbows on his knees and looked at the ground. 'What about him?'

'Well, we haven't heard much, but people say … and you said … he was a bit out of control or something.'

'Yeah. He did some stupid things. Dangerous really.' He looked up. 'But he didn't deserve —'

'No. No. I know. So ... what? Tell us about him.'

'OK. Tim.' He sighed. 'He was a good guy, he really was. But he got ... disillusioned.' He clenched his fists and stared at the bony wrists. 'It started in the last few years of school. There's a fair bit of pressure.' He stopped and thought again. Then he sat up. 'His sister was going out with a guy he didn't like. And his mother was ...' There was a sour smile. '... going out with a guy he didn't like. And his father had married this really young person and gone to Darwin and, I don't know.' He lost his train of thought. The hands unlocked and spread stiffly in the air. 'I mean you get really sick of being at school, you know? You get sick of uniforms and timetables and speeches about responsibility and being told you have the world at your feet and all the bullshit. Everyone does. But Tim seemed to get really bad. He started ...' He jerked his head if he was getting ahead of himself. 'One of the teachers had it in for him and, I don't know. He wanted a girlfriend. All these things get mixed up in your brain and you just see the bad side of everything.'

'I understand,' said Chess.

There was no way that was true but Jacob found it encouraging. 'He started reading stuff on the net and on the news and quoting it to everyone. If you go to enough rough looking places and try to find the worst thing you can, you'd be surprised what you turn up, behind all the shiny shops and the … bluebells.' He waved at a bit of unpainted lattice, up against the wall of Mike's garage. There weren't any flowers there but we knew what he meant. 'He kept saying the world was a rank unweeded garden. He really liked that. He said a lot of strange things.

'Mostly he talked about secrets. Especially the secrets of people at school, where everyone was supposed to be so pure. He said he was making a mental list of all the lies people told. My sister Anna. His mother. Her creepy boyfriend. Me. He just thought the whole world was corrupt.' He shrugged stiffly. 'It was part of his anger about his own life or something. Early on it was a bit of a joke, but then we got into the heavy study and the exams and the stress levels and it got more serious.'

For a minute Jacob seemed weighed down by his own sad thoughts. Then he said, 'When you're like that, when you hate everything, you start to love anything that's a bit dark — horror movies, pictures from wars. There's a kind of attraction. I don't know.'

'Like heavy metal,' I said. 'And Goths.'

Jacob laughed. 'Yeah? I wouldn't know really.' He looked at me with new interest. 'There aren't that many Goths in Beechworth.'

Well, they weren't that thick on the ground in Yackandandah either but I didn't want to go into that. What was I going to say? That I'd seen them on TV?

'Anyway, that was it, really. He started drinking — a *lot*. And smoking dope. And he kept stealing cars and driving around. He smashed a shop window with a trolley. You couldn't go out with him because it always ended in something like that. He stacked a car. Totalled it.'

'But your grandfather helped him?' said Chess.

'He talked to some of the people involved, paid for the damage or something.'

'Tim was lucky to have him.'

'Yeah. Maybe. We were half responsible, you know? He was living with us. Although Mum was talking about kicking him out.'

'I suppose no one knew what to do,' I said weakly.

Jacob gave a bitter laugh. 'Anyway, he started doing this art project. This big year twelve piece of work. He was going to do a model of the school and fill it with poisons. Real ones. I mean not spill them — put them into the model in little bottles or something. It was, you know, to represent the corruption of the place. So he collected all these poisons.'

'Poisons? Plural?' said Chess.

'Just things you can find around the place. Cleaning things, stuff you clear the drains with, and rat poison, that sort of thing. But one day he came in and said he knew this guy who could get him something more interesting.'

I said, 'Potassium cyanide.'

'Yeah.'

'Who?'

Jacob tugged at his T-shirt as if it had got twisted. 'No one. I don't know. Someone who works in a lab or something. In Queensland, Tim said, but that might not be true.'

'That's incredible,' said Chess.

'It's what he told me,' said Jacob stubbornly.

'What did you say about it?'

'What do you think? I told him not to be stupid.'

'And he didn't listen?'

Jacob twisted his face. He was straining to explain something he didn't really understand.

'In the end it came too late. He handed the art in without it. But when the bloke arrived he met him, like in a dark corner at night, and he bought the stuff anyway. He thought it was funny or something. He was kind of excited.' Jacob's head made a jerky sideways movement.

Chess said, 'So he had this cyanide and he didn't need it.'

Jacob didn't trust his voice to come out. His mouth pressed together in a tight line.

'What was he going to do with it?'

'Nothing. Make another piece of art. I don't know. Nothing he did was making any sense. It was all just theatre to him. Big gestures to make points. And he got a thrill out of it — meeting the lab guy in the car park, that sort of thing. He was … Look, at the risk of sounding like the school counsellor, he was just expressing his pain.'

'We all have pain,' said Chess disapprovingly. 'But we don't all go out and buy cyanide.'

'I'm not asking you to understand.'

'OK,' said Chess, 'so that's where the cyanide came from. And, correct me if I'm wrong, but there is also something else very significant in the story. You say Tim talked continually about other people's secrets. That would give someone a pretty classical motive to kill him. If he knew their secret. If the secret was bad enough.'

Jacob looked impressed. 'Yeah. That's what I think.'

'Tell us about the secrets.'

'I don't know. I think mostly they were just small things. Kids cheating at school, or teachers hooking up. Just stupid stuff. But he was talking about it a lot. He was yelling it out at the ball. He was going to expose someone's secret. The whole room heard him.'

'Pretty stupid, really,' I said.

'Yeah.'

Chess said, 'So a lot of people have secrets. And Tim was more or less threatening them all.'

'Yes.'

'Then it's going to be complicated, isn't it? To investigate this we would have to interview a huge number of people and cross reference the stories. It's going to be hard as billy-o.'

Jacob looked up when she said this and suddenly he looked more positive.

'But that's just it. That's why you have to see Elsinore. Because the truth lies in there. And it isn't complicated. It's simple.'

Chapter 9

'It's an exercise in logic,' said Jacob. 'When you hear the full story you'll see.' He sat back in his wooden chair and his face had more colour.

'It's opportunity, you see. That's what detectives talk about isn't it? Motive and opportunity? Well, with Tim talking about people's secrets, there might have been a lot of people with a motive to kill him. But opportunity narrows it right down. There are only a few people who could have got hold of the poison that night. It's going to be a straight process of elimination. It just requires a clear head.'

Chess's eyes shone. 'Maybe I should write this down.' She sprang from her chair and ran into the house, coming straight back with her notebook.

Jacob didn't look too sure about this idea. 'What if you just let me tell it once? You can do that later.'

'Yes,' said Chess. She locked her hands together on top of the notebook and leaned forward over them. Then she glared at him so hard he was probably wishing she was writing.

'On the night of the murder —'

'Just a minute!' Chess held up a hand. 'Can I make a suggestion? Just to make it easy for my poor brain.' She paused. That was meant to be funny. 'Could we keep it in strict chronological order? So far you've brought us to the time when Tim told you he had received the poison from an unnamed person.'

'He got it the night before the variety show,' said Jacob. 'He told me about it the next day. The afternoon of the show.'

'Really? And when you all went to the show, which was at the Beechworth Town Hall, the poison was left in your house?'

'It was left in a granny flat out the back, a separate little house, where Tim slept. He called it Elsinore. That's why I gave you the key. You need to look it over.'

'So this is how we're going to narrow it down? Yes, I'm beginning to see.' Forgetting she wasn't supposed to touch it, Chess opened her notebook. 'In fact I've already thought about this. The poison was administered through Tim's whisky flask. And in your email you said Tim had drunk from the flask earlier in the evening, so the poison must have been put in the flask during the show. So …' She drew a vertical line down her page, getting ready for a list. 'It's a matter of who could have got the poison out of your house, out of Elsinore, and then accessed the flask at the Town Hall.'

'It's even simpler than that,' said Jacob.

That felt like when a teacher says an essay or a maths problem will be simple. I never believe them either.

He said, 'We should go back to chronological order.'

Chess looked at him, pencil poised over the page.

'Don't write this down yet. Just listen.' Now that he was into the facts Jacob looked happier. 'As we were saying, Tim got the cyanide the night before the show and he showed it to me the next afternoon.'

'He showed it to you?' Chess looked shocked.

'It wasn't dangerous.' Jacob was amused. Better than being annoyed by Chess's constant interruptions. 'It was poison, not a bomb. It was in one of those white plastic bottles with a child-safety lid, like the pill bottles you get from the chemist. The day of the show, he showed it to me in his room.'

'Elsinore.'

'Elsinore. Then he put it in his undies drawer and we went out.'

'So someone —'

'No. Just wait. We got back about half past five. By then Tim's mother was around. She's living in Brisbane, but she'd started a thing with this Beechworth guy and she'd come down to watch Tim in the cabaret. Mum had invited her and the new boyfriend round for a drink before it started. When Tim and I got home everyone was already there and we went off to our bedrooms to get changed.'

'So who was in the house at this time?' Chess picked up the pencil.

'OK. So, the list of people there …' Jacob watched her write it. 'There was Tim's mother, Jane, and her boyfriend —'

'Who Tim didn't like.'

'Yeah.'

'What was his name?'

'Calvin.'

'Calvin? The guy at Luca's?'

Suddenly a lot of things became clear. This is why Jacob had wanted us to go to Luca's. To have a look at Calvin.

My eyes met Chess's. You could imagine Calvin as a poisoner. He had those dead eyes.

Jacob saw our faces. 'Yeah. Calvin Goldstone. Look, I'm not saying it was him. There are a few possibilities. I want you to work through it.'

'All right,' said Chess. 'Back to the list then.'

'So. Mum and Dad and Grandpa — Angus — were there. And Tim's mum Jane, and Calvin. And Tim. And me and my sister Anna. And Anna had a friend with her, Clare Bishop. She was also coming to the cabaret. They're about your age. Year ten.'

'Fifteen-ish at the time,' said Chess.

'Yes. Just let me tell you.' Jacob's eyes started to look hot and wet. This was the important bit. 'OK. So all these people were in the house. Tim and I were getting dressed in our rooms. When I was dressed I went out to see if he was ready. And while we were there Angus came to see us.' He paused. 'He had heard us.'

When he said this he sat back suddenly, as if it was some great revelation, and then he looked at us, waiting for our reaction. The he realised it needed more explanation. 'Earlier that afternoon! Angus was coming out to tell us something, but when he got to the door he heard Tim telling me say something — 'cyanide' or something. So he stopped and listened and heard about the jar of poison. He didn't want to burst in and make a scene. Maybe he needed to think about it. Probably he couldn't quite believe what he was hearing.

'But later on, that evening before the ball, Angus came out to talk to us about it.'

'What did he say?'

'He asked if he'd heard right and Tim said 'Yes' and showed him the bottle. It was labelled 'potassium cyanide' and 'poison' in big red letters.'

'I should hope so,' said Chess.

'So Angus said, "Is it real?" and Tim couldn't lie about that in case Angus just threw it in the bin or tasted it or something. So he said, yes it was real.

'Angus tried to give us a lecture. He isn't actually that scary. Really he seemed sad and worried about Tim. He asked Tim what the poison was for and Tim tried to explain about the art. Then Angus told us we were old enough to start behaving responsibly and did we have any idea how dangerous the stuff was and it wasn't a game.

'But then, while he was going on like that the two girls appeared.'

'That's —' Chess looked at her book. 'Anna, your sister, and Clare, a friend.'

'They'd more or less sneaked up behind him before he'd noticed, so they heard a lot of what he was saying. By the time Angus saw them they were just standing there stunned and Anna was kind of giggling. So Angus had to ask them to come and join us. He finished the lecture but then he didn't seem to have any idea what to do. He said you couldn't put cyanide down the sink or the loo or throw it into the garden because who knows what environmental damage you would do or what you would kill.'

'That's absolutely correct,' said Chess.

'He talked about putting it in the safe in Mum and Dad's room, but he didn't want anyone else to know about the poison so he couldn't really do that.' Jacob stopped, looking guilty. 'Actually you're not supposed to know there is a safe so forget I said that.

'In the end he agreed we had to hide it in Tim's room again, for the night, and dispose of it properly in the morning. But Angus said a drawer was a stupid place to hide it.' Chess nodded smugly. Jacob made a face. 'So he ended up hiding it behind some of the books in a big bookcase, right there in Tim's room. We all saw him put it in. We all knew exactly where it was.'

'And you were supposed to get it out in the morning.' Chess jabbed the end of the pencil into the book. 'But in the morning it was too late.'

Jacob was looking past Chess to the clothesline where a red shirt and some underpants were jumping around in the breeze. 'After Tim died we told the police about the poison and they searched the house. The poison jar was still there but the cyanide powder was gone. There was just a little bit of it sprinkled on a table.'

Chess said, 'Someone had come back that night with another container, and poured it in.'

'The point is, you see —'

'Only five people knew where the poison was,' said Chess in a thrilled voice. She started writing on a new line. 'Angus, Jacob, Tim, Anna, Clare.'

'The person he bought it from knew he had it,' I said.

'Good point,' said Jacob. 'But they wouldn't have known where he put it. When the police got back to his room that night the place hadn't been searched. And there was no time for anyone to search and then tidy up everything. And I'll tell you why.' He was picking up again. He leaned forward.

'Just a minnie,' said Chess. She help up a finger on her left hand, scribbling madly with her right.

Jacob froze and then shut his mouth. Our eyes met, but we didn't comment. To give her time, he looked down at his feet and the sharp black shadows of the chairs.

Finally Chess said, 'OK.'

'OK,' he repeated. 'Now listen to this bit. It's crucial. After the poison went in the cupboard, everyone left Elsinore. Three of us, Angus, Tim and I went immediately to the Town Hall. We had to set up Tim's act and Angus's drum kit and it was going to take a while. We were together all that time and there were other people there too. Then Angus was on stage all night and Tim and I were talking to people at the cabaret. Apart from trips to the toilet and things, we had alibis. No one had time to go to the house and back again.'

'The two girls, then.'

'After we left the granny house the girls went back inside for food and photos.'

'With your Mum and Jane and Calvin.'

'They all stayed for about an hour. But they were all together and, like us, once they got to the cabaret they were with other people all night.'

'Those alibis are a bit hazy. If everyone was running around at the cabaret it's hard to prove you never left. Except for Angus, if he was on the stage.'

'Yeah, maybe. But there's something else. Something that makes it all impossible.' He pointed at Chess's notebook as if this was a fact that should go in there. 'When everyone left for the Town Hall, someone else stayed behind in the house.'

'Who?' said Chess, excitedly.

'Calvin's kid was staying at our place for the night.'

I said, 'Calvin has a kid?' He didn't seem the parent type.

'I know,' said Jacob. 'But yeah, he does. Paz. And Paz was going to stay at our place while his father was at the show.'

'Why?' said Chess.

'It was something he cooked up with Tim. He doesn't like babysitters. I mean he's about thirteen or something.'

I was getting confused. 'He cooked it up with Tim?'

'Tim didn't like Calvin but he and Paz were pretty good mates, and Tim had said Paz could stay at Elsinore that night and play his Play Station. He had some new fantastic game or something. So at the time everyone left this kid went straight out to Tim's room and stayed there.'

Chess gave a little gasp.

'Yes,' said Jacob. 'He was sitting right in front of the cupboard all night playing his game, and he was awake right up until the police arrived at half past one to search the place.'

Chess nearly jumped out of the chair. 'But this is hugely significant. The only possibility is that the poison was removed in that short time between you all coming out of Elsinore and everyone leaving. Is that what you're saying? And that is a window of about half an hour. And in that little window there was no time for an outsider to get in, search the place, empty the poison into another container, tidy it up again and leave without being seen. So it must have been a person who knew where the poison was.' She looked at her book. 'One of the five.'

Jacob said, 'Angus and Tim and I didn't have any time at all. We went straight to the hall. We were together up until the show started and after that I was talking to people all night and Angus was on the stage. We didn't have time to get back to the house to get the poison.'

'And the only other people who knew about it, were …' Chess started a new line in her book.

'Anna and Clare.'

Suddenly, as if he was trying to get away from what he had just said, Jacob stood up. He stepped down onto the weedy lawn and went to the clothesline. He yanked at one of the wires. The red shirt jumped around as if it was struggling to get free.

Then he came back. 'Look, I'm not saying they took it. Obviously they're not murderers or anything. But they've got no brains. Especially Anna.' He stared at the old paling fence. 'They must have moved it, hidden it somewhere for a joke. Maybe they took it to the Town Hall or left it in the car or something.' He looked back at me. 'But I'm pretty sure they haven't told the police that. So how can the case get anywhere? Do you see?'

'What did they tell you?'

'Anna won't tell me anything. I'm her brother.' He started massaging the fingers of one hand. 'Look, I don't know. It probably isn't as simple as it looks. There'll be other things you'd come across as soon as you started asking questions. It just needs to be sorted out, that's all. It needs someone logical. Someone who can think rationally and won't get confused.'

Chess stood up. 'You want me to talk to them.'

'No,' I lifted a hand. 'No, Chess, OK?'

Jacob was nodding. 'I tried to get them to talk to you last night.'

'Those two girls?' I said. 'At Luca's?'

'That was Anna and Clare?' said Chess. 'The main suspects?' She glared at me. 'I knew we should've found out what they wanted.'

'We didn't know who they were.'

'Well, never mind now.' Chess's expression said she had to put up with my stupidity all the time. 'We'll just have to find them again, that's all.'

'And what?' I said nastily. 'You're going to interview them?'

'They didn't seem too bad.' She was lying. She hated girls like that. She turned back to Jacob. 'Actually, they probably wouldn't tell me much, but I'm sure Matt could handle them.' I started shaking my head but no one was looking at me. 'If Matt could charm them maybe they'd tell us something. Unfortunately there is one major obstacle.'

'What's that?'

'We've been sent here for a rest. If people suspect we're becoming involved in another mystery we'd be taken straight back home. And prolonged contact with your family would be taken as suspicious. If we're going to talk to your sister we need to wangle it so we meet them without anyone knowing.'

'You wouldn't have to see her at our place,' said Jacob. 'Anna's never home anyway.'

'It'd be too risky for her to come here though. Mike could easily find out. In any case he'll probably ask us what we're doing every day. We need a cover.'

'OK.' Jacob thought for a minute. 'What were you planning to do this afternoon?'

Chess shrugged. 'Matthew has ambitions to watch as many films as possible.'

They both looked at me. Then they looked away again. This thing had its own momentum now and they didn't want to be slowed down.

Jacob said, 'What if you decided to go to a ghost tour? Would that be considered normal?'

'Yeah,' I said. 'For ten-year-olds.'

'Oh, but we could do it,' said Chess, enthusiastically. 'We went to the open garden. Mike already thinks we're desperate for entertainment.'

'Right,' said Jacob. 'They have them up at Mayday Hills.'

'That's the old mental asylum,' said Chess to me. 'It's a fascinating —'

'Chess, I know.'

Jacob said, 'Go in the front gate and follow the signs to the Bijou Theatre. You don't have to actually do the tour. Just wait around the door. I'll text Anna. Make it two o'clock. There's bound to be a heap of kids around then. And if you just happened to run into a few people and get talking …'

'Perfect,' said Chess.

'You saw Anna last night? She's got blonde hair with streaks in it.'

'Oh we'll know her.'

And then, having decided all that, they picked up their chairs and headed back inside.

'Hang on a minute.' I stood up, grabbed my chair and followed them.

I couldn't believe this. A few minutes ago we were arguing about whether to even talk about the murder and suddenly it was all settled and Jacob was leaving. I put my chair back in place and stood facing them across the table. 'I haven't agreed to this.'

They looked at me as if I was speaking Martian. I sat down at the table, a big demonstration that this conversation wasn't over. And to drive that point home I picked up two pikelets, one in each hand. Oh yeah. I was having breakfast. Take that.

Now I didn't really know what to say. I looked down. 'We can't rush this,' I said to the pikelets. 'We have to think about what it might be like.' I looked up. 'Asking about a murder — it digs up a lot of bad stuff that wants to stay hidden. And people try to stop you. It's not a nice thing to get into.' It sounded weak. I remembered my big ideas the day before, about being involved and helping people.

Jacob could have gone into all that obligation stuff too. But he had a better answer. 'Everyone thinks I did it.'

There was a stunned silence.

'That's …' I was going to say it wasn't true but I remembered Mike's face the night before. Smug, half amused half disgusted. '*That's what I've heard.*'

'It's true. The whole town thinks I did it.'

My right hand shoved its pikelet into my mouth. It was as if it wanted to stop me saying anything.

He went on. 'I mean if you ask them they'll say they don't know but when they look at me, when I talk to anyone or walk into a shop — anything — it's there in their eyes. Have you any idea what that's like?'

He was gripping his chair again and now his hands had that whitish powdery look that means the skin is really dry, and underneath that they were a light purple. I don't know how much that told me about his emotional state —probably nothing — but it made me feel sorry for him. And once that starts it's hard to control. Suddenly I was thinking all the old 'Poor thing' ideas again. It would be bad enough having a friend die in front of you, and actually having handed him the thing that did it, and then having to see his parents, and be just swamped by how devastated everyone was. How much worse would it be if everyone thought you did it?

Chess and Jacob were standing quietly, letting me think all this through. I sucked the pikelet off the roof of my mouth. I heard myself saying, 'I guess we could go and stand around at Mayday Hills.'

They immediately started moving towards the door.

Mike's front path was about two metres long, surrounded by woody lavender and geraniums with long stalks and no flowers. There was a sparrow pecking at the hard ground. I threw it the second pikelet.

Under the trees there was a late-model Subaru Outback. Jacob moved towards the gate.

'Just a minute,' said Chess. She gave him a long hard look. 'You don't think it was Anna, do you?' She narrowed her eyes. 'Who do you think it was?'

He held his hands up and took a step backwards. 'Whatever I think, I might've got it wrong. I want you to come to it clean and find out for yourselves.'

But look,' he took another step towards the car. 'You don't have to commit. Just say you'll do one thing. That you'll go and meet two girls.'

'OK,' said Chess.

He went to his big shiny car and we stood at the fence watching while he backed out. I was wondering what we'd been dragged into and trying to tell myself we could handle it. Beside me the sparrow was standing over the pikelet, furiously shaking its head from side to side. It seemed to have its beak stuck.

Chapter 10

Mayday Hills sits on high ground above Beechworth. There are some big white buildings there, and a shady garden where we had picnics when I was a kid. It started as a mental hospital and it's been a lot of other things, but when Chess and I got there everything looked closed. At the entrance there was an old fashioned fence made of white wood with big knobs on top. It was slumping over at the end, where the gate had been ripped away.

As we went through, an old brown van went past. It rumbled around a turning circle, then stopped and the two people in it sat staring at us. One of them was big, like the guy at the Langtons' open garden. I couldn't be sure it was him. He was just a shape through a car window, and before I could say anything to Chess, they drove off. I told Chess about it but she wasn't really listening.

The signs to the Bijou Theatre took us down a long road, past big sloping lawns covered in trees, and then up behind the buildings. I'd heard people talk about the Mayday Hills asylum before and, like I said, I'd had picnics out the front, but up until now I'd had no idea of the size of the place. It wasn't just the backs of the white buildings. It was more like a whole town. There were cottages and houses scattered over a wide area, all old and shabby, with rickety verandahs and tiny dark windows. Some of them had labels — 'Store', 'Kiosk' and, oddly, 'Toy Shop'.

We ended up in a big empty car park and stopped.

'Jeez,' I said.

The building ahead was high, looming over us, derelict and sinister. The upper floor was dark pink and the paint looked as if someone had had a go at sandpapering it off. There were a lot of tiny windows leading to empty rooms. Right around the ground floor there was a covered walkway. Here the windows were boarded up and the doors had gone powdery with age.

Chess went to stand near a closed double door under another sign that said 'Bijou Theatre'. There were a few kids waiting for the ghost tour, running or standing around, shoving at each other, dropping chip packets, but despite them the place seemed quiet.

'Jeez.' I tried a laugh. 'There's no real need for a ghost tour, is there? The place is creepy enough on its own.'

'What do you mean?' said Chess.

I couldn't explain it. Through a gap I could see more of the empty buildings, more low walkways, more shady gardens and more of the small, blank windows. It felt ... Creepy isn't really the word. What this place made me feel was bigger than that. It was something to do with dying, and sadness, and years of lost time. You had the sense that the empty rooms went on forever.

Chess looked around for the girls from Luca's, then she got bored and pulled out her phone. Since Jacob left, she'd been Googling everything she could – images of the charity night and things about Rawdon School and the Langtons and Calvin Goldstone. She hadn't found anything useful yet, or she would have told me.

Two kids near us were doing zombie walks and laughing about mad people locked in small rooms. Not that long ago I was like that, able to make dumb jokes about stuff without realising how sad it actually was.

'Matt.' Chess was frowning at me. 'Just try to remember why we're here.'

I made a grunting noise. I still wasn't sure I even wanted to be here. I knew I'd agreed to help Jacob, and Chess was hopeless in the real world and needed someone to look after her, but now I was wishing we could drop the whole thing. I wasn't sure what I wanted. The truth is, my thought processes aren't always that clear. Most of the time they aren't even processes.

After a while the two girls came walking into the car park and saw us. The sunlight showed up the orange streaks in Anna's hair. She looked at Chess.. In the light coming off the walls and the phone Chess's face was a sickly colour. Anna nudged the other girl, Clare.

Look. No one ever said I'm a saint. It gets really old to be forever classified with the geeks and at times like this I don't always behave well. I threw a hand over my eyes and dragged it down my face, miming being annoyed by Chess. Even as I did it I knew I was being a traitor. But Chess didn't notice. She was scribbling something in her book. And maybe, in the cause of helping Jacob, she wouldn't mind.

OK, she would mind. And it didn't help anyway. Anna's sneer just widened to take me in and Clare looked unimpressed

Or maybe it had helped a bit. Anna's expression faded into a smirk and they came towards us.

I said, 'Hello.'

Today Anna was wearing a padded jacket in bright yellow-green with bits of black on it. The jacket was short and tight and under it she had a short tight singlet.

'Jacob sent us,' I said. 'He wanted us to meet you.'

Clare said, 'Matthew and ... Chess?' She bobbed down, trying to get into Chess's line of vision. When Chess looked up she said, 'I'm Clare.'

She had her hair done in sticking-out pigtails. Her eyes were ready for a laugh, but not in the same way as Anna. Ready for a nice laugh.

'So you're from Sydney,' said Anna.

'Yeah.' I said this quickly to stop Chess arguing.

I don't know where she got that idea from. Maybe Jacob told her. He probably thought it would give us some credibility. With someone like Anna Sydney is even more exciting than Melbourne and definitely better than Yackandandah.

'What part?' said Anna, with hard eyes.

If you're going to lie to someone it's important to answer with no hesitation and casually, as if it's no big deal. 'Cronulla,' I said. 'It's near Bondi.'

Which was probably not right, but they were the only two places I could think of. Out of the corner of my eye I could see Clare raising her eyebrows but she didn't say anything.

Anna seemed satisfied. 'Well it would've saved a lot of time if you'd talked to us last night.'

'Sorry.' I didn't mean it. If they'd really wanted to talk to us they could have done it out at the tables, like any normal person. But I didn't want to start an argument. 'I didn't realise who you were.'

'Is this going to take long?' Anna looked at her watch. The jacket squeaked and pulled tight around her elbow. A child's parka, too small, the colour of a tennis ball. 'Because we've got a thing. Haven't we, Clare?'

I knew other girls like this. Human Instagram. They made a big deal out of small events, talking as if everything they did was super-exciting, daring you to keep up with them or be labelled boring. Sometimes I try to draw Chess into conversations but today I didn't bother. She was never going to be friendly with these two. We were here for more important things and hopefully she'd be happy to listen and absorb everything.

Anna said, 'Jacob thinks we're just going to drop everything. It gives me the shits, it really does. Just because he has no life. Just because he doesn't want one.' She tossed her head, a movement that included a quick glance down over her front.

'He's OK,' said Clare.

Anna pulled a face. 'All he does is mope around all day — with Mum behaving as if he's about to die. I don't know how long he thinks he can keep it up.'

Clare said, 'He's had a rough time. He was right there when …' She glanced uncomfortably at me. 'We can't know what things are like for him.'

'Exactly,' I said. 'It's that Confucius thing, isn't it? Never criticise someone until you've walked a mile in their shoes.'

'Yeah right,' said Anna.

'That way, when you do criticise them, you're a mile away. And you have their shoes.'

Clare rolled her eyes. But for some reason Anna made a squeal of over-done laughter. She pushed me in the chest.

At least she'd stopped whining about Jacob. I seized my chance. 'There's a few things I need to ask you. Can we sit down somewhere?'

We found a seat in the courtyard, facing a low wall around a bed of ferns. Anna and I sat on the seat. Clare sat on the wall and Chess went on the ground, up against it. She bent her knees in front of her, showing that she wore thick socks with her running shoes.

Leaning on the wall beside her there was an old concrete plaque that said, *'THIS GARDEN IS DEDICATED TO ALL THOSE WHO HAVE LIVED AND DIED HERE.'*

I got a little bit of that spooked feeling again. Who dies in a garden?

'OK,' said Anna. 'Jacob says you want us to tell you about Tim Williams.'

'Yeah.'

'So what are you? Some kind of …' She stopped and made another tense little wiggle of her head.

'We're no one. We're just friends.' She still looked suspicious. 'Chess knows someone from your school.'

'Who?'

Chess said, 'Jeremy Smith.'

'Oh,' said Anna. She liked him. Lucky. She glanced for a millisecond at Chess and then back at me. 'Really?'

'And Jeremy's starting a blog. About unsolved cases.' I was lying my head off now. I waved a hand to show the details weren't important. 'For some subject. You know the kind of thing.'

Anna nodded.

'And we're stuck here for a week with nothing to do. So I told Jez I'd look into it. Tim's death might be something he could write about. I mean it seems pretty ... out there ... And it does seem to be the only thing anyone ever talks about round here.' I hoped that sounded like a Sydney person. 'So we ran into Jacob and we were asking him about it and he said you had a better idea. What people were saying. Around the town.'

I could have saved my breath. Anna didn't need persuading.

'Well we tried to talk to you at Luca's. We were sure it was you. Jacob described you really well.' She gave a meaningful look at Chess. 'He said you wanted to talk to us, and then you wouldn't. I couldn't see the problem.'

I said, 'Mainly it was the person outside in the alley.'

Clare looked at me sharply. 'What person?'

'Stomping around. We heard them kick a rubbish bin or something.'

'There wasn't anyone outside,' said Anna.

'Of course there wasn't,' said Chess. 'Matthew has a vivid imagination.'

But there had been, and the fact that they'd denied it worried me.

Now, because Chess had spoken, Anna was giving her a long blank look. I had to distract her. 'Well,' I said brightly. 'Here we are now. Talking.'

Anna was still looking at Chess. 'So,' she said, quiet and mean. Then she turned back to me. 'What exactly is it we're supposed to tell you?'

'I don't know. Everything. I mean it's probably not easy for you to talk about it. It must've been bad.'

'It was.' Anna instantly forgot about Chess. The story about the death of Tim was something she loved telling. 'It was ho-orrendous.'

'And you were both there?'

'Yeah!' Anna made her eyes wide, exaggerating the horror. She looked at Clare but Clare wasn't joining in so she turned back to me, shaking her head. 'God it was just the worst night.' She didn't really feel anything. She had described this a hundred times before. 'Tim was staying at our place. He was Jacob's best friend.'

'What was he like?'

'He was lovely,' said Anna. 'I mean insane, but really he was just this nice sweet guy.'

'You hated him,' said Clare.

'Clair-uh!'

'You called him a loser.'

Anna did another little ducking motion with her head and brushed at something on the green jacket. 'That's just things you say.'

Clare turned to me. 'He was basically OK. But he had started going pretty wild. He used to get really blind. He stole a car and wrote it off. And he graffitied the school walls.'

'Oh yeah,' said Anna. 'So ba-a-d. Except it was Shakespeare.'

Clare ignored her. 'There would've been other kids with him but they always seemed to get away.'

Anna said, 'Jacob stopped going around with him because there'd always be something going on. Plus Tim'd be really friendly and the next minute he hated you. He called Jake a spoilt wanker and then he'd go, oh Jake come out with me, and Jacob would be like 'no way' and then sometimes he'd have to go because they were mates and he wanted to keep Tim out of trouble you know.' She looked at a ring on her thumb and gave it a twist. 'But it was impossible.'

'Angus said he was unhappy,' said Chess.

Anna hissed.

'He was different,' said Clare. 'He really thought about things and knew a lot of stuff and he was funny to talk to.'

I said, 'Did you talk to him on the night of the ball?'

'Yeah. I sat with him for quite a while. I was probably the last one he had a conversation with.' Her face was genuinely sad. She wasn't trying to put it on.

'Did he say anything?' I said.

'What sort of thing?'

'I don't know. Anything that might be a reason for someone to ...'

She thought for a minute. 'He talked a lot about secrets.'

'That's what Jacob said.'

'He was in this crazy mood. I told the police all about it but I don't think they paid much attention. He kept saying he would like to disappear. He hated the world. He kept leaping up and yelling at the whole room, threatening to tell someone's evil secret and he said something about it on the stage, too.'

Chess wriggled her feet excitedly.

I said, 'He didn't say whose secret it was?'

'No. Lots of people I think. Like I said, he was in this mad mood, as if he was angry about something, but he kept trying to laugh about it. He said something about a crab going backwards.'

'What did that mean?'

'Nothing. Nothing really meant anything. Except one thing.'

'Yes,' said Chess eagerly.

'At least, it seemed to be significant to Tim.' Clare looked at Chess, as if she might be more help than Anna and me.

'What?' said Chess.

'He said 'one may smile and smile and be a villain.' He said it twice. Yelled it out.'

'Really?' I said. 'One may smile and smile…'

Chess started writing it down.

'… and be a villain,' said Clare.

'Who was that about?'

'He didn't say. He was quite into English. And drama. I think it's Shakespeare.'

'*Hamlet* again, I suppose.' Chess pulled out her phone to Google it.

'As if that matters,' said Anna. 'He was just a psycho.' She said this nastily, as if it was Chess she was insulting.

Chess had gone the dark colour, getting angry as well as embarrassed.

'Look,' said Clare quickly. 'Don't get too caught up in it. Tim just liked things that sounded good. He probably wasn't talking about anyone in particular.'

'Yes,' I said. 'But he must have known something serious, about some real villain, mustn't he? Because that person killed him.'

'Well, yeah. That's the theory.'

We fell into a sad silence.

'If you want the truth,' said Anna, 'he was actually extremely annoying. He'd had so much alcohol.'

'Oh, and you hadn't?' Clare smiled but there was sharpness in it.

'No.'

'You nearly made yourself spew.'

'Not that time.'

'It's every time,' muttered Clare.

Their eyes met and it started to look a bit serious — the kind of bitterness you get between people who used to be friends.

Anna glanced cautiously at me. 'I don't do that any more.'

I really wasn't interested. And I was starting to worry. If these girls were going to fight we wouldn't get anywhere. 'So what actually happened? Did you see him drink the poison?'

'Not really,' said Anna, resentfully.

Clare said, 'There were so many people there. By the time we realised something was going on, he'd fallen down and you couldn't see anything.'

'Penny Lusk saw it,' said Anna. 'He was thrashing around. He was red and gasping and he made a kind of gargling noise. His eyes rolled back until you could only see the whites, and his mouth fell open and he started dribbling.'

'Ohhh.' I didn't know what to say. Chess had frozen.

'Disgusting,' said Anna, flatly.

This was a bad place to be told a story of death. I looked around at all the walkways, the locked doors and the narrow windows. Everything looked closed off, abandoned, unfriendly.

I could feel Chess glaring at me in the hard way she does when she wants me to do something. Slowly I started remembering what we were here for. According to Jacob these girls were the only ones who could have got at the poison. It seemed bizarre, but I thought I might as well treat them as suspects. I started to look for a motive.

'So Tim knew some people's secrets and we don't know whose.' I gave a smile, trying to look admiring. 'What about you, Anna? You seem to be the kind of girl who has a lot of secrets.' That sounded sleazy. I hurried on. 'Maybe Tim was talking to you.'

She flicked at the end of her hair. 'Oh, I might have secrets. Quite a few actually. But Tim didn't know them.' She rubbed her hands across the seat then noticed the bird poo on it and snatched them up.

'So,' I said quickly, 'Tim knew secrets about a lot of people and we don't know who. Anyone could have had a motive. It's going to be hard … for Jeremy Smith's blog … to draw conclusions about who murdered him.'

I was planning to lead from here into the real thing we came to talk about, which was what happened at the Langtons' place before the show and how the poison could've been taken out of the bookcase.

But Anna surprised me. 'Oh everyone knows who did it.' She paused, enjoying the effect of her words. 'It was Calvin.'

Chapter 11

Chess crossed her legs and leaned forwards, chin up, listening. Clare looked at her curiously. She was starting to wonder exactly who we were and why we were so interested in this murder. Our story about Jeremy's blog was pretty weak.

'Calvin?' I said.

It hadn't occurred to Anna to wonder anything. She was enjoying this. 'You know who I mean. The waiter. Tim's mother's boyfriend. He's her ex now, but he was with her at the party. She was all over him. It's so gross when old people behave like that. But everyone knows it was him. He hated Tim.'

'Enough to kill him?'

'Maybe. If Tim was going to expose some guilty secret.'

'What makes you think Calvin has a guilty secret?'

'Have you met him?'

I wasn't going to agree straight away. 'I thought he was OK.'

Anna screwed up her face. 'Have you seen his car?'

'Anna.' Clare laughed. 'Not everyone has money you know. Some people are happy without it.'

'Oh fine. But he's not happy, is he?'

'He's not cheerful,' said Clare. 'Happy is different.'

'Anyway,' said Anna, turning back to me. 'It was definitely him. The police can't prove it but I know he did it.'

'How?'

'Because he was the only one who could have got the stuff.'

Chess made a sudden movement. I knew why. According to Jacob these girls were the only ones who could have got the poison.

A group of kids came around the corner and went through to the next courtyard. They were all talking and laughing at the same time, the kind of conversation where you can't really hear the words, so it sounds like a kind of excited howling.

Clare said, 'Perhaps we could start at the beginning.'

I gave her a tiny grateful smile. She seemed to like it.

And now Chess decided to speak again. She looked only at Clare. 'Jacob told us the logistics. Around six o'clock the poison was put in a bookcase in Tim's room and only five people knew where it was. Tim and Jacob and Angus and you two.'

'That's right,' said Clare. She opened her mouth to go on but Chess interrupted.

'And Tim and Jacob and Angus immediately left the premises and were together until well after the start of the cabaret. From that point they had alibis. Angus was on the stage. And none of them told anyone where the poison was.'

Clare nodded.

'But you two stayed longer at the house. And from the time your group left for the Town Hall, there was a boy sitting in front of the bookcase. And he stayed there all night. So that means the poison had to have been taken in the hour while you were still there.'

'What are you trying to say, Chess?' said Anna.

Chess swallowed hard.

'Well, you're pathetically off the track. For one thing we were not the only ones who knew where the poison was.'

'You're saying Calvin knew?'

'Yes. I am saying that.'

'You mean you told him?'

'As if.' Anna turned to me. 'I reckon he heard us talking. After we saw the cyanide we went back to the house and he was hovering around the kitchen.

Clare and I were saying something about keeping cyanide in a bookcase. Just to ourselves.' She raised her voice defensively as if we'd criticised her. 'Well, it was pretty surreal. I mean trust my family. Anyway Calvin was standing there. And he's just the sort of person who would listen to private conversations.

'Secondly.' She looked at Chess again. 'No one took that poison before we left. We were watching the granny house the whole time. The back of our house is all huge windows that look directly out at it. We were eating pizza with our fingers right there and then we were having photos taken in front of the windows. And a light was left on out there so you could see the granny house clearly. And we were always together.'

'Even Calvin?' said Chess.

'Calvin was taking the photos.'

'So he couldn't have stolen the poison.'

'Not then obviously.' She gave Chess another withering look. 'He went back later. You just haven't got that point, have you? He's the only person who could have.'

'Why?'

'Because the kid sitting in Tim's room all night was his son.' Anna was sick of sneering at Chess now. She turned back to me. 'Calvin's the only person the kid would lie for, isn't he? He must've come back, taken the stuff and told his kid not to say. It's the only way it could possibly have happened. Any moron could see that. So if you want to find out what happened, I suggest you talk to Calvin.'

'Where do we find him?' said Chess.

He lives in Warner Road. Have you got a little map?' She spoke as if Chess was mentally retarded. 'It's just down the hill from here. Some broken down old place. Not even a house really. More like a fire station or something. And the back of it is completely knocked down. You'll see it. Calvin works at Luca's on Sundays but they don't open until five.' She smiled grimly. 'Visit him. Ask him your questions.' She laughed. 'I'd love to see it actually.'

Three boys went across the grass near us. Trailing behind them was a little girl in a white tracksuit. She called out, 'Nathan! Listen!' She was holding a pamphlet for the ghost tour. The boys went into the door of the theatre. In the big bubble of silence that followed them, I heard the girl say, '*All that we see or seem.*' At that point she saw us sitting there. She stopped and looked me right in the eyes as if she was telling me something. '*Is but a dream within a dream.*' Then she stuck her arms out as if she wanted to fly, and ran to join her friends.

It sent a cold feeling down my spine. I told myself to concentrate. It was just a little girl spouting poetry.

'So,' said Chess. 'You maintain that Calvin hated Tim Williams so much he left the cabaret show and went to the house to get poison, then he took it back to the Town Hall and found a way to get it into Jacob's whisky flask. And he forced his son to lie about it.'

It sounded so simple when it was put like that.

'So why hasn't he been arrested?'

Anna said, 'How would I know? I suppose they can't prove it. I think he will be arrested soon.'

Or was there more to it than that? We had only just started this. Suddenly I had a feeling there was a lot we didn't know. Some large feeling, something to do with what the little girl had said and something to do with the empty buildings. I felt like there was a lot going on around us that we couldn't see.

Anna sucked in a breath and slung a little bag over her shoulder. 'Well ... just so the whole afternoon won't have been wasted, we're going down to meet some people at Zamkazan. Come on, Clare.'

Clare stood up.

'Wanna come?' Anna was looking firmly at me, not including Chess in the invitation.

For a second I actually thought about it. This was exactly what I would have wanted, to get in with some kids in Beechworth. Even if one of them was a pain, it would have been a start. I might have ended up finding other people. And Clare seemed nice. More than nice. For a second I even started telling myself that Chess would be happy going off and doing some of her own stuff.

But at that point my eye was caught by an object in the grass. Someone had dropped a book. I went and picked it up. I looked back towards the theatre door but all the kids had gone in.

It was a magic book. *Glorio Mephisto's Encyclopedia of Card Tricks.*The cover had the face of a man and a pair of white gloved hands. Around him there was a pack of cards, swirling through the air in the shape of a giant question mark.

'I'm gonna go.' Anna turned and walked away.

Clare waited a second but I just stood there staring at the book. The man's face was looking straight out of the page. His cheeks were flat and square and his eyes were droopy, outlined in black. But he had a powerful gaze, penetrating and kind of mesmerising. It was the look of someone who has some special type of knowledge, held deep inside his head, who knows something you'll never know.

'What is it?' said Clare.

For a second I stared dumbly at her. Then I showed her.

'Did someone drop it?'

I looked vaguely at the grass where I'd found it. 'Yeah. I suppose so.'

'Is there a name?' Clare took the book and opened the front cover. Then she looked at me. 'That's funny.'

Her face darkened and, like me, she looked around at all the quiet walkways and windows. 'That's really weird.'

I took the book back from her. Inside the front cover, in pencil, someone had written a name:

Tim Williams.

Chapter 12

'There! That was them again.'

'What?' said Chess.

'The van again. Up there. Weren't you looking?'

We were coming out of the Mayday Hills grounds and starting down the road towards town and the brown van I'd seen earlier had just gone slowly past us.

I said, 'When we got here they parked and stared at us. It was the guy who was hanging around in the garden. I think he's in that school photo. Anyway, they meant us to see them. It was threatening. And they're still here. They're hanging around.'

'Do you mean that old brown van?' Chess pointed down the road where the van had turned left and disappeared.

'Yes, Chess. You saw. They wanted us to see them staring. Who does that?'

We were heading towards that corner now, going past a garden of clipped bushes and swept paths. There was no one in sight. I looked nervously over my shoulder.

Chess spoke calmly. 'Were they actually staring at us? The second time?'

'The passenger looked this way.'

Chess smiled and nodded. She thought I was being an idiot. But I wasn't. Or maybe I was. After the atmosphere at the mental asylum, and finding that book, I had a weird feeling – that there was a lot of important stuff going on, just out of sight and all around us.

But I wasn't going to let myself lose it. I tried to focus. I focussed on a branch of purple flowers leaning over a fence and took a breath.

'All right.' Because of the nerves, I still sounded annoyed. 'Don't worry about it.'

We went past the corner where the van had gone and, of course, there wasn't anything there. The next corner was Warner Road. We turned into it.

It wasn't hard to find the place Anna had described. Number nineteen was not a real house at all. It looked more like a miniaturised community hall. Over the front door it had a brick porch with an arch, and on that there was a sign that said Wallace something and some dates. As Anna had said, the back of the building had been knocked down. From the side, we could see there was a bit of normal house and then a white fibro bit and then the building just ended, as if it had been chopped off.

'Could someone live here?'

'It'd be breezy,' I said. 'Let's go and see.'

'Well, yes, all right. But first — a few points on strategy.' Chess stopped walking and looked at me. 'This will be the second time we've seen Calvin. Obviously Jacob sent us to Luca's to observe him. Anna considers him to be a serious suspect and I think Jacob does too, don't you?'

It was very quiet here. Somewhere I could hear a lawn mower, which is usually a nice safe sound but I couldn't see where it was coming from and …

'Concentrate,' said Chess. 'We need to work out what we're going to say to Calvin. What's our goal for this interview?' She frowned at me. 'Come over here.'

We went across the road and stood outside a normal-looking house, looking back at Calvin's place. Next door there was a long building that looked like an old hospital or school. It was having some kind of major renovation. It looked as if everything inside it had been pulled out and chucked in the garden and then weeds had grown up through it all. Around it there was one of those temporary builders' fences, but it was Sunday and there wasn't anyone working.

'You know what?' I said. 'I'm starting to think this isn't a very good idea.'

Chess stamped a foot. Actually stamped it, like a bad actor. 'Don't be ridiculous.'

'I still reckon there's someone watching us.'

'Who?' She gestured wildly up the street. 'Where are they?'

'It just feels wrong.'

'Honestly!'

A car came along the street and turned into a driveway. It was yellow and contained only a very short white-haired woman.

'OK. You're probably right.'

Back at the intersection, another car had turned into Warner Road. It was a Commodore, one of the really old models.

'Come on,' said Chess.

There was plenty of time to cross. We stepped out into the road.

And then I stopped. In the old half-wrecked hospital next to Calvin's, just near the gate, there was a fridge, standing open, with a stack of old gutters leaning up against it. From behind that a man appeared.

He was tall and bulky, wearing a green rugby top with a light-coloured logo on the chest. It was the bloke who'd stared at me in the Langton's garden. This time he wasn't nearly as neat. His tracky pants were too low on his belly and sagged at the knees. His head looked large and bony and he was wearing one of those tight white beanies that look like a condom for the head. That exaggerated the big bones of his skull and the thick neck and jaw. He was looking in our direction.

I stopped in the middle of the road.

'What?' said Chess.

'That's the guy.'

'What?'

'It's him,' I hissed through my teeth.

The driver of the white car bipped angrily and frowned out the window as he went around us. The beanie guy came through the gate and stood facing Calvin's house. He shoved his hands in his pockets.

'He's just a builder or something. He's waiting for someone.' Chess didn't sound sure. But she straightened her shoulders. 'Come on.'

As soon as the car was out of sight Beanie turned his head our way. He took his hands out of his pockets. And that was enough for both of us. We turned to go back. Then we stopped again.

There had been a movement. A few houses away from where we'd been standing there was a big hedge and then a gateway under a little wishing-well roof. Just as we turned, someone had ducked back behind the hedge. There was something obvious and kind of stupid about the movement — Jim Carrey playing a spy — but that didn't make it any less scary.

Then, as we stood there, he stepped back out to the footpath and looked at us. He was short and chunky and stood with his arms slightly out from his sides, like a Russian weight-lifter. We turned back to Beanie. He was still staring straight at us.

And then just as I was calculating our chances of running like mad, we heard a voice say, 'Excuse me.'

Beanie turned around and looked behind him. Someone had appeared from up the side of the hospital. It was a woman in a dark blazer. She had white stockings and business-type shoes and she was carrying an iPad. Her hair was sprayed into a big round helmet.

Beanie tried to ignore her.

'I'm sorry but is that your vehicle?' The voice was clear with a hard edge that made it carry right out to us. 'You can't park in the middle of the space like that. Other people need access.'

Beanie turned to look at her.

'If you're helping with the pipe work you can park in Cork Street.' She stood there staring straight at him until he started moving and then followed him back up the side of the building.

I turned around. The other bloke had gone too. Chess and I backed the few steps off the road and watched while the brown van came out through the temporary fence and drove away.

'Right,' said Chess. 'Come on then.'

'What?'

'Let's find Calvin.'

'Chess, those guys —'

'It probably was nothing to do with us.'

'No. It definitely was.'

'What? What could they want?'

'Well I don't know.'

'And besides, they've gone.'

'Yes, but — '

'And if they do constitute a danger to us, then we're probably better off getting inside as soon as possible, wouldn't you say?'

Chapter 13

The porch of the Wallace building was littered with crisp brown leaves. The button for the door-bell was corroded to a white colour and wouldn't push in so I knocked, making a sound that echoed hollowly in whatever was behind. Nothing happened for a while, then the door was opened suddenly.

It was Calvin. He stood very still holding up a piece of toast, as if he was just about to take another bite. And he stayed that way for longer than was normal, his face set and expressionless, taking us in.

'I really hate Promite. Do you want this?' He thrust the toast forward.

Dumbly we shook our heads. Chess unhooked her bag from her shoulder and held it in front of her. It was a signal that we wanted to come inside. For a second Calvin stared at it the way he'd stared at us. His face was thin today and stretched tight across the bones, so that his mouth seemed to push forward from his cheeks. He rubbed a hand hard over the fuzz on his head then stepped back and let us in.

We went into a corridor of grimy white paint with one door on the left and two on the right. Past the doors, the walls ended. There was a roof over a big empty space and no back wall at all. Calvin took us into the room on the left which was huge. It had two old armchairs and a TV on a table against the wall but they were all a long way apart. They looked separate and unused and lonely, like things in a museum. There was one window covered with a dusty venetian blind. Through holes in the ceiling we could see wires and woodwork and empty spaces.

Up in a far corner, sitting at a scratched table, was the kid from the Langtons' garden. The one with the magic trick and the bright orange hair. Calvin muttered 'Paz' and something about being back in a minute and went towards an open doorway. Through there we could see a microwave on a bit of old bench. It was another room with no back wall.

Paz was facing us but looking down. In front of him there was a book, held open with the end of a chopping board and while he read it he was fiddling with a coin. He had one elbow on the table with the forearm going straight up and with his other hand he kept scooping the coin off the edge of the table, rubbing it on his forearm and letting it drop. He didn't seem to know he was doing it. He kept reading the whole time.

Through the door we could hear Calvin making kitchen noises. I could see a sparrow near his feet.

Paz glanced up at us, looked back down, scooped up the coin again, rubbed it into his arm and removed his hand. The coin had disappeared. He put his hands flat on the table and stared at us.

At that point Calvin came back. He had a new piece of toast, this one with just butter.

'Welcome to the Goldstones'.' He looked around. 'Pretty bloody depressing, isn't it.'

'No, it's nice,' said Chess quickly. 'Are you renovating?'

'We're security.' He turned away. 'Come up here. I'm late.'

He led us back out to the corridor. There must have been a shower somewhere because the air was damp and smelled of shampoo, although I don't know what Calvin could've used that for. We found him in the second room on the right, another big white room. This one had a mattress on the floor.

Calvin went over to the window. 'Paz's got the heater in his bedroom because he says he needs to do homework.' He lifted the toast to his mouth, sneered at it and dropped it into a waste paper basket beside the mattress. 'He won't live with his mother. Not that you can blame him.' Instead of a doona, the bed had an opened-out sleeping bag, bright blue and old. Calvin tugged at it, straightening out a lump. 'It's a complete con. He never uses his room. He just sits out there all day.' He looked past us, through the door. 'He's a clever little bastard. Watches people, you know? Very irritating to live with.'

I huffed a tiny laugh. Calvin turned his gaze to me. His eyelids were half lowered. 'And his taste in music is right up his arse.'

Chess and I glanced at each other. It was impossible to find an answer to that. But I was starting to see one thing. We didn't have to worry too much about how to approach Calvin. He wasn't the kind of person who expected small talk.

So I thought I'd jump right in. 'What we're here for —'

'I know what you're here for.' Calvin's lips turned down at the ends. 'Little Miz Langton. What's she been telling you?'

'Ms —?'

'Anna Langton. You saw her an hour ago, up at the ghost tour.' He saw the looks on our faces. 'Paz was there. Didn't you see? No? He must've had a hat on. I told him. You can't have hair like that and get away with things.' He stopped as if he'd forgotten what we were talking about, then remembered. 'He was there with his mates. Not that he's got any real friends. He's too serious. And too nosy.'

'The reason we're —'

'Murder,' said Calvin. 'You're investigating the murder.'

'How do you know that?'

Calvin shrugged. 'Not hard to work out. With your background and the way you were going on last night, talking about the Langtons. Then meeting Anna. Twice.' He folded his arms and leant back on the window sill. 'I suppose with your recent triumph in Yackandandah you fancy yourselves as experts.' He hissed through his teeth.

'Not really,' I said, weakly. His attitude was making me more curious about how he fitted into things, but it was hard to know how to take it from here. I had the feeling whatever I said he'd interrupt.

'Yes.' Chess stepped towards him. 'Something like that.'

Calvin stared at her with lowered lids and a sour mouth. 'All right. And Ms Langton's been accusing me, has she?'

Chess dropped her bag on the bed, making an airy little whump into the sleeping bag. 'She said we should ask you a few questions.'

He did another miserable laugh and shook his head, as if he couldn't believe how ridiculous this was. 'What sort of questions?'

'OK.' Chess gave a little wiggle, preparing herself for a long discussion. 'On the night Tim Williams was killed, you attended the variety cabaret as partner to his mother. You were her …' She didn't have a word for it.

'Yes.' Calvin's eyes were like a window with the blinds down.

'What about Tim? How did you get on with him?'

'He didn't like me.'

'Why not?'

'I don't know.' He looked back at Chess. 'Do you like me?' When she didn't answer he muttered down towards his hands, 'I'm gonna go to that charm school and ask for my money back.'

'Nevertheless,' said Chess in her worst know-all voice, 'the world is full of bad relationships. They are not in themselves enough to provide a motive for murder.'

'Well, I'm relieved you see it that way.'

'That's not to say you didn't have a motive.' Chess stepped towards him. 'Apparently, for several days before he died, Tim was saying he knew things about people — people's nasty secrets.'

'Stupid kid.' Now, just for a second Calvin sounded sad.

Chess didn't notice. 'It's a classic motive really. Someone may have killed him to prevent their terrible secret coming out.'

Calvin lifted off the windowsill and half-turned, scowling out at a scraggy bush.

'Do you think that could be the case?'

He made a sad little noise through his teeth. 'Yes. I think it could.'

Chess nodded in a satisfied way, as if she had extracted an important confession. 'In particular, at the charity show that evening he shouted something out across the whole dance floor. He said, "*One may smile and smile and be a villain.*"'

She left a long pause here. Calvin turned around sat back on the windowsill, staring down at his hands. 'It's *Hamlet.*'

'You know the phrase,' said Chess, accusingly.

'I've seen the Mel Gibson movie.'

'Apparently Tim said it as if it meant something.'

'Well yeah. It probably did. Just not in the way you mean.'

'What then?'

Calvin's mouth made a little sad grimace. 'Sometimes a play or a movie or whatever just gets through to you. You know? It makes you feel you're not the only one.' He waited, saw we didn't get what he was saying and went on. 'For Tim it was *Hamlet.*'

'What about *Hamlet*?'

'Well, if I remember right, Hamlet was this young guy who thought everything was corrupt and he was generally pissed off. And he was confused and couldn't work out whether or not he wanted to die. So he went around making a lot of trouble for everyone and in the end someone poisoned him.'

This was how Jacob and Anna and Clare had described Tim. There was a silence in which we all thought about him.

'But that's not what he meant by the line, is it?' said Chess. 'Whether or not he could identify with Hamlet isn't really the issue.'

'You tell me,' said Calvin.

'He was accusing someone of being a liar and a villain.'

Calvin gave her a thoughtful look that had a touch of admiration in it. 'Look. Beechworth people are like people everywhere. There are all kinds. Tim knew things about teachers and shop keepers. And what about Helen Langton? Or Jacob and Anna, the dear little innocent things? Tim could've been talking about any of them. One may smile and smile and be a villain.'

'It could have been you.'

'Have you seen me smile yet?' He dragged some air in through his nostrils. 'OK, look. We can talk about the night of the poisoning. I really don't care. But first of all, just let me tell you one thing.' He looked at me. 'You shouldn't have anything to do with this. It's dangerous.'

'In what way?' I said.

Calvin laughed sarcastically. 'Well, let's take a wild guess — that meat-head hanging around my front door for example, could he have had anything to do with it?'

'Do you know him?'

'Grif Griffiths? Don't let the charm fool you. He looks like a brainless thug because that's what he is.' He sighed. 'In fact a lot of people involved in this are dangerous.'

'Except you of course,' said Chess.

Calvin raised one eyebrow. 'I have my moments.'

'But you don't really think Anna's dangerous,' I said. 'For example.'

'Well she's no Einstein, and a Code Four bitch … sorry.' He sighed and thought for a minute. 'No. She'd like to think she was dangerous but she isn't. At least she's nothing compared with Grif. That's my point.'

'I'm not afraid of people like him,' said Chess.

'Well that's just stupid.'

'I'm sure you'd like us to give up. I'm sure you don't want to be asked questions about that night. I'm sure you wish we'd just go away.'

'No. Well, yes. But that's not what I meant.'

Chess said, 'All right. Thank you for your concern. The warning is noted.'

'And we agree,' I said. 'Big No to danger.'

Chess's eyes narrowed. 'But I'd still — seeing as you don't mind — I'd still like to hear about your movements on the night of Tim's death.'

Calvin stared at the wall. There was a place where a poster had been removed, leaving Blu-tak marks.

He said, 'OK. If you're going to let Jacob Langton manipulate you into some stupid detective game, I can't stop you. I can only give you my opinion. Just be careful, that's all.'

'Would you please tell us the events of that night? Your version.'

'All right. Firstly …' He was talking resentfully, as if Chess was somehow making him tell her this. 'Anna and her little mate were talking about cyanide and a bookcase. Fair enough. But I did not immediately make a plan to come back and steal it. I didn't have a reason. And I don't think that quickly. I didn't even take it seriously. It sounded like all their conversations, completely meaningless. At the time I didn't even realise exactly what they were saying.' He paused and looked at Chess. 'But I can't prove that.'

'Knowledge or the lack of it is generally difficult to prove conclusively.'

'Is that right?' he said drily. 'So. We all did photos and we went from there to the show. No one had time to go out to Tim's room and we would've seen them if they did.'

'That's not relevant,' said Chess. 'What we're interested in is the possibility that someone returned at a later time.'

'And Anna reckons that I've come flying back from the Town Hall and got the poison and made Paz lie about it.'

'That's right.'

'And she doesn't think the police would ask me about that?'

'No one seems to know what the police are doing.'

He laughed. 'Yeah. You're right there.' He rubbed at his head, leaving a red mark. 'OK. Look. I had no opportunity to come back to the house from the Town Hall. Apart from a couple of two-minute toilet breaks, I spent every second of that ball with Jane Williams. She never left my side. This story will be confirmed by Mrs Williams.' He looked coldly at Chess. 'That's Mrs Jane Williams, the victim's mother.'

'And your girlfriend.' Chess blushed at the word.

'What's your point? If she loves me she might lie to protect me?'

'It's possible.'

'Even if I killed her son?'

'It might be unlikely.'

'Unlikely!?'

'It's not unprecedented,' said Chess. 'Women have been known to lie for men they loved.'

He curled up one end of his lips. 'Unfortunately for that theory, Mrs Jane Williams never loved me like that. And even if she did, she doesn't now. As a couple we are no more.' He shook his head and stared at the floor. 'Fortunately for me she didn't let that get in the way of the truth. She told the police I was at her side the whole night and I'm definitely innocent. She's gone back to Brisbane but I'll give you her phone number if you like.'

Chess thought for a minute. There was something she wanted to ask. She sent me a pleading look but I didn't know what it was. She took a deep breath. 'Why did you break up?'

Calvin made a pained face. He waved a hand. 'Just part of life's strange mystery. At the charity night Jane was so crazy about me she couldn't part with me for a second. And now it's over.'

'There must be a reason.'

'Oh!' His voice was high and hard. 'A reason!'

In the other room Paz had switched on a radio, or maybe it had been on the whole time and now I was aware of it. Some pop song came through the door, muffled by distance in that way that makes any music sound sad and lonely.

Calvin said, 'Have you ever had a boyfriend?'

'No.'

He sighed again and now behind the resentful manner you could see real pain. 'She doesn't think I'm supportive. I'm not supportive. We were just having fun together. Nothing bad was supposed to happen.' He sighed very sadly. 'I couldn't help her, that's all.'

'Did you try?'

'I didn't love her.'

There was a shocked silence.

'What do you want me to say? Maybe things are simpler than this in Yackandandah. Tim was a good kid. It's very *very* sad. How's that supposed to turn me into a saint?'

'It isn't,' I said.

But Calvin wouldn't be comforted by me. The whole connection with the Williamses had been bad for him and he didn't want to be forced to think about it. He took a step towards the door. 'Anyway I'm late, so if you've finished …'

But Chess hadn't finished. She had a calculating look in her eyes. 'So you and Paz are innocent.'

Calvin went past her. 'We're "two, two the lily white boys".'

'In that case you'd be hoping someone would find the murderer.'

He stopped in the doorway. 'I hope someone *else* finds the murderer.'

'You said yourself, you didn't mind us asking questions.'

'Only because I can't stop you.'

'And similarly you won't mind if we talk to Paz.'

He opened his mouth in a silent 'aah', recognising he had been trapped. Then he made another hissing noise through his teeth but he couldn't think of anything to say.

Finally, as if he'd completely forgotten about the whole of the previous conversation, he spoke to me. 'One of life's romantics, that's Paz's problem.' He pointed to the wall beside the door. 'See that stain? He reckons it looks like a pine tree.'

It was weird the way he changed subject. It was some kind of trick — a way of keeping us confused or hiding things.

The stain he was looking at was rust-coloured and vaguely triangular.

'It's a three-eared dog, isn't it? Anyone can see that.' He pointed to a jagged edge. 'Got a bit of acne, maybe, and the tail's bent, but that's what it is.'

I gave an uncertain laugh but Calvin had already left the room. We followed him up the corridor. As he went through the front door we could hear him still muttering. 'But it's not a pine tree. That's just stupid.'

'All right.' Chess called after him as if something had been agreed. 'Thank you.'

Then the door slammed and we were left in the airy, empty house, with Paz.

Chapter 14

You would never have picked Paz for Calvin's son. He was pale and plump and he had all that bright red hair. Today his T-shirt was yellow with a row of green stars around the middle.

He stopped reading, pushed the book next to a notebook and pen and watched us come in. In his hands he had a pack of cards and he was shuffling them without looking. He kept doing it while he spoke. 'Don't worry about Dad. He's like that with everyone.'

That was like his father — the abrupt jump into a topic with no mucking around.

'He is quite a sour puss,' said Chess.

'It's not his fault. He's had a lot of disappointments.'

You have to feel sorry for a kid who needs to make excuses for his parents — I knew a few of those including, come to think of it, me.

'No. He's good.' I laughed. 'You should see my dad.' My father was the grey beard, straw hat type. He wore tie-dyed T-shirts and loose surf-brand shorts with flowers on them.

Paz didn't smile. 'He thinks he's an anarchist. But his problems are psychological not political.'

It was a funny way for a kid to talk. And Paz had thick lips and a soft lisping way of speaking that made it even stranger. While we were talking he'd been moving the cards, rolling them over and over, passing them, one at a time, from the top of the pack to the bottom with clean little clicking sounds.

'We came here to ask questions.' Chess stepped closer to the table.

Paz gave her a long stare. There was another thing that reminded me of his father. The closed look in his eyes. Actually there was a difference. They both hid their thoughts but Paz was more watchful. If Calvin's eyes were like windows with the blinds down, Paz's were like one way glass. You couldn't see in but he could see out.

He'd had the same expression in the Langton's Garden the day before. And the thought of that made me remember. He had been standing with Grif Griffiths.

It was very quiet. The room was full of grey shadows with whitish light coming from the open doorway.

Chess said, 'Your father said we should talk to you.'

'He thinks I should have more friends.'

I said, 'What about Grif Griffiths? Is he a friend of yours?'

He looked at me with his mouth open.

'I saw you with him yesterday in the Langtons' garden.'

'No he's not a friend.'

'Never mind that,' said Chess. 'We came to ask about Tim Wilson. Your father said it would be OK if we talked to you.'

Paz nodded. 'He lets me fight my own battles.'

'Why would it be a battle?'

He gave us the blank stare again.

We were doing it all wrong. This kid didn't know us and he had played a key part on the night of the murder. He would've been asked about it a million times. If we were expecting him to go over it all again, we'd have to give him a reason. At least he'd have to feel he knew us a bit.

I said, 'You're good at that.' I nodded towards the cards in Paz's hands and edged closer, getting between Chess and the table.

'Yes.'

'Do a lot of magic?'

'Oh yes.'

'We found a book about magic at Mayday Hills today.' I got the book out of Chess's bag and pushed it across the table. 'It's got Tim Williams's name in it. You were mates of his weren't you? Did you drop it while you were up there?'

'Keep it. You might find it interesting.'

He pushed the book back and we looked at the magician on the front. One hand was out in front of him, palm upwards, drawing unseen powers from the air.

I said, 'I saw you at the Langtons' yesterday. Did you and Tim do magic together?'

Paz gave me a wary look. 'Tim had a more theatrical style. I like small tricks with cards and everyday objects. Street magic. It's less commercial. It's anti-commercial. I'm a populist.'

'Is that what you're doing now? Practising tricks?'

His eyes went to the cards. 'You can't start with tricks. You have to work on the fundamentals. It's very laborious.' When he used the big words he exaggerated his own lisp, almost as if it was a joke.

'Can you show me a trick?' I used this question to sit down. Close up I could see his hair was dyed unevenly and waxed into ragged tufts.

He seemed to be thinking about my question. He put the pack in one hand and squeezed it, causing the cards to fly one at a time into the other hand. It made a sound like a bird fluttering. Finally, bringing his chair closer to the table and putting the cards in a perfect pile in front of me, he said, 'I'll do you one of my old ones. It's called Can I Trust You?'

Was there a message there? I didn't know, but it felt like progress. I leaned forward and smiled. Beside me Chess pulled out a chair and sat down.

'You mean Can We Trust You?' said Chess. 'Surely you're the one who's going to try to trick us?'

Paz ignored her. He started dealing the cards onto a pile, face down. 'Tell me when to stop.'

The backs of Paz's cards were covered in white masks. After five or six cards I opened my mouth but Chess put a hand on my arm to make me wait a bit longer. She left it there until about ten more cards had been dealt and then, with a smart air, as if she'd now made it hard for Paz, she said 'Stop'. Chess was that sort of person. If you say you're going to trick her she'll automatically try to ruin it.

But Paz wasn't worried. His eyes met mine with a tiny smile. He flicked up the next card, holding it out so that we could see it and he couldn't. 'Hold it and don't tell me what it is.'

I took it. The card was the King of Clubs.

He pushed the notebook and pen across. 'Write it down.'

Chess held the book below the level of the table. Then, before she wrote she turned her back so there was no chance of him seeing the pencil strokes.

With another small smile at me Paz looked the other way. When she turned back he said, 'Keep the page where I can't see it. Put the card back.' Still looking away, he held out the pack for me. I put the card back in and he shuffled them and put them down again. 'OK. Now I'm going to find the card for you.'

With one smooth movement he fanned the cards evenly out, face down. Then he stared at the backs of them.

I was secretly thinking this was a bit weak. He couldn't see what Chess had written, that was all just a distraction. But it wouldn't have been hard to have the whole pack pre-marked. I was pretty sure Chess was onto this too. And she wouldn't be tactful about it. When the trick was finished she would inspect the card carefully in front of him.

Paz was moving his hands in the air above the cards, as if feeling for some secret vibration. Soon he grabbed one and held it up for us again so that he couldn't see it. 'This one,' he said, grinning.

It was the seven of hearts.

I shook my head.

'Oh.' He was surprised. 'Really?'

'That's not it,' said Chess.

Paz pressed his lips together. He thought for a minute. 'OK.' He stared at the back of the offending card, frowned and put it face down to one side. Then he picked up the pack, shuffled them and spread them as before.

But it was all going wrong. He touched the back of a few and then looked up with a hurt look. 'I can't ... I don't get it.' His voice was small and weak. His colour rose and now you could see how young he was. Finally he looked over at the face down seven. 'It wasn't that one?'

'No,' said Chess.

It was getting embarrassing. He looked at her. 'Are you sure?'

'Yes.'

'Perhaps we could just ... Could I see what you wrote?'

From her lap Chess produced her piece of paper. She unfolded it, showing the words 'King of Clubs'.

'Oh-h-h.' Now, something had annoyed him. 'Hang on.' He looked carefully at Chess's face and then at the face down card. He put a hand to it. He lifted one corner and peeped. Suddenly he sat back and folded his arms. 'Well fine,' he said. 'If that's the way you want to be.'

'What?' said Chess.

He looked disgusted. He pushed the face-down card towards her. 'You don't look like a liar.'

'What do you mean?' Chess was annoyed. I turned the card over. It was the King of Clubs.

Suddenly Paz was grinning.

I laughed. 'Get it Chess? He can't trust us.'

Chess narrowed her eyes. She was looking from the spread pack to the single card and then at her piece of paper, but she couldn't see how it had been done.

Finally she decided to admit she was beaten. She even managed to sound admiring. 'That was very good. It really was.' She returned the card to the pack and pushed it to one side. 'Now. A few questions.'

Paz was studying her, as if he could see her mind working. His father had said he watched people. He used all those big words. But a minute ago he had seemed young and confused. The kid was a born actor. One minute he was the little boy then suddenly he was the smart operator, and he slipped easily from one to the other. You couldn't work out which was the real Paz and which was the act.

Chess said, 'You saw us at Mayday Hills around two o'clock, with Anna Langton and you told your father about it.'

Paz picked up his cards again and started fiddling with them.

Chess said, 'Did your father tell you what he thinks we're doing?'

'You're trying to find out who killed Tim.'

'Yes, we are.' Chess looked at me. 'And as you no doubt know the biggest question is, who could have removed the cyanide from the bookshelf in Tim's room?'

Paz watched his moving hands.

'And, just to jump right to the crucial point, it's pretty clear that no one could have taken the poison before everyone left the Langtons' for the Town Hall.'

There was a silence. From the kitchen came an electronic hum, then a shuddering sound with a few bottles clinking together. An old fridge starting up.

'And Anna says you were sitting in Tim's room from the time everyone left until they all got home again, that is, right through the time Tim was actually being poisoned.'

'I was.'

'Then you must have seen who came for the poison.'

'No.'

Chess sat back. 'Well, you do see what a difficulty that causes, don't you? We have an impossible situation. Either the family are wrong, or they are lying, or you are.'

'I'm not.'

Chess gripped the sides of the table, thumbs underneath, fingers out in a row. She leaned over them. 'Of course, we'll go back over everyone's stories again —'

'Can I just say ...?' I tried to make my voice gentle. 'We know it's not your dad. He has an alibi and the police would definitely have checked all that. But if it's someone else, if you're protecting someone, Paz, if someone came back and got that powder and you know who it was, that means you're one of the key witnesses. Do you see?'

Paz was doing harder exercises now, splitting the pack, making the two halves swap places, all with one hand.

'It's a very dangerous position to be in.' I tried to shock him. 'Chess has the burn marks to prove it.'

He glanced at Chess's arms, hidden by long sleeves, and then back at me. 'Is that why she's always so angry?'

'Angry?' Chess said that in an angry way which made me smile. And for a second I wondered. Was that what he saw, behind her tough act?

Paz looked steadily at her. 'I'm not protecting anyone.'

'Maybe you left the room for a while,' said Chess. 'Went to the loo or something.'

He put the cards on the table. 'The toilet was in the next room. I left the door open. I would've heard if anyone came in.' He paused and went on. 'And yes, the Play Station was making a noise but I only did a wee. Even if they'd been really quiet there wasn't time for someone to get in, unlock the bookcase, pour the stuff out of the bottle into something else, shut the cupboard and get out again.'

Like I thought, he'd gone over this a hundred times before.

'And you didn't go to the house at any stage?' said Chess.

'I had snacks with me. Water, blankets, snacks. I had it all with me.'

'You couldn't have —'

'I was playing *Bloodborne*. You don't fall asleep.'

His quiet confidence was starting to get to Chess. 'You do see, don't you, that there is one more possibility? That you're lying to save yourself. That you took the poison, ran with it to town, or stole a car, or passed it to someone.'

'I can't run that far and I can't drive.'

He was perfectly polite but the shortness of his answers made them sound stubborn.

'And this is what you've told the police?'

'Yes.'

Chess looked at me. 'No wonder they're not getting anywhere.'

'Yep.'

'So what are we left with? A jar of extremely deadly poison which somehow …' she waved a hand, '… *dematerialises* from Tim's cupboard and magically *rematerialises* two kilometres away, inside a room full of people.'

I wanted to tell her getting mad wouldn't help. The kid was obviously lying to protect someone, or else he was intimidated.

Paz jumped subjects again. 'Tim liked magic. He saw me performing in the street one day and asked me to teach him some. That's how I met him. That's how Dad met his mother.'

'Well that's nice,' I said lamely.

'Not really. Their relationship was dysfunctional.' Paz's hand went to the cards again. He fanned them out in one hand then closed them. 'Tim wasn't happy. He hated the world. Sometimes he didn't want to exist any more. He just wanted to disappear. I mean we all get like that, don't' we?' He looked at me.

'I suppose.'

'I made a trick in his honour.' He said it uncertainly, again like a young child afraid of rejection. Or was he just acting? 'Would you like to see it?'

'Yeah, why not?' I thought if we watched another trick he might decide to talk to us. At least it might give Chess a chance to calm down.

He said, 'I call it the Elsinore Vanish.'

'Why?' said Chess. 'Why Elsinore?'

Paz smiled at a secret joke. 'Doesn't matter.' Then he hurried on. 'OK. Please point to a card.' He spread the pack out again, face down.

Like before, he held swept the cards into a pack, holding up the one I chose so that he couldn't see it. Three of spades.

'Now watch closely.' He put the card back in the pack. Then he shuffled and put the pack in a pile face down.

There was something in his face that reminded me of the picture on the cover of the book — a look in his eyes that meant he knew things other people didn't, that he was in charge. This was why he liked doing tricks, I thought. It put him in control.

'Tim was learning to make himself disappear,' he said quietly. 'His stage trick was very basic but he was trying to work out how to improve it. He practised a lot with cards.' He looked up with a faint smile. 'And he taught me. The card you saw it's in there somewhere, right?'

'Yes.'

'Put your hands over the pack.'

I did what he said, covering it so that it was completely hidden.

'Good. You have big hands.' He nodded for a while, looking at me, then he quietly sat back. 'OK. That's it.'

'What?'

'It's done. It's gone.'

'What?' said Chess.

Gently Paz removed my hands. He spread the pack out again, face down, then lifted one end so that they all flipped over like dominoes. I scanned the row of red and black letters. There was no three of spades.

'It's over there,' said Paz, as if it was no big deal.

'Over where?'

Paz pointed. Beside the door there was a row of three hooks holding an umbrella, a green supermarket bag, and a worn out raincoat.

'In the coat pocket.'

This was impossible. Paz hadn't been anywhere near the coat. I searched his face for signs that it was a joke, but he was deadly serious. 'I'll go and get it if you don't believe me.' He started to rise from the chair.

'You stay right there,' said Chess suspiciously. 'Matt will go.'

I didn't really want to. Fair enough, Paz could make a card disappear from a pack, but this one would have to fly through the air. But they were both staring at me so I went over there. I didn't know what I was going to find. It obviously wasn't going to be the three of spades. Hopefully there was going to be some other surprise that made it funny.

Chess came over with me, watching closely. In the first pocket I found twenty cents and a packet of Extra chewing gum. In the next a short blunt pencil. In the inside pocket there was an envelope. I looked enquiringly at Paz.

'That'll be it,' he said casually.

The envelope was old, stamped and addressed to Calvin and torn open. Inside was a playing card with white masks on it. I turned it over.

It was the three of spades.

Paz sat back, looking quietly satisfied. 'The Elsinore Vanish.'

Chess looked at me, frowning, then went and sat back down. 'I presume there's a point to all this?'

Paz shook his head.

Chess said, 'Well that's very nice. But let me tell you that poison did not disappear from the cupboard by magic and fly across town. Somebody took it out and they got it to the Town Hall and into Tim's flask and they did that by some normal human method. It is not impossible because it happened. And it if seems impossible, then either there is some fact we don't know, or somebody is lying.'

Paz was looking young again, confused.

'So thank you for the entertainment. But I am not going to be distracted by games. I'm going to get to the bottom of this. All it will take is a bit of thought. I'll work it out logically and then I will understand.'

Paz was shaking his head. 'You're not supposed to understand.' He looked at me for support. 'It's magic.'

Chapter 15

'Well it's all becoming pretty obvious, isn't it,' said Chess. 'I didn't think it would be this easy.'

'What?' I hated it when Chess said things were obvious.

'I've never met such a self-satisfied kid.'

'I wonder what you were like at eleven.' Actually I could remember.

'He's lying. Someone did come to the cupboard. He's protecting someone.'

'I guess so.'

'He's obviously a very good liar.'

I had thought that too. Good actor, good liar. 'Maybe.'

'Or else there's a secret back way into the cupboard, so that the person could have got the poison and technically he didn't see them. Tim loved magic.

Maybe he had his cupboard set up like one of those gadgets conjurers use. So Paz can say he didn't see anything. But he knows about it. He's evasive. He uses tricks to avoid answering questions, the way his father uses rudeness.'

For the rest of the walk home Chess lectured me about how we should have got more out of Calvin or Paz and how I'd been no help and how we had some serious thinking to do. Of course I didn't really listen, mainly because I was worrying about what Calvin had said about Grif Griffiths and looking around for the brown van.

That night Mike was cooking us a leg of lamb and I was looking forward to it. It's something I've noticed about older people. It doesn't matter what they do for a job, it doesn't even matter if they don't like cooking, after the age of about forty they all become brilliant at roasts, as if it's part of the ageing process or something. When we got home Mike had already started. He'd cleared the tiny kitchen table and put out woven place mats and a vase of flowers. The garlicky herby smell made me want to rip the meat out of the oven and just start gnawing at it.

Pretty soon he had Chess washing beans and broccoli, which was pretty funny because she can't stand either of them. Mike was tasting some chocolate sauce in a pan on the stove. He asked me to finish setting the table.

While I rummaged in the cutlery drawer he said, 'Before I forget, Matt, your dad rang. He's buying a tent, got it ordered through a shop here. He's got a mate in Beechworth? Someone Gray?'

'Bruce Graeber.'

'Yeah that was it. Bruce Graeber at the outdoor shop. The tent's arrived and your Dad's coming to the shop tomorrow at eleven. He's going to ring you. He thought you might like to meet for a coffee or something.'

'Yeah. Great.'

Mike heard my lack of enthusiasm. 'Can't get away from him, eh.'

'He's always been like that. Mum says it was his favourite song in the seventies. '"If You Leave Me Can I Come Too?" She thinks it's hilarious.'

I turned to the table. Now Mike was looking sideways at Chess. 'So Chess.' Suddenly he didn't sound so relaxed. 'Speaking of fathers, how are things going at your place?'

Chess had the beans in a colander under a running tap. She rummaged through them vigorously.

'Well, thanks.'

'How's the new house? The new-old house?'

'We're getting there.'

'Good!' said Mike, too brightly. You had to feel sorry for him. He obviously felt he should talk to her about her life, but I could've told him it wasn't going to be easy.

'Did you get all the problems sorted out?'

'The roof is fixed. Not the plumbing.'

'Is there anything I could do?'

'No thanks.' Chess had both hands under the water now and was kind of scrubbing. These were going to be the cleanest beans in Australia. 'It's very nice of you to have us here.'

'No. My pleasure.' Mike was stirring away at his sauce. He took a breath. 'And Dad?'

'He's good.' Chess seemed to realise the beans had had enough. She tipped them into a bowl and reached for the broccoli.

'Is he home at the moment?'

'No. He's off,' said Chess.

We all knew what that meant. Her father went away for four or five days at a time, drinking.

'When did you last see him?'

Chess didn't have to think about it. 'Friday the ninth.'

'Two weeks ago?'

Mike pulled the sauce off the heat and turned around to face her. He was right to be surprised. Two weeks was unusual. I hadn't realised it had been that long. It meant things were getting worse.

'It's OK. There's less housework when he's not there.' That's something Chess often says when people show signs of being sorry for her. She tried a laugh that didn't really come off. 'It's hard for him. It's been hard since my mother died.'

Mike nodded. 'I'm sorry about your mother, Chess. It's very tough.'

Chess's mother left her father when Chess was three. She died overseas somewhere when Chess was seven.

'It's OK.' Now Chess seemed to realise how short her answers were. She added, 'I was too young to remember much.'

This was a lie. I had a fair idea Chess remembered a lot about her mother. She just never talked about it.

Mike nodded understandingly, although he didn't understand. He turned to put some plates in the griller above the oven. But when he straightened he kept the conversation going, thinking it might help Chess to talk about it. A lot of people make this mistake.

He screwed his face up as if he was trying to remember. 'What was it? Cancer?'

'I don't know.' Chess turned off the tap and looked him straight in the eyes, almost as if she wanted to shock him. 'I don't know how she died. No one will tell me.'

It had worked. Mike was completely stunned, and hurt by the aggressive way she said it.

I'd seen this before. Chess was trying to show that it didn't worry her. But it sounded as if she was angry with him for asking. Or maybe Paz was right. Maybe somewhere deep down she was angry about the whole crappy deal. I'd never thought of it until he said that.

Anyway, whatever the reason, Chess talked in a tough way and she didn't realise how much this upset people. Or perhaps it was deliberate, a kind of warning — try to talk about this and it will always be worse for you than it is for me.

'That's no good,' said Mike gently.

'I don't let it worry me,' said Chess.

Mike had stopped doing anything. For a second he just stood there in his stripy oven gloves, staring at Chess. I could see what was going through his mind — how weird she was to be so blank when she talked about her disastrous parents. He was now wondering what he could say to make it easy for her to express her feelings.

Like I said. A lot of people make this mistake.

Chapter 16

By the time we got to bed I was amazingly tired. I needed something old and familiar so I setup my wobbly TV and watched two episodes of *Friends*, reciting all Joey's lines, until the insides of my own eyelids were starting to seem interesting. Then I turned it off.

But the day wasn't over. Just after I'd wrestled my way into the floor-bed there was a tap at my door. Chess came in without waiting to be asked and in the dark she tripped over the end of my mattress. It didn't slow her down. She squeaked 'Oops', got her balance and turned the light on before I was even sitting up.

She was still dressed, as if she'd been busy with something. As if she didn't feel like going to bed. I thought maybe it had something to do with the conversation about her parents. Maybe she needed to talk about it.

But of course that wasn't it. It was the mystery. Her very own private puzzle. Since we had left Calvin's flat she'd been more wired than ever, stimulated by all the things she'd heard. Now she was waving her phone and notebook at me.

'I thought we should just go over things.'

I sat up and blinked at her.

'We've been told so much. I think we need to go through it all, get our thoughts in some kind of coherent order, work out how far we've progressed and formulate a plan of action.'

There was probably something I could've said about privacy, but nothing came to me. I reached over and got a T-shirt off the bed springs.

While I put it on Chess edged around, squeezing her feet along beside the mattress, then she sat down on the springy wire netting of the bed frame. The TV did a graceful roll onto its face.

That got me out of bed. Chess leapt up, putting her feet on my doona, and together we set the telly up again, then she carefully lowered herself onto the steel frame. I pulled over my black and white fake-fur cushion that I took everywhere and shoved it behind me.

I hadn't actually agreed to anything, but she wasn't worried about that. 'I've been reading that book on logic that Angus lent me. I think if I can follow that pattern — small syllogistic steps — maybe then I could show him what I've got. He'd help, I know.'

'I didn't think Angus wanted us to get involved.'

'That was Mrs Langton. He lent me the book and asked me to email him. I think he's very worried about the situation.'

Chess stopped and wriggled her bum on the narrow bar. 'The first thing we need to discuss is those two thugs. Calvin called the big one Grif Griffiths. I can't find anything Googling people called Grif or Griffiths associated with Rawdon Grammar or Beechworth. And you can't Facebook stalk someone with a name as common as that until we get a first name. So are we worried about them?'

'Not really.' That was a lie but I wanted it to be possible for her to sleep. 'I reckon they did too much staring. They were trying to look scary and trying too hard always wrecks it. And it doesn't really work when you've got a big Santa Claus gut. And the little guy, he's just the classic small man. The way he stood. It's like, 'I'm so muscly I can't get my arms down'.'

'So we don't let them put us off?'

I pulled a face, trying to be braver than I felt. 'Nah.'

'Good.' Chess patted her notebook. 'So the problem of this murder — first there's something I don't understand.'

'Only one thing?'

'It's Jacob. Why did Jacob send us to see Anna and Clare? He tried to imply they were the only suspects. He must've known they weren't able to get the poison that evening. He must've known they were going to lead us to Calvin.'

I'd thought about this too. 'Yeah. I think he did.'

'Then why send us off in the wrong direction?'

'Because, like he said, he wants us to get out there and meet everyone and see everything and slowly come to our own conclusions.'

Chess frowned. 'Are you saying Jacob knows who did it?'

'Yes.'

'Why wouldn't he just tell the police?'

'Maybe he can't prove it.'

'Why doesn't he at least tell us what he knows?'

'We might not believe him. You know ... when you find a murderer it's usually hard for everyone to accept. He wants us to go over the whole thing from the beginning, so when we do come to the truth we'll believe it and we'll be convincing.'

I thought of something else. 'And maybe he isn't sure. Maybe he wants us to come to the same conclusion as him so he knows he's right.'

Chess thought about this for a minute. 'Well,' she said. 'We better get on with it then.'

'Yeah.' I looked at her book. 'Take it away, Sherlock.'

I handed her my Totable Attachable Night Bed Illumination, which is a torch made in Vietnam with a bit of thick wire on the end.

Chess put the torch on the bed. 'The way I see it, there are two possible threads of enquiry. Motive and opportunity.' She straightened her back. 'As far as motive goes, it's fairly obvious. Tim knew someone's secret. The trouble is, anyone could have something they're ashamed of.'

'True.'

'So it would be more profitable to think about opportunity. That allows for complete rationality and it narrows things down. In fact we seem to have arrived at an impossible situation. But …' She held a finger up. 'It's important to remember that everything we know has been told to us by other people. If the stories are inconsistent, if the picture they paint is impossible, it means only one thing. Not that a handful of poison slipped out of a cupboard unseen and flew across town of its own accord …' She pulled a face to show how stupid that was. '… but that someone is lying.'

'And how are we supposed to know who that is?'

'I agree. It's hard. Especially when you meet a lot of new people. And when they are so eccentric, like Calvin and Paz, or when they're snooty Barbie girls —'

'Clare isn't like that.'

Chess narrowed her eyes. 'I knew you'd like her.'

Chess didn't really like anyone our age, even though some of them were nice to her. She'd learned not to risk it.

She went on, 'What I'm trying to say is the personalities can be distracting. We need to sort through everything people have said. Pick out the facts.'

She waved the notebook again, proudly this time. 'I think I've made some progress.'

She left a little silence. I don't know what for. Applause, maybe? A chance for me to beg her to go on? Instead I gave her a little yawn to remind her it was sleeping time. She shoved the notebook at me.

> Saturday 14th November 2015
> The Night of the Remember November Charity Cabaret
> Early Evening Langton House
> 6 pm
>
> ---
>
> Poison is hidden in Tim's cupboard
> Seen by Angus, Jacob, Tim, Anna and Clare
> Angus, Jacob and Tim go to Town Hall. They all remain together until cabaret begins.
> Anna and Clare are together with Calvin, Mrs Williams and Mrs Langton until they leave for hall
> NOTE: No opportunity for anyone to retrieve poison at this time unless extreme collusion.

I said, ‘Collusion?’

‘If a lot of people are together it makes it unlikely they did anything. You can almost imagine two people agreeing to steal poison and kill Tim. But for Mrs Langton, Mrs Williams, Calvin and Anna and Clare all suddenly to cook up an idea like that on the spur of the moment and then agree…’

‘It’s impossible.’

‘Exactly. In fact the improbability of collusion must escalate exponentially with each person added. Wouldn’t you say?’

She had said that last bit to annoy me. I scowled at her.

‘Therefore …’ said Chess, turning the page.

<u>Conclusion</u>
Poison retrieved **after** everyone left for the ball.

Chess frowned at me. ‘It’s reasonably simple so far, isn’t it?’

‘I dunno,’ I said. ‘Are most of your murders more complicated than this?’

She made a face. ‘We must remember it’s early days. I’m sure there’s a lot more to this story than meets the eye.’

She was getting that ‘let’s play detectives’ tone.

‘Chess —’

‘So, on to the cabaret. Five people knew where the poison was and once they were at the Town Hall they could have told anyone. That completely opens the field of possible suspects. Either someone left the ball, got the poison and returned without anyone noticing, or they phoned an accomplice who got the poison in to them somehow. Then they found Tim's flask and put the poison in without anyone seeing. We should really inspect the Town Hall and see what would be possible.' She took the book back, turned a page and wrote:

NEXT
* Inspect Town Hall

'So, now we come to Paz.' She paused for dramatic effect. 'He maintains he was in Tim's room in front of the cupboard for the entire duration of the variety show. This leaves only two possibilities. Either he's mistaken or he's lying.'

Suddenly she looked down at me. 'He was evasive, wasn't he?'

'I thought he was trying to tell us something. With his disappearing trick. He left that book for us to find. One of us should read it.'

Chess sighed. She knew I didn't mean me. 'Yes. All right. But what about those other things he said. Saying we weren't supposed to understand?'

'Nothing. He just wanted us to leave him alone or something.'

'Hmmm.' Chess frowned at me and then stared at her notebook. 'Right. Well, possibility one — he's mistaken. Maybe he left the room and forgot, or underestimated the time he spent in the toot, or fell asleep without realising it. All seem unlikely.'

She looked pointedly at me, waiting for me to agree or disagree. I gave her a tiny nod.

'And then we have the question, could someone have sneaked up while he was in the toilet or asleep? Or got into the back of the cupboard somehow? We need to go and see Tim's room.'

'Yeah. That'd be good really.' I was interested in Tim and curious to see what sort of place he slept in.

On her page Chess wrote:

* Inspect Elsinore

She waved the notebook. 'Finally there's the possibility that Paz is lying and he knows perfectly well who took that poison.'

I shrugged.

'And the person he's most likely to lie for is his father.'

'Calvin says he has an alibi. He was with his girlfriend all night.'

'We need to check that. I forgot to get Mrs Williams's number.'

'And if Calvin is the murderer, why would he go out and let us interview Paz alone? Wouldn't he be more protective?'

'Maybe he doesn't think we're a threat. He doesn't think we're capable of solving this.'

'Then he's in for a nasty surprise, isn't he?'

Chess gave me just the tiniest flicker of a grin. 'Anyway, we need to talk to Paz again.'

She wrote:

 * Reinterview Paz

Chess was happiest like this, working deep inside her head, shuffling symbols, looking for connections. That was something I realised after the last murder she solved — puzzles were a kind of safety for her.

Chess was looking at me. 'I know what you're thinking.'

I made a mock guilty face, trying to be funny.

'But I don't want to talk to Mike about my parents and I don't want to think about them and I don't see why I should. Things like that only hold you back.'

I shrugged. I wasn't arguing. She'd said all this before.

'Angus's logic book has inspired me.' She was holding the notebook, looking at it as if it was some kind of prize. 'I know who I am now and I know there are others who agree with me. Being a creature of reason and logic and very little emotion is a strength. It means I can help people. You just need to accept that and let me get on with it.'

She put a hand on the springs behind her to push up off the bed, then leaped lightly across the mattress and left. The TV rocked gaily around for a bit and then rolled onto its face.

Chapter 17

It must be easier in those other worlds. Take any of them —Star Trek, say, or The Hunger Games, or even Jason Bourne. Life is so simple for them. When bad things start to happen the hero can just deal with it. You don't see him ducking into the shop for milk, or slipping away to finish an essay, or weeding his grandmother's marigolds. He can concentrate on his clues or his evil megalomaniac.

Meanwhile, back on planet earth, I had a message to ring my mother. It was the morning after our little midnight meeting and I used Chess's phone and Mum made me hang up and she called me straight back. This meant Chess wasn't paying and we could spend as long as we liked chatting about important stuff — their pottery stand at the Country Creatives Festival (successful) and their attempts to train the dog to poo next to the compost bin (not). With the entire Langton angle out of bounds I didn't have much for her. I told her about Mike's house. And what I'd been eating. She likes to hear that.

Eventually she got to the real point of the phone call, which was to tell me that Dad would meet me at twelve o'clock outside the Four Winds Outdoor and Country Clothing Store. She also gave me a message for Chess.

I didn't pass the message on straight away. I was going to have to pick the right moment.

When I put the phone down Chess was at the kitchen table looking at her notebook. We were going to follow the plan, first item: checking out the Town Hall. After some food we headed out.

It was one of those fresh airy days, full of blossom and irritated sparrows. Everything looked clean and soft. Chess was happy. She had a plan, things to investigate, questions to ask, and a book to write the answers in. I sighed. My news was going to prick that bubble.

There were a few cars parked along Mike's street, but there was no one else on the footpath. A breeze was making leaves dance around. A block ahead some flowery branches were sticking out across the footpath and flapping in the wind. There was someone there, in flickering sunlight and shade, someone small with bright red hair.

'That's that boy,' said Chess.

She liked calling Paz 'that boy', to show she wasn't impressed by him.

I wasn't actually sure it was him. This kid looked too small and his clothes weren't brightly coloured. I was about to call out to see if he reacted, but for some reason I didn't. My mouth opened and closed. Then the kid seemed to hear something. He turned to look at the garden behind him and disappeared.

'It was him, wasn't it?' said Chess.

'I don't know ...' My voice wavered. I told myself not to be stupid. There was nothing strange about what had happened. A kid had come to the street and been called back by someone. But now I was aware of all the houses and their empty windows and I was thinking people might be watching us. My walking became stiff and self-conscious like a performance.

Across the road, a house had a sign that said Chorleywood Medical Clinic. A woman was leading an old man up a ramp towards the front door, while a little girl waited on a square of grass. The girl had a dog on a lead. She dropped the lead, cried 'Fetch!' in a reedy voice and threw a stick to the edge of the grass. The dog sat down. I grinned.

But my breath still wouldn't go smooth. It was like it had been at the open garden and at Mayday Hills. Once you decide something is wrong, everything starts to feel threatening. In the next garden a tap was dripping. A screwed up chip packet went rolling past our feet. A woman in a tracksuit came out of a driveway, glancing at us as she passed. She got in a car and drove away.

And now there were people behind us, young blokes by the sound of them. I didn't know where they came from but I could hear them, mumbling jokes and laughing in short grunts.

Somewhere behind us the little girl squealed, 'Where did you go?' I turned and saw her disappearing around the back of the medical place.

'Chess,' I said. 'Chess, do you think …' But then I stopped.

'What?'

'Nothing.'

A car passed us from behind. It was an old station wagon with rusty iron roof racks and there was just one person in it — a tall thin person with no hair. Calvin? All I could see was the back of his head.

This was stupid. A lot of people had hair like that.

Then I heard another car behind us. This time it came out of a side street and, by the sound of it, took the corner way too fast. There was a screech of tyres. We turned around and as we did, the blokes behind ran at us. I just had time to register that one had a beard and that the car was a dark brown van when they went past me, bumping me aside and scooping

Chess up. They had her in the back of the van before I'd even moved.

Then they were gone and I was alone in the quiet street.

For a second I was frozen. Body, mind. Numb. Across the road a face appeared at a window. It scowled as if the noise had been my fault. Then it disappeared and all the silent little houses just sat there behind their gardens, as if nothing had happened.

A whole series of actions crowded into my head all at once. I should yell. Would anyone come out? If they did I had nothing to show them. I could bang on a door, ask for a phone, ring the police. I could run, but where? I could go back to Mike's …

I didn't have time to think anything else. Back up the road, from the same place as last time, the van came again. It roared past me, screeched to a stop, swinging from side to side on worn suspension and, like a spiteful square creature that didn't like what it had eaten, it spat Chess out. A hand gave her a shove and she went down on her knees on the gravel. The door slammed and the van roared off.

Without knowing I was moving I came up beside her. 'Chess! Chess!'

I had to hook her under an arm to get her to her feet. She tucked her hands under her armpits. One side of her face was going red and there were grimy patches on both knees. 'Chess!'

Chess spoke quietly and flatly. 'Same brown van.'

'I saw.'

'There were three of them.' She sounded cross at this, as if it was cheating in some way.

I didn't want to hear the details. All I wanted to do was get away from there. 'Come on. We'll go back.' I put a hand under one of her elbows and pulled, looking all around for signs of the van returning.

Chess shook me off and took her hands out from under her arms. But she couldn't keep the shake out of her voice. 'It was about the murder. About Tim. They pressed my face into the floor.' She touched her cheek, feeling for damage. 'They said give up and go home.'

'So let's ...' I had to stop for a jerky breath. I took another sideways step towards Mike's place.

But Chess didn't budge.

'Chess we need to get off the street. They might come back.'

So that she wouldn't have to answer she brushed herself down again, bending forwards to study the dirty patches on her knees.

'Chess!' I bent down too, trying to force her to look at me.

She talked to her knees.

'And Matt?'

'What?'

She straightened. 'You were right about the big tummy. He was a complete porker.'

Well whatever it takes. If the thought of Grif's gut was going to help her to deal with this, that was all right. She wiped her face with a sleeve and then pulled out a hanky and went over it again, hard.

'Can we go?'

She waved the hanky up the street. 'Once we get to Camp Street we'll be almost at the Town Hall. We'll be safe there. Then we can discuss this calmly.'

She was right. The Town Hall was as close as Mike's and there would be people there. 'Come on, then.'

It was all I could do to keep from running. I started off at a fast walk and Chess followed. We went past the bushes where I'd seen the kid who might have been Paz. There was no one there.

We went around a corner and got a block closer to the main street before we stopped. There were a few shops near us now and cars parked, and up ahead we could see the roundabout, the post office and traffic.

'All right,' I said. 'We should go to the police.'

'What?'

'Those guys. They always know where we are. They were at Mayday Hills and Calvin's and I reckon it was them waiting outside the toilet at Luca's. And now this.'

Chess was the colour of yesterday's pasta. She had her grazed hands pressed together in front of her, but she was keeping tight control of herself. She licked her lips and kept her voice steady. 'If we report this they'll ring your parents and we'll be going back home.'

I didn't have anything to say to that.

'They didn't hurt me. They were just trying to scare us. They want to stop us asking questions.' She brushed at her cheek as if she could wipe away the damage. 'They're worried about us. In a way that's a good sign.' Now she was actually looking proud of herself, as if getting shoved into a van and half smothered was a win of some kind.

'Yeah, fine, but it's not worth the risk is it? I mean this time they let you go with a warning but what's next?'

'If we keep going we'll find out.'

'No —'

'All right. All right. I agree with you.' She was completely OK now. It was amazing. She was even getting boring. 'Obviously from here on we have to be careful. But this is the middle of town and there are people everywhere. We can at least look over the Town Hall. Then we can go and meet your Dad.'

And in a way, now that I was calmer, I half agreed with her. Beside us in the street a car stopped to pull into a park and there was a little tour bus behind it full of people. No one was going to get us here.

Chess said, 'Are you OK?'

'You're the one with gravel in your hands.'

Chess looked down at the heels of her hands. There wasn't any gravel actually stuck in them but they were dented and there were small streaks of blood. She rubbed them hard together. Then her chin went up.

'Gravel, grazes, rocks, having your lunch mashed into the mud. It's nothing new really, is it?'

I grimaced. 'Not for you I suppose.'

Chess raised her voice as if they might be listening. 'These fellows aren't sophisticated. In terms of methods, I can't see a lot of difference between them and the average eleven year old. So I don't see why they should scare me.' She wiggled her puny shoulders and tossed her pointed head. 'I have been bullied by experts.'

'All right.' I started walking. 'Good speech. We go on.'

OK, so this was a big mistake. That's easy to see now. Looking back, it's obvious we should never have kept going. But — how can I explain it? Stories somehow feel different when you're inside them.

And I didn't realise. That's my other excuse. I had no idea how bad it was going to be.

Chapter 18

We came to the Town Hall from the back. It was built on sloping ground so here it was three storeys high. The ground floor was made of rough stone with three double doors, like you'd see on an old warehouse. Two had padlocks but one was open and we could hear voices inside.

Chess said, 'Our first objective should be to learn all the ways in and out of the room where Tim died. There might be access here to the main floor.'

'All right.' I wasn't sure if we could just walk into these back areas but I tried to sound confident and led the way to the open door.

Inside we found some old prison cells lined in wood, with cobwebs and tiny high windows. There was a little tourist party here, listening to a bloke with a waistcoat and a beard telling a story about bush rangers. They ignored us. Squeezed into one corner there was a narrow spiral staircase. I went a short way up but at the level of the ceiling it was blocked by boards. 'No access there,' I said.

Chess had a look too. 'All right. Let's go around.'

At the front the Town Hall was only two storey but it was impressive, built in grey stone with tall arched windows arranged in pairs. Inside, it was a typical old building — stained glass over the door, a patterned tiled floor and a lot of dark wood. There were quite a few people around. At the doors that led into the main hall there was a sign that said, 'Health and Wellbeing Expo'. A bloke went past us carrying some kind of musical instrument in a case and after him came a girl in orange tights and red boots carrying cartons. They went up the three marble steps into the hall.

Chess was taking photographs of two flights of wooden stairs, one leading up and one leading down, so I waited. On one side of the entry area there was a door that led to a tourist information centre and shop and beside that, on the wall above a rack of pamphlets, there was big map of Beechworth. I went to look at it. And I started to see something.

'Chess —'

'Let's go in.' She went into the main hall and I followed.

We stopped just inside the door. The hall was full of people, setting up tables and noticeboards and moving chairs around. In the middle of the room, getting in everyone's way, there were two women discussing the layout, pointing at heaters and lights. One was holding a clip board and the other had a stack of flyers in a rubber band.

I glanced at Chess. She was focussed and intense. Too intense. She had the stiff look of someone who's holding something in. You couldn't blame her, after what had just happened. But she wasn't going to talk any more about the attack and now that we had come here there was nothing else to do but keep going.

Chess started going around inspecting everything, taking photos of the walls and windows. The hall had arched ceilings, wooden panelling, honour boards and clunky lights shaped like bent umbrellas. It was junky and daggy and heavy and comfortable. All the windows had the blinds pulled right down so that the light spread out softly into the big space.

One end of the room was taken up with a low stage. We went towards it, the floorboards moving and creaking under our feet. It wasn't like a theatre stage with wings and curtains, just a platform that went right up to the walls. At the left there was a tiny flight of stairs. On the stage there was a young guy connecting computers and speakers and two other people were moving a cardboard cut-out bee, while another person waved their fingers at them saying, 'More ... more ... stop.'

I had a thought I sometimes have. Other people seem so ... planned. They seem to think about their days — about their lives — and make decisions and have reasons for those decisions. Sometimes I wonder if people are just pretending. I seem to go through life in a jumble of vague ideas and feelings.

Chess had a plan. She had written it in her notebook. Or maybe she was just pretending too. Maybe the notebook was a way of convincing herself that she was in control.

She caught me looking at her. She held my eyes for a second then said, 'Three ways in and out.'

It took me a while to realise what she meant. At the far end of the room, through all the people, I could see a huge official-looking table and behind that there was a set of double doors. There was smaller door in a corner. The other way out was the main door. There was no way off the stage except forward into the room.

Chess was looking around as if she was memorising everything. 'We need to picture what it was like.'

The bee people had gone and come back with some cardboard trees and flowers. They smiled at us as they went past.

Chess looked up at the stage. 'I wonder exactly where Tim was standing when he died.'

Died … I tried to get my head around it. This was a place where a murder had happened, like that corner on the country road, like the pool where we'd found Debbie.

But that wasn't right — it wasn't like them. Those places had atmosphere. You could feel it as soon as you got there. Their terrible history hung in the air somehow, like ghosts. Here, with all the activity around us, there was nothing. The wall behind the stage had fake pillars, painted dark pink and decorated in gold. People were pushing the brightly coloured scenery around, grunting and laughing. Behind me the room was full of noise and busy chatter.

Then, close to us, one calm voice said, 'Hello, Jessica.'

Chapter 19

I whirled around. Angus Burden was there, hands together on his stomach, round forehead shining in the dim light.

'I thought I might find you here.'

I started to go towards him but Chess stepped sideways onto my feet, which sent us both stumbling around. Eventually we managed to get in front of him. Angus looked a bit surprised by our way of doing things but he was smiling politely. He was wearing a pale checked shirt, a brown tie and a woollen jacket with leather buttons.

He said, 'So like all of us you're curious about the place.'

I said, 'We weren't … We aren't …'

Angus said, 'No, no. I understand perfectly. There's something about a mystery, isn't there? An unknown is like a sore in the mouth. It's very difficult to leave it alone.'

Someone was crawling along the bottom of the stage, taping wires to the floor. Angus backed shyly out of their way. 'I'm so sorry.' They ignored him.

He looked around at all the activity, frowning as if the people shouldn't be here. 'I haven't been here since the night Tim died. Poor old Tim.'

'Yeah.'

'A terrible thing. A troubled boy.' His voice was soft. I remembered he had spent a lot of energy trying to keep Tim out of trouble. 'But,' he lifted his voice, 'are you sure it's a good idea for you to be here? The police haven't finished their investigation.'

I said, 'We're just …'

Chess put a hand on my arm. She didn't want me to mention Jacob. She said, 'We thought we might be able to offer a new perspective, as outsiders. As experienced outsiders.'

'Oh yes.' Angus looked thoughtful. 'Anything we could do to speed up the police's progress would be good. It would certainly help Jacob.' He sighed. 'But could I ask you, I know it is none of my … could I just ask you to leave him out of it?'

'Oh yes,' breathed Chess, blushing. 'Absolutely.'

'Poor old Jake. He's been completely knocked for six by this whole thing. Well, who wouldn't be? He needs to get away to university next year.'

'Definitely,' I said.

'He has such great potential. A much better brain than I ever had. It would be a tragedy for him to waste another year.'

'Oh yes,' said Chess.

'But maybe there's no harm in someone new applying their minds to our local puzzle.'

'No,' said Chess eagerly. 'There's no harm at all.' She waved an arm at the room. 'We wanted to see how it was all laid out.'

'Excellent idea,' said Angus. 'I'm convinced the solution to this little ... awful mystery ... I'm sure the answer lies in exactly that. The geometry and the geography of things.'

'That's what I said.' Chess looked at me, wanting me to confirm that.

I said, 'Actually it's funny you should mention geography, because I was looking at a map —'

'Motives are just too vague,' said Chess. 'We need to concentrate on simple clear facts. Apply logic.'

Angus said, 'If there is anything I can help with ...'

'Well there is, really. Yes.' Chess stepped towards him. 'We came to see how easy it would be for someone to sneak away from the variety night and then come back with the poison and then get it into Tim's flask. As you say, that's the key to everything. But we don't know exactly what was happening here that night — how it was all set up.'

'Oh I see.'

'Maybe you could tell us?'

'Oh. Well. Yes. Let me see.' Angus turned and sat back on the edge of the stage. 'The room was very crowded, completely crammed with tables. The lighting was dim. There were acts on the stage all night and that, of course, was brightly lit. I was in the band.' He pointed to the front right-hand corner of the stage. 'We played accompaniments to all the acts. For the comedy sketches I used my cymbals and drums. Then in the intervals we played dance music. The dance floor was small, squashed in here at the front.'

Chess said, 'Can we go up?'

She led the way up the four steps, onto the stage. We went across the front, out of the way of the people working, and looked out over the room. Chess said, 'So how was it when Tim died? What happened exactly?'

Angus nodded with a sad face. 'Ahhh. Goodness. Well … Late in the evening … Tim was up here next to the band, doing his magic show.' He pointed to the centre front of the stage. A few people glanced up at us but they must have thought we were planning part of the expo and looked away.

'The act was based around the notion of disappearance. It involved the use of the trap door.'

'The what?'

Angus smiled and lifted his eyebrows. For just a second he looked alert and happy. 'Come and see.' There was only one guy on the stage now. We edged past him and the cardboard trees to a back corner. 'Below the stage is a set of stairs. It was used to bring prisoners up from the cells in the days when the Town Hall was a courtroom. It's blocked off now, as you can see, but this panel will lift up if unlocked from underneath.'

We could hear the tour going on under our feet, soft voices and a burst of ghostly laughter.

Angus said, 'Tim used this for his disappearing act. I persuaded the administrator to unlock the trap door, just for the night. Nobody knew it was open. Most people have forgotten it's here. For the trick, Jacob was hidden behind a curtain and he disappeared by jumping through the trap door. Then he reappeared at the main door and ran up to join Tim. He was carrying Tim's flask, which had also previously disappeared. That was part of the trick.' For a moment his lips pulled into a strange shape and then went loose again. He took a breath.

'It was all simple stuff but we were having fun with it. The plan was that at the climax of his trick Tim would also go behind the curtain and through the trapdoor. But he wasn't going to come back. I didn't realise at the time but apparently he was actually going to leave town.' Angus's voice went soft and sad. 'He was going to make himself permanently disappear. I don't know why.'

Jacob had been sad about that too.

I said, 'In a way he did disappear.'

'Oh dear.'

We all stared at the trapdoor listening to the muffled voices coming up from under the floor. I was thinking about Tim's tricks, his love of magic, the delight he would have had planning his disappearing act. There was something about that story that made his death even sadder.

After a minute Angus turned to the front of the room. 'Well at least you've had a chance to see the place.'

We looked around at all the busy, purposeful people and slowly we absorbed some of their energy.

After another moment Chess said, 'There are three ways in and out of this room.' She pulled out the notebook and started pointing at a plan she'd drawn.

'Plus the trapdoor,' said Angus.

'Yes! And several ways to get in and out of the building.' She held the notebook where Angus could see. 'It was completely feasible for someone to sneak away and then bring the poison back into the building.'

'Yes I think so too.'

'You were on stage all evening.'

'Except for short toilet breaks.'

'So you have an unassailable alibi.'

Angus shrugged and nodded.

'And also you were in a position to see the movements of the other suspects.'

'Suspects?'

'Only a few people knew where the poison was: Tim, Jacob, you, Anna, Clare Bishop and possibly Calvin Goldstone.'

He pushed his hands into his pockets and looked thoughtful.

'Did you see anyone go out?'

'As I said the room was dimly lit and crowded. I could see people on the dance floor. Anna danced nearly all night with some of her more unsavoury friends. She has taken up with a rather rough crowd I'm afraid. There's nothing I can do.' He drifted into silence, frowning, then went on. 'And I could see Tim's mother, Jane. She danced a lot.'

'With Calvin?'

'I don't think Calvin dances. Most often she was with a local jewellery maker, Peter Lord, nickname Byron.'

Chess nudged me hard in the ribs. Angus went on, 'So I'm sorry. It would have been possible for anyone to leave the room without me seeing.'

The woman with the clip board was alone now and she was looking at us. She had white-blonde hair and rectangular red glasses. She adjusted the glasses on her nose and started coming across the room.

Angus said, 'Of course in order for someone to poison Tim's flask it was not necessary for them to come back into this room. The flask had been confiscated by Calvin earlier in the evening. It spent most of the night out in an office in a back corridor.'

'Yes.' Chess hadn't drawn that on her map.

'Would you like to see?'

We smiled at the clipboard woman as we went past. Angus led us out and along a short corridor to a room in the front corner of the building. It was a tiny office with a desk and filing cabinet squashed into it and a kitchen bench along one wall. It had a closed up, polishy smell. We all shuffled in and then, finding there wasn't much to see, shuffled back out again.

Chess said, 'Anyone could have got in there.'

Angus said, 'There is something else I need to tell you.'

As he said this a very fat man carrying a plastic kettle edged past us in the narrow corridor.

Angus said, 'Do you think we should finish our discussion elsewhere?'

Outside it was still windy. Angus led us to the garden beside the hall. It was a tiny park of raked gravel paths under trees that were so enormous that all you really saw were the massive trunks. They made it very shady, which would have been good in summer. In September it was dismal. There was one of those little round bandstand things and a fountain that looked as if it had been spewed up by a faulty concrete mixer.

We found a pair of wooden benches and sat down. For a minute no one spoke. On the far side of the gardens there was an old church made of grey stone, dark-looking, under more of the big pine trees. A man in a bulky knitted jumper came out of a back door to look at a fallen branch. Angus watched him with a worried expression until he went back in.

I said, 'Is everything OK?'

Angus nodded. 'I want to give one small word of caution.' He spread his hands on his knees. 'It's generous of you to take an interest in Tim's death but it's only fair to warn you …' He stopped.

'What?' said Chess.

'There's a local boy. Although that isn't really the word for him any more. I wasn't entirely clear with you before because I didn't want to worry you. I saw him at the open garden and I do know who he is. His name is Simon Griffiths.' Chess immediately started Googling the name. 'For a time he was at school with Jacob and Tim but in year ten he moved to Melbourne. The boys have told me about him over the years. He left under something of a cloud.'

The wind was lifting puffs of dust from the gravel paths. In the garden beds, plants were whipping around.

'What kind of cloud?' Chess could talk and search the net at the same time.

'Apparently he was something of a bully. And this developed into quite serious violence. He was close to being expelled but he went to boarding school in Melbourne and I believe soon after that he dropped out of school altogether. By all accounts he has become involved with gangs down there. Drug dealing.' Angus moved his back stiffly on the seat. 'Late last year he started turning up in town again, staying with his parents, who are very decent people. They run a gallery. I think Simon sold some drugs in the town here.'

'I can't find anything much. One assault charge in a newspaper report.' Chess lowered the phone.

Angus said, 'The important thing for you is that I think he had something to do with Tim's death.'

'Why do you think that?'

'Small things Tim said. Whispers around the town. Of course if there was anything definite I would take it to the police. Anyone would. But so far there seems to be nothing concrete. I just have the impression that Tim knew something about this Griffiths boy's activities and threatened to expose him. And I think there was someone else involved in

Tim's death, too — someone local who was working with Griffiths selling the drugs.'

'Calvin Goldstone.'

Angus looked horrified that Chess would say the name. He glanced around. 'I'm not sure. Not at all sure. All I'm saying is, by the way Tim was behaving in his last ...' Angus's breath caught. He coughed. ' ... during his last days ... oh dear ... he might also have been threatening to expose ... this person.'

'And then he was killed.'

'Yes.'

A woman went past us with a raincoat flapping at her legs and a scarf streaming behind her.

Angus said, 'Worryingly, I think Griffiths is in town at the moment. I think I saw him in the street yesterday. So I would proceed with caution.' Angus studied Chess's face. Out in the daylight we could see that one of her cheeks was red. His eyes went down to her dirty knees. 'And I suppose ... if Griffiths had something to do Tim's murder ... a person like that might be prepared to commit further acts of violence to avoid discovery.' He waited for her to say something.

Chess's face was blank and stiff. 'We'll be careful.'

He lifted his chin. 'I don't mean you to be unduly afraid. This is Beechworth, after all.' He gave a feeble laugh. 'I would just avoid walking alone at night, that sort of thing. But if you feel threatened in any way, go straight to the police.'

'Definitely.'

I don't know if he believed her but he didn't say anything else about it.

Behind the woman with the scarf there were a couple of youngish guys in jeans and leather jackets. They were frowning at the ground while they talked, as if they were planning something serious. Suddenly one of them gave a laugh, one of those loud businessmen laughs that always scare me for some reason.

I said, 'Can we be a bit clearer? Grif Griffiths is involved in drugs. Calvin was working with him. Tim Williams was threatening to expose them.'

Angus said, 'I didn't say it was Calvin Goldstone.'

'No but Chess did.'

Chess nodded. 'Calvin and Paz deflected our questions with rudeness and silly tricks.'

I said, 'No. It doesn't feel right.'

'What does that mean?' Chess was annoyed. I wasn't supposed to have ideas of my own.

'It doesn't fit with the way Paz is. He isn't nervous about his father. They aren't sharing any big terrible secret. They're relaxed together.'

'We hardly saw them together.'

'It was enough.'

That made Chess even madder. 'But that's just vague feely stuff.'

Angus said, 'I think Chess is right. If you're serious about finding Tim's killer it's important not to be distracted by imagined emotional states.'

Chess said, 'Exactly.'

Angus said, 'I suspect that, when we eventually find it, the solution to this mystery will be startlingly simple. As we said, you must stick to concrete facts. Entrances, exits, pathways, front doors, back walls.' He seemed to know Chess found this sort of thing reassuring.

Chess said, 'Unfortunately, so far the physical arrangement of things hasn't really helped.' She had lost the fierceness and the bottled-up fear. She was more relaxed and more positive. 'It would have been easy for anyone to get in and out of the Town Hall and easy to find Tim's flask and put the poison into it. None of those things narrow down the list of suspects at all.

I said, 'Actually there is something in the geography.' They both looked at me. 'Can I tell you my thing now?' They still just goggled at me, so I went on. 'I was looking at the map of Beechworth. Up until now I hadn't realised where things actually are. When someone else is driving you, you don't really pay much attention. To get to Langton House we drove around in a big circle, and we went in another big circle to get to the Bijou Theatre at Mayday Hills. But when you look at a map you realise Langton House backs onto

Mayday Hills. I saw the trees and the old wall from the garden that first morning. I just hadn't made the connection. And when we walked down from there to Calvin's house we went the long way. But you could actually cut straight through. It isn't far.'

Chess said, 'What are you saying?'

'Calvin's house is on a direct line between Langton House and the Town Hall.'

'And?'

'Paz could easily have walked to the Town Hall. Or he might've met Calvin half way, at their place. Calvin said he was with Mrs Williams all night, but Mrs Williams danced a lot with other people. His alibi doesn't hold up.'

Chess said, 'So that is consistent with the idea that it was Calvin who killed Tim.'

'Well, yeah. Maybe.' For some reason I just couldn't see Calvin doing any of it. I couldn't see him involving his son. Paz wasn't wary of his father. It just didn't seem that way. But I'd already been told these were vague and useless feelings. 'Really, anyone who was reasonably fit could've run from the hall to the house and back again.'

At that point I had a vague memory of a pair of running shoes, but Chess was making one of her impatient little noises and I lost it.

Chess said, 'So once again we haven't narrowed the field of suspects.'

'But thank you, Matthew,' said Angus. 'It is a valid point.'

Around the fountain a bed of strappy plants was churning in the wind. The leaves blew upwards and I saw a lizard, suddenly in the light. For a second I could see every scale and its bright eyes. Then the leaves dropped back. When they lifted again it was gone.

Chess sniffed. 'Motive doesn't narrow the field either. Tim was threatening to expose secrets but anyone in the town might have a secret.' She was staring into air. Not in a vague way, she was concentrating, as if what she was saying was written there. 'The most important thing is the question of how the poison got out of Tim's room. It was locked in a bookcase. Five or six people knew of its existence. And Paz was sitting in front of the bookcase all night.'

She brushed at the dirt on her pants, making it worse. 'This is crucial. If we want to know who killed Tim we need to find out what happened in his room that night.'

Angus said, 'I'm glad you've come, Jessica. You're just the person for this. What we need is someone who won't be distracted by spooky atmospheres and how people seem.' He edged forwards on the seat. 'Being an outsider is also an advantage. Your clarity is not spoilt by all the local gossip. Stick to small simple, irrefutable, logical steps. You'll be surprised how far they can lead you.'

'I always do.'

Normally this would be annoying but I was happy. Chess has had a lot of people trying to help her over the years and she's always resisted. Independence is a big thing for her. But Angus talked about things she really cared about. He had helped Tim Williams and Jacob with study and with life. Maybe one day he could help Chess decide what to do with her big brain. He could advise her about uni courses, things like that. And he was a funny old guy. Gentle and humble and sad, and pompous in a way that was peculiar and not annoying.

Also, if Chess had someone in her life she actually admired, then that would take the pressure off me.

'That's what I have to work out,' said Chess. 'How they got the poison out of the cupboard.'

'Oh yes. This is all so difficult.' Now Angus seemed to be getting tired. He looked sadder than ever. 'It just doesn't make sense.'

That reminded me. 'You said you had something to tell us.'

'Yes, what was it?' said Chess. 'What do you know?'

He looked down at this hands. 'One small detail on the night of Tim's death. At the variety cabaret. A movement. The thing is, it was so small ... But I believe I saw something pass from one hand to another.'

'Do you mean one person? From hand to hand? Or two people?'

Angus frowned at her. He had the out-of-focus look Chess gets when she's thinking.

'Do you mean like magicians? Sleight of hand? A trick of some kind?'

But now he went a bit dithery. 'Oh no. Or maybe, yes, thank you, Chess, maybe that describes it.' He was looking older. His mouth had gone soft. He looked as if he was about to cry, or topple sideways. 'I'm so glad you're here. I wanted to say …' He gave a shaky laugh. 'The problem is, a preconceived notion … A rumour will colour everything you see and hear.'

Chess said, 'But it isn't a rumour. You saw something.'

'I can't be sure.' He stood up. 'Best to keep it to myself for now. And it's time for me to get out of your way.' He was feeling stronger. He smiled down at Chess. 'Come and see me. But first follow your investigation as planned. Don't be discouraged by smoke screens. Ask your questions again. If there are lies, stories will change. Examine people's answers for inconsistencies. When you think you've found something come and see me. I'll tell you then what I saw. If your suspicions match my own … then maybe we'll have something.'

Chess looked frustrated, but all she said was, 'All right.'

She opened her mouth to add something but, without giving her a chance, he turned and left.

Chapter 20

Angus headed off towards Loch Street, but it was nearly twelve o'clock. We had to go to the Four Winds Outdoor Shop. We started walking towards the main street. Ahead of us at the front of the gardens there was an old stone horse trough and beside that, in full daylight and definitely him this time, was Paz.

'Aha,' said Chess under her breath. 'Got you.'

Paz had his back to us and he was with a group of kids but they moved away. Paz looked in our direction.

'Come on,' said Chess. Not hearing my protest she charged over there.

Paz had a paper cup of chips. He watched us with the same expression as before, as if he thought we were going to say something interesting.

But Chess didn't waste time. 'You're following us.'

He shoved a chip into his mouth then tipped the box towards Chess and wiggled it, offering her one.

She ignored him. 'We see you, you know.'

You couldn't really blame her for being aggressive. Paz had been there when she got pushed into the van.

Paz didn't seem to mind the way she was. He watched her calmly, chewing and swallowing. 'It's the hair, isn't it? Dad says I look like a traffic light.' He was lisping again, through thick lips.

'Are you working with this Grif person?'

There was a flicker of recognition, immediately followed by wariness.

'Are you helping him? Is that how they know where we are?'

Paz looked at me. 'What does that mean?'

I tried to sound apologetic. 'It's just that we saw you. In Finch Street. And just after that Chess got thrown into a van.'

'And you saw it happen,' said Chess. 'You're watching us.'

'I'm keeping an eye on you. It's not the same thing.' Paz put the last few chips in his mouth and screwed up the box.

Chess folded her arms. 'It makes you an accessory, you know.'

'It makes me a student of human nature.' He was a funny kid. He sounded as if he spent a lot of time with adults, not the way Chess did, more arty or something. Now he smiled. It wasn't a nasty smile. There was a hint of apology in it. 'It was Dad's idea. He's worried about you. He wanted me to watch and call him if there was any trouble.'

'But you didn't call him.'

'Yeah. I did. But you were chucked back out of the van before he got there.'

'So if you're trying to keep us out of trouble, you completely failed.'

'I didn't say I was good at it.' He suddenly looked interested. 'What'd they do to you?'

'None of your business!' Chess was outraged. Then she looked thoughtful. 'So you're not helping Grif to follow us?'

'No way.' He looked at her directly. 'Look, I try to get on with everyone and not be judgemental. But that doesn't mean I get involved in their anti-social behaviour. I wouldn't help Grif Griffiths with anything. He's an anarchist. I did see you get thrown into that van but it was a long way away. I phoned Dad but there was nothing else I could do.' Here he put a slight emphasis on the word 'I' and threw a glance at me.

I said, 'Chess we have to go.'

'Oh yes.' Chess looked at her watch as if she was surprised to find it was still morning. 'We're going to meet your father.'

'Right-o.' Paz threw his rubbish in a bin and left us.

'Yeah.' We started walking.' And Chess ... There's something I have to tell you. About meeting Dad today.' It was time for my big message. This was not going to be what Chess wanted to hear, on top of everything else, but I'd run out of time.

'Yes?'

'This morning on the phone, Mum told me ...'

'What?' she said impatiently.

'Your father's coming too.'

Dad and Alec were waiting for us outside the shop. Dad had on the floppy shirt with yellow trains on it (which, believe it or not, is not his worst one) and faded green pants and surf sandals. Alec was in black pants and an unironed white shirt. His black hair curled up around his neck. He was thinner than last time I'd seen him and healthy looking and he'd had a shave.

It's always embarrassing meeting your parents in public. There's nothing that can be done about that — even if your parents are relatively OK, you still feel vaguely ashamed, worrying if there's something about them you're not seeing.

But there's one thing I've learned about this and that is that it's much worse if you let the embarrassment show. The best thing is to be nice to them, look straight at them and pretend they're normal people. Then you've got half a chance that no one else will look too hard.

But even though I know all this, it's still weird meeting my father in strange places. I never quite know what to do. Fortunately, even though he thinks of himself as fairly new age, Dad doesn't really hug that much. And shaking hands is something neither of us ever do with anyone. So we just said 'Hi'.

That didn't matter. Later on Dad would find a reason to put a hand on my shoulder and we both kind of knew that. We couldn't have said it at the time. We knew it without knowing we knew it, if that makes sense.

I suppose daughters are different. I would think it's fairly common for fathers and daughters to hug each other, but with Alec and Chess there was no way. They were much worse than us. Neither of them was comfortable out here on the street, Chess because she didn't understand shopping, and Alec because he didn't understand daylight.

And having to meet each other made it much worse. They were stiff and their 'Hi's had a half-swallowed sound. I felt bad for Chess. She had enough to worry about without this.

I turned to Dad. 'How's Robert?'

'Robert is good.'

'Did you see the new glaze?'

'The mottled blue ash. Yeah.'

'Good?'

'Yeah. Really good.'

If this sounds jerky and nervous it wasn't. Now that we'd got past the greeting problem we were fine. That's just how we talk. Dad never uses long sentences and when I'm with him I don't either.

'He's got a good set up. Very, very neat.' Dad made a regretful face. Being messy is one thing he'd really like to change.

I just laughed. He knows I think it doesn't matter.

He smiled ruefully and then tipped his head towards the shop window. 'Do you want to come?'

'Yep.'

Dad turned to Chess. He must have already discussed this with Alec. 'Do you two want to ...?'

He was going to suggest they go for a coffee or something, but Chess didn't let him finish. 'I'd like to see the tent.' She took a step forwards, not looking at her father. 'We'll come too.'

Alec met Dad's eyes. This wasn't what they'd planned. He hadn't seen Chess for over a month. But if he suggested anything now he'd be setting himself up to get rejected.

Four Winds was a huge shop with racks of walking clothes and long tables covered in knitted things. Bruce had done Dad a favour, getting this tent cheap from somewhere. It obviously wasn't an item he usually dealt in. We went up the back and Bruce gave Dad a tent in a bag and they talked about camping equipment and fishing and New Zealand. I listened and Chess and Alec pretended to listen. Eventually Bruce had to go and serve some other people and Dad took his tent to an empty space at the back of the shop and started pulling it out of its bag.

Chess wandered off towards a wall of coats and pants and Alec tagged after her.

Dad pulled the tent out of its bag and arranged the different bits on the carpet. He knelt down, half-unfolded the fabric, peered at one of the zippers, then pulled the poles out of their bag. I sat on the floor next to him.

Dad rubbed his hands thoughtfully along the group of poles. He said, 'Are you enjoying yourselves?'

It took me a second to realise he was talking to me, not the poles. I said, 'Yeah. It's good.'

'Seen any of Mike's movies yet?'

'Not really.'

He gave me a sideways look. But he just looked back at his poles, pulled one apart on its little spring and let it snap cleanly back into place. Then he put that down and started inspecting the seams on the inside of the tent's fly.

The sounds he was making and the plasticky smell reminded me of our previous camping trips, with borrowed gear. I wouldn't want to do it too often but now and then these trips are really good. We don't do anything, we just walk somewhere, put up the tent and make food and then sit and talk.

Actually we don't even talk much. Dad and I go into the bush to look at the sky and be quiet. The silence is the point. You sit there and let it come into you.

But today we were in a shop, and Dad had things to say. 'You went to see the Langton boy.'

'Did Mike tell you?'

Dad made an apologetic face. 'It's a big responsibility, having other people's children.'

'But we aren't children.'

'Matt.'

'OK. I get it.'

'So how was it?'

'What? Seeing Jacob?' I thought for a minute. There was a lot I couldn't tell him. 'He seems a bit … I dunno … stressed. He liked seeing us.'

Dad looked down at his pole and gave it another flick. 'You won't get in too deep, will you?'

'We're all right.'

'Yes. You are. But this Jacob has a lot of other people to look after him. You need to know your limitations. Especially Chess.'

'Chess?' I laughed. 'She's all right. She's always been all right. I'm the one who's the fruit cake, remember?'

Dad laughed too, and this is where he put the hand on my shoulder. 'OK. Well, just take it easy. That's all.'

So if Dad had come here to check up on us that was now done. He knew there was more I wasn't telling him but he could see we were OK, so he wasn't going to interfere. That's the way conversations with Dad go. The words are always pretty simple but all these important messages pass underneath.

He rubbed some tent fabric between his fingers. Dad is a potter. It's important to him how things feel. I stood behind him, looking down at the worn out soles of his sandals and the frayed patch at the end of his pants, and couldn't help smiling. One of Dad's biggest problems is that, although he hasn't got any money, he loves things that work well. This tent was an expensive one. I knew it would have a star-view window and fabric that breathed and triple-taped seams, because he'd already told me a hundred times that these things were important. He'd save money in other ways. When we went to Mount Feathertop we'd be eating noodles and lentils, and we'd probably have to push the car for the last five ks, but the tent would be perfect. When we put it up it would go swish rustle click, and those little sounds would be the best part of the whole weekend.

After a while he sat up. From here at the end of the shop we could see Chess staring intently at a thermal T-shirt. Alec was next to her, looking stooped and weak. He said something and Chess answered vaguely.

Dad said, 'I suppose you can't blame her for being like this.'

I felt I had to defend her. 'It's not Alec. She's always like this in shops.'

'Hmmm.'

'OK. They've got problems but she hasn't got time to sort it out now. She's got too much to do.'

Dad nodded. He thought I meant Year Eleven.

Chess had picked up a pair of walking shorts and was heading for a curtained off change room. There was no way she meant to buy them. They weren't her style of clothes and they'd be way too expensive for her. She just wanted to hide.

"She's met this old bloke who talks to her about logic and she's got a book about philosophy. And she's writing a lot of stuff in her notebook. That helps her deal with things.'

'Yeah.' Dad nodded. 'But one day that's going to stop working.' He put the tent back in the bag with a whispering sound, then he ran a hand over the bag.

'What do you mean?'

'Nothing goes away,' said Dad. 'You have to deal with things eventually.'

When we came out to the front of the shop, Chess was still in the changing room and Alec was hovering outside it, flicking through a rack of polar fleeces. He was maybe more wrinkly around the mouth than last time I'd seen him and the bags under his eyes were worse, but his skin was a good colour and his hair was clean. I wondered if he'd been drinking that morning. You can't usually tell with him because you can't always smell it on his breath. And he actually looks sicker and drunker when he's drying out. He wouldn't have had any in the car that morning with Dad there but he might've had a few before he left home.

As soon as she heard our voices, Chess came out. Without saying anything she charged across the room.

Alec trotted after her. 'Do you want those? I'll get them.' He tried to put a hand on the coat hanger but she pulled it away. 'Come on, Chessy. My shout.'

'I don't like them.' Chess shoved them back on a rack and headed for the door, with Alec almost running to keep up and Dad and me following.

'I'd like to, you know,' said Alec. 'I'd like to get you something.'

Chess didn't stop until she was outside the shop. Dad said a quick word to Bruce about ringing him this arvo and we followed them out.

On the footpath Chess was making little restless stepping movements with her feet, like someone who would like to run but doesn't know what direction. And Alec was still talking about the shorts he wanted to buy. 'I can, you know. I've got money.'

Chess moved over to glare at some jumpers in the window.

Dad said, 'Well, thanks Matt.' He was overdoing the cheerfulness. 'I'm glad you saw it. Let's both think about it for a day. I'll call you tomorrow.'

Chess and Alec were in one of those family things — quiet and savage and very deep.

Dad said, 'Bruce is going to show me another cheaper kind. He's being very helpful. I'll have to give him a teapot.' That's a kind of family joke.

While he talked, without meaning to, he frowned at Chess. This sulky act was new for her and he wasn't impressed. But he could see her side as well as Alec's and the look he gave her was sympathetic.

Alec was still trying to make her talk to him. 'It'll be good to be back, Chess. I'll get things sorted out for us.' His voice had gone husky. 'I'll get the roof fixed.'

'It's already organised,' said Chess. 'Tony Barrett should be there tomorrow. I gave him a key.'

This made everyone remember that Chess hadn't known when her father was coming home.

I wasn't impressed with her either. Big deal, her father had left her alone for long periods and she'd had to do all the housework for the last six years.

None of that was new. How was this meanness going to help?

Again Dad rushed in to fill the uncomfortable silence. 'Well. We'll be off then.'

'OK.' I knew what he was thinking. There was nothing either of us could say that would make this any better. If he was going to talk to Alec and Chess, which he probably was, this could be done back in Yackandandah.

We had the thing again, where we didn't want to hug or shake hands and couldn't think what else to do, so we quickly said, 'Bye,' and then Dad and Alec turned to go.

Unfortunately Alec couldn't leave it. He took about three steps and then turned back. To make it worse he had to talk loudly to cover the space between him and Chess.

'I'll see you at home then. On Friday?'

Dad tugged at his arm.

'Saturday,' said Chess.

'I'll do you a tuna casserole.'

'OK.'

There was a tiny softening in Chess's voice. Alec took a half step towards her. But as soon as she saw this Chess said, 'Bye!' and she whirled around and started walking quickly away.

Dad tightened his grip on Alec's arm and gave it a pull. Alec shook the hand off with a sudden swinging movement that made him stumble sideways. He stayed on his feet but a few people stared. While he was getting his balance back, Dad managed a final smile at me and an eye-brow move that recognised how terrible Alec and Chess were and how helpless he and I both were, and then he got Alec moving away across the road.

Chapter 21

At least Chess hadn't seen the stumble. I caught up with her a few metres down the footpath. I was trying to think of the right thing to say when I realised she was slowing down, looking at something up ahead.

We were near an arty jewellery-and-other-stuff shop and it had a major sale going on. There were people outside pointing at things in the window. Just past that, standing near some wooden benches with her phone clamped to an ear, was Anna.

When she saw us she waved and started coming through the crowd. She spoke into the phone. 'OK. Thank you.' She made the last word long and fakely sweet. She hung up, held the phone between two painted fingernails and dropped it into a shiny white bag. 'Who was that?'

She nodded across the road where Dad and Alec were walking away. There was a careful look on her face, as if she was ready to laugh but wanted to get some information before she let that show.

I looked her in the eye. 'The one with the beard and the shirt was my father. He's an artist.'

I learned to say 'artist' a long time ago. You couldn't say he was a potter because it sounded ridiculous. Artist was near enough and it explained away the weird dress habits.

Anna kept her face very still. 'What about the other one? He looked —'

'He's my father.' Chess was fierce and she'd spoken too loudly.

Anna saw a weakness. She made a snorting noise. 'No kidding.' She looked faintly disgusted. 'Is he an artist too?'

'He's an alcoholic,' said Chess.

'God,' said Anna with a look of horror. She looked after the dads, who were now well up the road. 'So they just let him ... walk around?'

I don't know what she thought an alcoholic was.

'He only eats people on Thursdays,' said Chess.

Anna didn't have any answer to that. She looked Chess up and down, letting her eyes rest on the smears on the dirty white jeans. 'Did you fall over?'

'Not exactly,' said Chess.

Anna decided to ignore her. She turned to me. 'That was Jacob.'

For a minute I didn't know what she meant. Then I remembered the phone.

'He's been looking for you. So I rang him when I saw you. He wants you to go up to the house with him.' She didn't ask if that was going to suit us. 'Come over here a sec.'

She walked us back towards the bench where there was a girl and a guy I didn't know. Not Clare. It was the girl with black hair that we'd seen outside Luca's. The guy had his hair shaved up the side with a pony tail on top and a stud in his nose.

Anna said, 'He's only around the corner. He'll be here in a minute.' She glanced at her two friends. Her face had gone blank again but her lips were pressed tightly together as if she was holding back a smile. She'd already told them about Chess and they'd have fun discussing her after we'd gone. She said, 'Jacob told me you're from Yackandandah.'

We'd said we were from Sydney. 'Yeah.' The best way to handle this was to look her straight in the eye again — a look that said, 'So I'm a liar. What are you going to do about it?'

'Have you lived there all your life?' said Anna.

'Not yet.'

Suddenly Chess said, 'Do you know Grif Griffiths? Simon Griffiths?'

They did. Instead of mocking the way she had burst out with it, they all looked at each other nervously.

Chess said, 'He's driving around in a brown van with a long wheel base, a scrape on the left rear bumper bar and a clunk in third gear. What's he up to?'

The guy said, 'Ask Anna.'

Anna said, 'Ro-ove!'

'She's one of his customers.' The guy was smiling and scowling at the same time. 'Or an agent or something.'

'Fuck off.' Anna turned to me. 'It's not true.'

The guy said, 'Maybe just once.'

Anna sat down on the empty bench and plonked her bag down hard on the ground. She spread her fingernails and looked down at them.

Chess said, 'Did Grif know Tim Williams?'

'Tim knew him. Yeah.'

I was thinking hard. Anna knew Grif too. She had bought something and sold it on. Was that true? Did Tim know? Did he threaten to tell? She would've been expelled.

Anna looked up and opened her mouth, about to ask something but thinking first. But before she had a chance to speak, Jacob's Outback came around the corner with the window open.

'Here he is.' She'd lost all the smartness. She was watching us thoughtfully. 'Off you go.'

Jacob stopped in the middle of the traffic for us to climb in.

'Grif Griffiths,' said Chess.

Jacob moved his hands higher up the steering wheel and squeezed, making the veins stand out.

'He used to go to your school. He's trying to stop us asking questions.'

'Just stay out of his way,' said Jacob.

'We're trying to. But he always seems to know where we are. Did Tim know about him? The drug dealing? Is that why he was killed?'

'You're not there yet,' said Jacob.

'What does that mean?'

'You don't know everything.'

'Well that's true,' Chess's voice got harder. 'But it's becoming increasingly obvious that you do.'

I could've told her he wasn't going to answer that. We were driving back to his place. Between the houses, over the big gardens, I got glimpses of the Mayday Hills parkland and an old brick wall.

Chess wriggled in her seat, edging around to face him more directly. 'Why don't you just tell us?'

'I'm helping you.' Jacob's profile was serious and determined. 'Time to see Tim's room.'

A short time later Jacob, Chess and I were in the Langtons' house, lined up along a huge floor-to-ceiling window. We could see a courtyard paved in large pale squares, with the house on three sides. In the middle there was a black iron table and chairs and a gigantic pot holding a bonsai tree.

The garden wasn't looking as perfect as it had for Saturday. The paving was scattered with curling leaves and bits of twig. There were more leaves on the table and a forgotten mug, and one of the chairs had a newspaper blown up against the back of it.

On the far side of the paving there was a lawn and past that, behind some flowers but still clearly visible from the house, was a brick building, tiny and square, almost like a country cottage.

Chess turned and looked behind us. 'So on the night Tim died, you and Tim and Angus left for the town hall and everyone else was in here having drinks.'

The Langtons' family room was huge, with leather arm chairs and a half-size pool table. The far wall had white shelves with a TV and hard drive and music system. Near the windows the wall was lined with stone, lead-grey, streaked with dusty white.

'Calvin was taking photos of the others in front of the window somewhere.' Chess turned back to the window. 'They had an uninterrupted view of Tim's room. Especially if the light was on over the door.'

While she talked she made spiky little movements with her hands and fingers. Meeting her father hadn't been good for her. In a way, it was worse for her than getting thrown into the van. She'd gone back to the way she'd been at the Town Hall — tense and trying not to show it.

Jacob didn't answer. He was staring out at the little house, lost in thought. 'It's a crucial point,' insisted Chess. 'It means it was impossible for anyone to take the poison before Paz took up his position in Tim's room. You do realise that, don't you? They all left for the Town Hall but then someone must have come back for the poison.'

Outside there was a gust of wind and a cloud of papery seed pods came swirling into the courtyard.

Jacob wasn't thinking about what Chess was saying. He took a step towards the door. 'Come to the granny house.' It was weird hearing him say that — a name from a happy childhood. As we walked across the courtyard he said, 'I always thought I'd be out here for my year twelve but Tim needed somewhere to stay. His parents are old friends of Mum and Dad.'

The granny house was symmetrical, with a window each side of the door, like a doll's house. Above the door there was a homemade sign, a piece of pine that someone had burnt letters into.

'*Elsinore*,' I read. 'What's the point of that?'

'It's just something Tim did. His name for the place.' Jacob produced a key and led us inside. He didn't think the sign was important.

But Paz had used the name for his trick. The trick was a tribute to Tim. Or maybe it was connected with this room.

Jacob hustled us in and pulled the door shut. 'There's no one here. Mum's shopping and Angus is at some old guy's place. But we better keep it quiet in case they come back. I don't want anyone knowing you're in here.'

Instead of opening the curtains, he turned on a light. We were in a small room with a saggy arm chair facing a TV and a PS4. Up against a wall was an old bookcase — the antique kind with two wooden doors on the bottom, then a wide drawer, and two glass doors on top, showing shelves of books.

'That's where the poison was.' Jacob spoke quietly, almost whispering. 'They found a bit of the powder spilled over there.' He waved to a small table near the door.

'Way over there?' said Chess sharply.

The table had a lot of stuff on it. Gadgets for magic tricks.

'Yes. For some reason whoever it was got the poison out of the bookcase and took it over there to empty it into their own container.'

'That's strange,' I said. 'Why would he do that? Why not just take the jar?'

'And, more importantly, how?' said Chess.

I thought it again. Chess was too focussed. Her face looked strained and her eyes were wet. She was trying to use the puzzle to forget all the other stuff, but today it wasn't working so well. She said, 'That's really the big question, isn't it? How did the murderer get the poison out of here? Paz insisted he didn't see anyone all night. So we need to work out if that's remotely possible. Or to confirm he's lying.'

She went to the bookcase and started running her hands over the wood. The glass doors had a little key hole with the key in it. Chess opened them and started tapping away at the woodwork. She pulled a few books out and felt the back wall of the bookcase, peering in to see what she could in the bad light.

'There's no false back.' Jacob tried a smile. 'No secret openings through to the wall, no shelves that slide magically into a hidden space.'

I turned my attention to the Play Station. There was a pile of games on top of it and a controller neatly beside them.

Jacob knew what I was thinking. 'The police went over the place but we put everything back more or less where it was.' He touched the top game lightly with his fingertips. 'His mother won't come here. She said she feels as if the place is haunted. She said it feels like one of his stupid tricks. His mirror box. Tim came into this house and never came out, but when you look inside he isn't there.'

He pulled his hand off the game quickly. 'Mum doesn't want to pack it away. We feel a bit …' He took a breath. 'We feel we should leave it exactly as it was. His parents will come one day. People need time.'

In the car he'd been in control but now, surrounded by reminders of Tim, his mouth was going loose. 'We don't feel as if we have the right …'

At this point his phone beeped and he grabbed it from a pocket, looking relieved to have something to do.

I looked through the games: *Bloodborne, Dark Souls, Kings Quest, Valiant Hearts, Call of Duty: Ghosts*.

Jacob put his phone away. He waved a hand timidly, as if movements that were too large might disturb the air. 'Keep it quiet, OK? Just in case?' He started to go out and then came back.

'There's something else you should know.' He looked very intense, as if he had some big secret to tell us. 'The lid was back on.' He looked at me waiting for a reaction. 'The spilled powder was on that table near the magic gear and the bottle was back in the bookcase with the lid back on.'

I had no idea what he was getting at but he seemed to want some kind of answer. Chess had finished inspecting the bookcase. Now she was scanning the books.

'So ... the murderer was very tidy?' I said.

He went out without answering, shutting the door carefully behind him.

At the sound of him leaving, Chess stepped back from the bookcase. 'What did he say?'

I repeated it for her.

'Is that significant?'

'Jacob doesn't know what's significant and what isn't. He's not dealing with this very well.'

Chess nodded. 'That's why he needs us.'

I looked at the low table near the door. It had Tim's richly coloured cylinders and boxes. And there was also another magic book, *Mephistos Encyclopaedia of Disappearance*. I went over and picked it up. 'Maybe there is something significant about magic.'

Chess made a little sniffing noise. 'Don't be silly, Matt. That boy uses tricks to avoid answering questions. That's all. We need to look at the physical arrangements and proceed with small, logical, provable steps.'

Quoting Angus made her happier and calmer. She went to inspect the window and the wall at the back of the room. I looked at the low table. Jacob wanted us to know the powder had been spilt here. Of course there was no powder on it now.

Five red cardboard boxes of different sizes, a piece of rope, a pair of giant dice, and the blue and gold tubes that were in the photo of Tim. They had some kind of weird name. What was it?

But none of that could be important. I turned my back on it.

At one end of the room a door stood open, showing part of a bathroom. I had a quick look in there. Toilet, shower, basin. The room was tiny. If Paz was having a wee he'd be almost level with the door. It would've been impossible for someone to get to the bookcase and out again without him seeing.

At the other end of the room there was a dark red door, partly open. Next to that was another small table, holding a bowl of bananas and apples, and an open packet of Nobby's nuts — and I realised something important. It had been a long time since breakfast.

Chess was lifting a poster off the wall to look behind it. It didn't occur to me that it was strange to find food here, in a room no one ever went into. I peeled a banana and took a huge bite. Then, while I was manoeuvring that into a chewable position, I shoved in a couple of nuts. Even with the salt, the nut and banana flavours went together quite well, which was lucky because these experiments don't always work. I kept eating and looked around.

Through the partly open second door I could see a dim light, with some dark shapes under it. I elbowed the door wider and went in.

I was in a narrow bedroom. The light was coming from a desk lamp, one of those ones on a folding stalk, like the Pixar lamp, and it was pulled down close to the surface of the desk. I went over and lifted it higher.

The desk still had all Tim's books on it. Standing up along the back were a few text books, a thesaurus and three files marked Bio, Maths and Modern History. On the left there was a pile of paper and plastic folders and, next to those, a lap top.

For some reason the sight of this desk gave me a cold lump in the stomach. I stood there looking at it, wondering why. Then I realised. It was exactly like my desk. Not exactly like. For one thing I haven't got my own lap top, but it was the same kind of thing. And the bed beside it, neatly made, with a lumpy doona and an Indian cotton blanket with a snagged thread in one corner — it was all, in a weird way, familiar. I started thinking of that first school photograph Chess had shown me, Tim's round face. And the photo in the Langton's lounge room, Tim doing his silly tricks, looking so pleased.

And now, suddenly, out of nowhere, it was possible to feel it. This was the place of a dead person. The stage hadn't had that feeling — it was here. And what you could feel — it wasn't ghosts. It was silence.

I hadn't worked it out before, but the road where Jeanette died and Debbie's black pool were full of it too — not the normal peace-and-quiet kind of silence, something more, something that makes you think of vast empty space, and time that goes on forever. The silence in this little house, *Elsinore*, went deep, as if it had somehow soaked into the walls, and now it was seeping out again, filling the space, like water vapour.

Tim Williams wasn't just some mystery, some puzzle to keep Chess's mind away from her father. He was real. He had a tiny bedroom and a desk full of stuff and a thick doona that he would throw off every night. He'd had a life. And someone had taken that away.

With Jeanette and Debbie I'd felt sad and then I'd felt rage. Tim deserved a bit of that too. For the first time I really felt it. I wanted to find out what happened, not for Jacob, or Angus, and not for Chess. For Tim.

I shoved the rest of the banana in my mouth, put the peel and the nut packet down, wiped some salt on my pants, sat down at the desk and started leafing through the pile of papers.

After a minute I had a bit of a smile to myself. I'd had the impression this Tim guy was a good student — intellectual and organised. But this was just like the pile on my desk, a big random jumble, all the subjects and assignments mixed up. There were lined A4 pages with class notes in scrawly handwriting, typed up assignments marked in red pen, old exam papers, and other pages covered in drawings and doodles. There were a lot of display folders, mostly half empty, with class notes and printouts from the net: *Imagery of John Donne, The October Revolution, Suspense and character in Gattaca.* Amongst all that there were large yellow envelopes with nothing inside and printouts from net sites about magic, and catalogues of conjuring stuff with order forms.

I wasn't really getting anywhere. One of the yellow envelopes had Tim's handwriting across the front: *'Crab Going Backwards — madness feigned and real in Hamlet.'*

Across one corner, in someone else's handwriting, *'Williams you bastard!! Hundred big ones. Next time I want a discount.'*

I rubbed my hands over the writing, trying to work out what it meant, then leafed through the pile again.

'Look in the lap top,' said Chess.

It was lucky I'd finished the nuts because I sucked in a lot of air. She didn't notice she'd scared me half to death, partly because she was so hyper-intense and partly because she never notices things like that. Now, without waiting for me to recover, she pulled the lap top towards her and felt for the ON switch.

She pressed a few buttons, stared at the screen, then opened the top drawer of the desk. With a little grunt of satisfaction she pulled out a scrap of paper.

'Luckily Tim was the sort of person who has to write passwords down.' She gave the piece of paper a little disapproving flick. 'I ask you.' With six brisk little taps she typed in 'HAMLET' and then watched as Tim's desktop appeared. I didn't offer her the chair. I sat back and picked up the bag of nuts.

Chess stooped over the screen, tapping keys and stroking the mouse pad, occasionally making little 'Ahh' noises, like a doctor listening to someone's chest. The screen flashed and changed. She scrolled down rows of emails, looked through folders.

Then she sat back. 'Oh my golly.'

She'd found a file called '*One may smile and smile and be a villain*.' In it there was a photo — a guy leaning on the bonnet of a car with a beer can, laughing. It was Jacob. Chess pressed a key. Another photo of the same car. This time one front corner was smashed. Jacob was in the driver's seat. He seemed to be struggling with the door. A third photo showed him climbing over into the passenger seat towards an open door.

'Tim emailed this photo to Jacob.'

I said, 'Photos of himself?'

'Jacob wants to be a lawyer. He couldn't afford to be caught drink driving or crashing cars. Maybe Tim was threatening to expose his secrets. It would give Jacob a motive.'

'You're not saying you think he killed Tim?'

'It's a theory.'

'But he asked us to come to Beechworth. He brought us to this room. He left the desk light on for us.'

'Maybe he wants to confess. Maybe he can't take the pressure.' Chess shrugged. 'You're the psychologist.'

'No. It can't be right.'

'We need to get home to think about it. This doesn't necessarily —'

Before she could finish, the other room lightened and a voice called, 'Hello?'

It was Mrs Langton and she was already inside. Chess and I leapt up. We went out through the door.

'Oh!' My voice had squeaked. I struggled to control it. 'Hello.'

Mrs Langton must have seen the light and come to investigate. She didn't know what to make of us being here. She came another step into the room, smiling warily as if she thought we might be insane.

'We were just looking at … around …' I started this sentence quickly and ended weakly which made me sound sounded guilty, as if we'd broken in to steal things. 'Jacob brought us here.' In a way this was dobbing him in because Jacob hadn't wanted her to know we were here, but it was too late to worry about that. Also I was in a panic. I was confused. Was Jacob Tim's villain? Could Tim have been threatening to expose Jacob's secrets? But Jacob had begged us to find Tim's murderer. So that didn't make sense. We had found out something massive and confusing and we had no time to think it through.

Mrs Langton frowned. 'Jacob? Is he home?' She looked behind her, back through the door towards the garden and the house.

Chess took that opportunity to leap back to the bedroom. I heard the lap top click shut. Mrs Langton stared at her. Now she definitely thought we were insane.

'Didn't you see him?' I said. 'I thought he was going to ...' I stopped.

'What?'

I couldn't think of an answer. I didn't know where Jacob had gone.

Mrs Langton said, 'Has he left you and gone off to watch the cricket?' She frowned. 'I didn't see him anywhere.' Her eyes went to the bowl of fruit.

'Would you like a banana?' I said. It sounded completely ridiculous, partly because I was offering her food in her own place, but mostly because as I said it I held out the bag of nuts, which made it look as if I didn't know what a banana was.

Mrs Langton stared at the nuts. 'No thank you.' I put them down. Then she noticed my first banana peel beside the bowl.

'I'll get that!' I leapt to pick it up and then leapt back into Tim's room to grab the other one off the desk. Then I stood in the middle of the room with a peel in each hand, looking frantically around for a rubbish bin. 'We thought it would be OK to eat something. We were going to clear it up.' She was staring at me.

'Jacob said he'd be back in a minute,' said Chess feebly.

I could see a bin under the bathroom sink. I started towards it.

'Wretched boy,' said Mrs Langton.

I whirled around. The banana peels swung gently.

But she was smiling. 'I'm really sorry he's treating you like this.' She looked at the desk light, now visible through the open door. 'I sometimes wonder if he's ... Jacob was very disturbed by his friend's death. We all were. I hope he hasn't got you two —'

'No,' said Chess quickly, without knowing what she'd been going to say. 'We're fine.'

'Well, I'm very sorry he's brought you here and just abandoned you. He's been quite peculiar and dreadful these days. I'll have a quick scout around for him and then I'll drive you home again.'

Chapter 22

'Tim had a wonderful collection of video games.' Mrs Langton led us out of Elsinore, locked the door and pocketed the key. 'Or so I'm told. Of course I wouldn't know anything about them.' She wasn't concentrating on what she was saying. As we got to the door she said, 'That jolly Jacob. People think he's wonderful but he can be a real menace when he wants to.' Then her voice lifted. 'Oh, here's Anna.'

Anna was in the family room, sitting sideways on a leather couch with her knees bent up in front of her. She had a book resting on her legs. She can't have been there more than ten minutes.

'Look at you,' said Mrs Langton. 'Always with a pencil in your hand.' She had that adoring, slightly fuzzy tone that she used for Jacob.

Anna looked up in an unfocussed way. As her mother waved us towards the chairs, she stretched her legs along the couch. This allowed us to see a large visual diary with some sketches on it. Anna had been drawing. Now she started again. Her pencil made a quiet scratching sound on the page, which is a sound I like. I leaned sideways to see what she was doing.

Anna's hand had polished nails and a ring on every finger, but it moved the pencil skilfully. And she wasn't drawing Barbie girls or big-eyed cutesy-pie cartoons. She was drawing cats. She looked up for a second. In a patch of sunlight in the corner, curled loosely against the warm stone wall, was a brown-grey cat. And now my surprise was joined by something else — something that might have been a bit like resentment. Because Anna's drawings were good.

'Cats,' I said.

'Are you drawing Pebbles darling?' said Mrs Langton.

Anna didn't look up. In a dreamy voice she said, 'I'm trying to get the movement … the angle of the ear.'

It was almost too much for me. I had this girl classified as a shallow clothes horse and not a nice person. But people who could draw were nice. They were intelligent and sensitive. They were me.

Chess wriggled, accidentally kicking the leg of the coffee table. At the sudden movement the cat got up, gave one of those up-themselves, shuddering stretches that cats do and walked stiffly out to the corridor.

The spell was broken. Anna looked at Chess and then at me and it was like a veil lifting. Suddenly she was the old self-conscious, hard-faced person. She did the stiff shoulder wiggle and clinked the bracelets on her left hand. 'And I am *so over* horses.'

At this point Mrs Langton said she would drive us home, but first Jacob should say goodbye and apologise for abandoning us. She went to find him.

Anna turned and dropped her feet to the floor. She put the book on the table and gave me a sly smile. 'You were totally sprung.'

'Jacob thought she was out.'

Anna looked out at Tim's house. Elsinore. 'Why did he take you there, anyway?'

I said, 'There was something he wanted us to see. He left a light on at Tim's desk. He left some bananas and nuts near the door to attract us over there.'

Anna curled a lip. 'What are you? Possums?'

I couldn't help a smile but Chess said, 'The lap top was plugged in, charging. And the password was handy. I think he wanted us to find out about some things.'

'What things?'

I said, 'There was a file about Jacob stacking a car. And I think he was paying Tim to do assignments for him. Tim knew a lot about him and he was threatening to tell.'

Chess said, 'Tim could have ruined Jacob's future.'

For once Anna forgot to sneer. She stared at her pencil.

I said, 'What we don't understand is, why would Jacob lead us to see all that? Is it some kind of weird confession thing? I mean I'm not saying he killed Tim or anything.'

It was such a huge thing to say, and I had said it in such an ordinary way, that we were all stunned. So for a minute we just sat there, staring out the windows.

It was a pretty view, like a painting arranged for the people inside to look at. A box-like house, a tiled roof, two square windows and a red door. On each side was a small tree, curved branches with clouds of blossom, and in front was the straight path, the lawn, the flower beds.

Elsinore. The Elsinore Vanish. A vanishing trick. A card had gone into a pile and then disappeared and reappeared across the room. I looked at the house again. It was like a box — a magician's box on a stage set.

'We're trying to work out what can have happened in there.' I looked at Chess but she had her intense closed-in look so I went on, working it out as I went. 'It was impossible for anyone to get the poison out of that room without Paz seeing them. If Jacob came and got it he must be threatening Paz not to say.'

Chess suddenly woke up. 'Of course it could have been you.' She narrowed her eyes at Anna. 'You bought and sold drugs for Grif Griffiths.'

'Once. Once!'

'Tim knew about it, didn't he? Now Grif Griffiths is threatening us, trying to keep us from finding something out. Is it about you?'

Anna snapped, 'Just wait a minute. Just let me think.' She tapped one finger onto the tip of the pencil, making little dents in her finger tip. After a while she looked at Chess and for the first time there was no scorn in her face. She looked confused, as if she was about to ask for help. 'There's something I have to tell you.'

There were voices and a high laugh and Jacob and Mrs L appeared outside, coming from the direction of the driveway. They came in through the glass doors. Mrs Langton was saying something about bananas.

Anna scribbled something on a page of her book. She tore the page out and shoved it at me. She said, 'Yes, of course you can have one of my drawings.' She was talking loudly for her mother to hear. She did one of her worst fake sweet smiles. 'Maybe I can have one of yours one day.'

As we walked towards the car with Mrs Langton, Chess and I had a look at what she had written.

'Post Office. 11 o'clock tomorrow.'

Chapter 23

After all that, of course we had to have another night session. This time I was actually quite pleased because I was going to worry about everything we'd learned anyway, and without Chess's help I was probably going to end up banging my head on the wall.

Some time around eleven, Chess came to my bedroom. She was holding a toothbrush and a little plastic soap holder. And she was in her nightie.

'We need to get this sorted out.'

I sat up and squinted my eyes. I was worried about Chess. Last time she'd come in here she'd been stimulated by her mystery. But tonight her face was pale and pinched and she was holding on to herself very tightly. At dinner she'd been so quiet even Mike, who had gone so badly with the personal questions last night, had asked her if she was all right. She'd said she was but it wasn't true.

'We have to be very careful. There are so many distractions.' She wrapped her arms around her stomach and for a second her face kind of collapsed.

'Chess —'

'Matt, no. It's important. We have to remember the difference between inductive and deductive reasoning and not jump too far.' She made a little movement with the toothbrush.

'OK. Let's get into it then. What are we saying? Jacob's now our man?'

Chess stood with one bare foot on top of the other. 'Well it all follows if you think it through.' She looked at the soap holder as if she wished it was the notebook. 'Tim did assignments for Jacob and he had kept evidence. Jacob was involved in some of the wild behaviour and the car crashes and the damage. And Tim kept photographs. He might also have known about Anna being caught up with Grif Griffiths.'

She was off now, thinking hard and fast. There was no room for thoughts about her father

'And then sometimes Tim got annoyed. On the night of the variety show he was full of bitterness and jealousy and rage against the world. And some of that anger was directed towards the "villain".'

'Actually that does fit, in a way.'

'What fits?'

'The fact that Tim was so angry when he talked about "the villain". It was because it was his friend. If he knew secrets about Calvin or someone else, I don't reckon he would have been all that upset. He would've been pleased.'

Chess shrugged and went on. 'Jacob had been working for years to get into Arts Law at Monash Uni and Tim could have ruined that. That gives Jacob a motive to kill Tim. Let's just run with that for a minute and see if it works.' She shifted her weight onto the other foot.

'Do you want to sit down?'

I waved at the metal bed frame but she ignored me. 'Say Jacob sneaked off from the Town Hall to Tim's room, bribed or frightened Paz into keeping quiet and ran back with the cyanide before anyone noticed he was missing. He laced the flask, then went to join Tim's act. And as part of the act he handed the flask to Tim, right in front of everyone.'

'All right,' I said. 'Here's where my problem starts. It's incredibly cold blooded. When Tim died, right there, right in front of him, Jacob had to fake surprise. He'd have to be a pretty good actor.'

'I don't think anyone there would have been watching Jacob's reaction. Everyone was panicking about Tim.'

'Maybe.' I sat back on the pillow.

'And now Jacob is pretending to go along with our investigation, while simultaneously trying to sabotage it.'

'But that's the other thing.' Now it was time for my really big objection. 'He didn't just go along with us. He asked us to come here. He was begging us to help him. Why would he do that?'

'Because he thought we'd do it anyway.'

'But it wasn't like that.'

Chess gave me a superior smile. 'Not this again.'

'There are some things you just feel, Chess. You just know them.'

'But someone *seeming* innocent is not reliable information. People who murder people are good at putting on false fronts. We learned that last time.'

I didn't have an answer to that.

Chess took a step further into the room. The nightie was short and lacy and showed her stringy knees. 'And furthermore, while pretending to go along with us, Jacob has an old school friend trying to scare us away.'

I was afraid the nightie might be a bit see-through. And even if it wasn't, there's something embarrassing about a nightie, no matter what it's made of. Just because it's defined as pyjamas.

I said, 'What about today? Why did Jacob lead us to Tim's desk with the light on and the lap top charged for us to find out about the essays?'

'Well I don't know.' Chess suddenly looked worried.

'No. Me neither. And then there's the question of Anna. She had secrets and knew Grif. It might have been her.'

'Maybe that hypothesis makes more sense.'

'It's hard to believe. She doesn't seem —'

'Agh!' Chess slapped the toothbrush and soap holder up and down in fury.

We looked at each other for a minute, listening to the night sounds, each waiting for the other one to have an idea. Finally I sighed. 'We're seeing Anna tomorrow. Let's leave it till then.'

'All right,' said Chess tightly. 'Let's say it could have been Jacob or Anna. Let's just move on to the crucial thing. Paz.' She stared at the wall, sticking up one finger. 'If Jacob or Anna left the ball and went back to that room and took the poison, Paz has to have seen them.'

'Well, that's weird, too.'

'Why?'

'Because he said the wrong thing.'

This was a big moment for me. Since I got to bed, I'd had a thought. And it was huge.

'If Paz knew who took the poison, but he didn't want to tell, all he had to say was he ducked out for a minute. He could say he went to the house to make a toasted sandwich and was gone half an hour. Or he could say he fell asleep. Then anyone could have got in there without him seeing.'

'Maybe he didn't think quickly enough. Not everyone is a convincing liar.'

'But Paz is a convincing liar.'

'And he is lying to us. Otherwise everything is impossible.'

Now I was feeling stubborn. 'Well I just don't think he was.'

Chess groaned.

'Here's a thing. Paz and Tim both liked magic tricks and Paz thinks the tricks are relevant. Doesn't it seem like that to you? He called that trick the "Elsinore Vanish".'

'He's laughing at us.'

'No. It was more like he was still doing tributes to Tim.'

Chess made another angry noise. 'It's all intuition. And it's nonsense. The only way any of this makes sense is if Paz is lying. If Paz isn't lying everything is just impossible.' She was really losing it now. 'This whole thing is a complete disaster! We've followed a trail and somehow, of all people, we've got to Jacob and Anna. But all we've established is that they both had motives for killing Tim. But *a lot* of other people could have had motives. And *no one* had opportunity. The field is still wide open. And at the same time it's still completely closed.' Her voice had gone high. 'So essentially we've got nowhere. We try to follow a line of thought and these ... big walls …' She made an angry chopping motion with the toothbrush. '… come down …'

I straightened the doona with a noisy flapping motion. 'I think we're just a bit tired. It might be important to stay open —'

'What does that mean, open?'

She was angry anyway, so I thought I might as well go on. 'I just think that sometimes you … we … use so much energy trying to control things it doesn't make it easier to think, it makes it harder. You know?'

She didn't know.

'If you're angry about your crummy life — '

'Well thanks very much!'

'— or afraid —'

'Afraid of what?'

'It might be better to just to go with that for a minute.'

'Like you, you mean? Be sensitive to feelings … how people *seem*. But then we end up with something that doesn't make sense.'

'OK,' I said soothingly. 'Well, maybe that's it, Chess. That's the thing we have to add to the equation. Things don't always make sense.' She tossed her head and stared at the door. 'Murder is very extreme. Extreme emotions are involved.' I'm no good at explaining things. 'Murder is about people. And people don't always behave logically. They do one thing and then they do another thing. They change their minds. And sometimes they do things for no reason at all.

'So intuition might be the key. When it comes to people, there are some things you just know. Inside. You just feel it if something is right.'

She almost laughed. 'I can't do that.'

'Well Chess, maybe that's what I'm here for.'

Which was completely wrong. What I was there for was to keep Chess out of trouble. I'd known that, back at the beginning. But now I'd got caught up in the whole mystery — the sadness, the fear, the idea that we'd cut a path through all the confusion and lies, point out a murderer, take away everyone's pain, the idea that I had talents Chess didn't have.

If I'd thought about it for a minute, I would've remembered the way it should be. Chess was the clear-eyed one who discovered hidden truths. I was supposed to look after her, to make sure nothing bad happened.

And at that I completely failed.

Chapter 24

At ten o'clock the next morning Chess came in with the phone. My dad wanted to talk to me. The conversation was too long and annoying for me to describe, but my half went like this:

'Don't come ... we're fine ... Chess is all right ... I *am* looking after her ... Dad. We're sixteen ... We don't need more cake ... No. Don't come.'

You get the idea.

At five to eleven we were standing under the arches of the post office on a corner of the main street, waiting for Anna. Behind us, down near the old court house, two tourist buses had arrived. There was a crowd of people gathering in front of us at the intersection, crossing the road and spreading out towards all the shops.

We were waiting for Anna to appear, but I was also watching for Grif's brown van. I would always be watching for it when we were on the streets of Beechworth. Last time he'd let Chess off with a warning but who knew what they would do next, if they realised we hadn't given up? I hadn't mentioned this to Chess but I suppose she was thinking about it too. She was quiet and still very tense.

There was a group of kids outside the bakery. As I watched one guy pushed the head of another one, putting him in a fake neck lock, while the others all made 'Whoa' sounds. When they straightened, they shoved each other and everyone laughed and swayed around. I grinned.

A voice behind me said, 'Hi.' I whirled around. It was Clare.

'Hi-i.' I started weakly because my mind had been a hundred miles away, and then, half way through the word I tried to sound glad to see her. It came out sounding fake. I could see that in her face. I cursed myself. It wasn't fake. I was glad to see her. At least I would've been if I'd had a chance to have a normal day.

Clare must've been as embarrassed as I was because we then had one of those out-of-order conversations that means people are just filling up the silence and not thinking about the words.

Clare said, 'How are you?'

I said, 'How are you?'

'Good.'

'What are you up to?'

'That's good.'

'Nothing much.'

At that point, realising I had actually answered my own question, Clare laughed, and I laughed too, and just for one tiny second everything felt normal.

'There she is,' said Chess.

Clare looked to where Chess was pointing and her face went stiff. Anna was across the road, outside one of the old banks. She was standing in the middle of the footpath with tourists jostling around her.

'We're meeting her,' I said.

Clare took a step back.

Anna didn't seem to have seen us. She was looking away, down past the bakery, peering at the approaching traffic, as if she was waiting for someone to come in a car.

Clare touched me on the arm. 'Can I tell you something?'

I looked at her.

'It's Anna. I just think you should know —'

'Look. She's not a friend. We just want to ask her something.'

'No. I mean … be careful. She's got a big chip, with her brother being everyone's hero and then everyone's prime suspect. It makes her …'

'We know what she's like. It's OK.'

'No. You think she's a lightweight, a pretender. But some of the stuff she does is serious.'

'Anna!' Chess called.

Anna didn't move.

'She didn't hear. *Anna!*'

Anna moved her head, looking around vaguely, but she didn't look our way.

'What's she playing at?' I said to Chess.

'I'll leave you to it,' said Clare.

I turned to her. 'Sorry, I just really have to do this.'

'It's OK,' she said cheerfully, and walked away.

So when I joined Chess at the roadside, waiting to cross, I was feeling pretty bad. I was feeling sorry about Clare because she was really nice. But at the same time I was also wondering what Anna was doing and also thinking about how important this whole thing had become and how I just had to finish it. When it was over I'd get back to being normal. I really would.

'Why can't she hear us?' said Chess.

'Oh she heard us all right.'

It was weird. One minute Anna was going to help us and now she was ignoring us. Maybe she just liked messing with people.

We were tangled up with a large group of tourists, all waiting to cross the road. Anna scanned past us for a second, across the top of the traffic. Then she sort of froze. She seemed to see something. I turned to look. Coming up Camp Street from the direction of the gorge was the brown van.

'Anna,' I yelled.

But she didn't need warning. She was already running, away from us, back up Ford Street.

'Did she see the van?' said Chess. 'She should stay here among all the people.'

There was a break in the traffic. 'Come on,' I said.

The van was behind two other cars which had stopped at the roundabout. That gave us a few seconds to get away.

'Matt, I think —'

'This isn't the time for thinking. Run.'

We got to the middle of the road, waited for a car and a ute, and made it to the other side. But Anna had moved quickly too. Already she was half a block away. Unfortunately these were the prime tourist shops, full of lace things and chocolates and soaps and half the stuff was out on the footpath and the bus people were looking at it. Through the crowd I could see Anna's blonde head, still moving away. We went as fast as we could, dodging people, trying not to lose sight of her. She kept looking behind her. After a few more metres she went to one of the little bridges over the gutter and peered down the road.

'What's she doing now?' said Chess.

We looked too. The brown van wasn't even there. Grif hadn't seen us.

'So what is it?' said Chess.

Anna turned again and, just for a second, she looked straight at me.

Chess said, 'It's us. She's leading us somewhere.'

We caught the flash of a smile.

'This is bullshit,' I said.

Anna was going past a plant shop now, big bright flowers in old-fashioned pots. She was in a clear patch, moving quickly. Chess and I were still caught up in the crowd, walking, dodging and weaving. I looked again. There was no sign of the brown van.

We got to the plant shop and started running. Anna went across a side road towards a couple of old churches. Finally she stopped.

We were outside Luca's now and nearly at the corner. 'Anna!' I yelled.

Anna was standing in front of one of the churches, beside a big sign and a couple of rocket-shaped bushes. She gave another smile, right at me this time, but then suddenly she looked tired and a bit confused, as if she didn't know what we were shouting about. She raised an arm, as if she was going to wave to someone behind me and then she glanced towards the door of the building and moved the arm in that direction. Then she turned and ran inside.

Chapter 25

The building wasn't used as a church any more. The sign outside said 'Youth Access Centre'. The big double doors were open and inside them there was another set, also wooden, with windows in them. As we came through one of these inner doors was swinging shut. We went banging into the building. Then we stopped.

There was only one person in the Youth Centre and it wasn't Anna.

We were in a high room, painted a kind of browny purple, with tall windows on either side and a double door at the back, also half wood and half frosted glass. The room was full of bright furniture — orange and pink couches and cushions with spots on them. There was a set of speakers up against a wall, a guitar on a bean bag, a set of table soccer and a quarter-size pool table.

Way up the back of the room, in a corner, there was a small desk and standing behind the desk was Paz.

Chess marched up to the doors at the back. They were locked. She shook the handle and then tried to see through the glass.

The room was very quiet. Any traffic was muffled by the double doors. It felt as if there was no one else in the building. On the table in front of him, Paz had spread a red cloth, an old curtain or something, thick, with a faded swirly pattern. On it he had a black briefcase, also pretty old, worn smooth at the corners.

He didn't seem surprised to see us. 'Hi guys,' he said, in his lispy, childish way.

Chess turned away from the back doors. 'Did you lock them?'

'They're always locked.'

'Where did she go?' Chess's voice was cracked and unnatural after the sprint.

'Who?'

'What do you mean who?' She turned and looked at every corner of the room. Her eyes fell for a minute on a tiny brass grate in the wooden floor. Then she looked at Paz again. 'Anna! Where did she go?'

Paz started getting some things out of his case and placing them carefully on the table. A pack of cards, a glass and two fifty cent pieces.

With a huff of impatience, Chess went up to him and looked under his tablecloth. Paz looked at me. The look was slow and direct, not really amused, but he knew something. This was some kind of game.

Chess glared at him. 'Well, she didn't just disappear.'

'Are you saying she vanished into thin air?' Paz waved around the room. 'That doesn't sound very rational.'

Chess realised he was mucking around with her. She took two steps towards him, watching him carefully.

'Go back,' he said quietly, nodding towards the street. 'Have a look.'

She hesitated a second, narrowing her eyes at him, then throwing back her shoulders in an irritated way, went back to the main doors.

I thought it would be best to leave her alone. I went closer to Paz. 'Sorry about her.'

'Chess is OK.'

I grinned apologetically. 'She takes a bit of getting used to.'

'No,' he insisted. 'I think Chess is ultimate. I mean she has a lot of worries, hasn't she? I bet she's not always like this. And I like the …' He waved towards the area around his waist. '... the pants ... and the little-girl plastic watch, and the way she just doesn't give a stuff.'

I nodded. He had surprised me again. As we got older Chess was becoming more accepted — not liked exactly, but accepted. But when I was his age it was only cool to be ... well, cool.

Paz reached into his bag again and pulled out some scraps of material, hankies or scarves. They had that intense sort of colour that means they'd feel really soft.

'What's all this about Paz?' I waved at the table of stuff and then at the empty room.

'This is about economics. The Beechworth City Council want to start a Youth Café. We are having fund raising events. We run school holiday workshops — art, magic, guitar.' He gave me a soft smile. 'The guitar is the most popular.'

I looked around at the room. A row of lime green chairs with chrome legs, a gum machine full of M&Ms. On the left, between windows, there was a giant pin-up board covered in photos — kids playing guitars, talking laughing, making faces at the camera.

Beside that there were two tall mirrors propped up on stands, facing each other. Someone had put one of the green chairs in between them. In the mirror facing me, I could see the chair's reflection, but I could also see a reflection of the other mirror, so that there was an infinite line of empty chairs, getting smaller and smaller.

Paz saw me looking. 'Forever mirrors,' he said. 'They're just for our amusement.'

Chess was moving around at the front door, coming in and going out. It was very quiet. I thought about the brown van again.

Paz said, 'I want to show you something.'

But I didn't have a chance to ask what he meant because Chess called me. I went to join her. Between the wood-and-glass doors and the outer doors there was about a metre of space. The outer doors opened inward and they were pushed back at right angles. Chess pulled one of them. Behind it was a small space, big enough to stand in.

'Anna could have hidden in there,' said Chess. 'We were coming up the street, so if she'd hopped into the side we were coming from we wouldn't have seen her.'

I said, 'And she pushed the inner door to make it swing, to make sure we'd go rushing in.'

'Then once we were inside she just sneaked away.' Chess made a frustrated noise, edged past me and went back to Paz.

Paz was folding a purple scarf. It kept slipping through his fingers.

'Oh very clever,' said Chess.

Paz made a snatching motion at the air in between them and opened his hand to reveal a fifty cent piece.

'But unfortunately,' said Chess, 'we're here for a fairly serious matter, and I'm finding it hard to take things so lightly.'

Paz put his coin on top of two others already on the table.

Chess took a step towards him. 'Obviously you and Anna cooked up that little trick between you.'

He lined the coins up with precise movements of his soft fingers.

'What possible reason could you have for doing something like that? I didn't realise you even knew each other.'

'We don't.'

'Well, what then?!' It was getting hard for Chess to stay calm. She made a jerky movement with her head.

'Paz,' I said gently. 'Do you know where Anna is? We really need to talk to her.'

He looked up warily. 'We decided I should talk to you instead.'

'You decided? When?'

'Anna came to see me last night. Dad was at work.' Paz glanced at Chess and then looked back at me.

I said, 'Why?'

Paz shrugged. 'She's like everyone else. She thinks I must know who killed Tim. The killer had to have sneaked back from the ball and got the poison while

I was sitting there.' He put his hands on his scarf, smoothing it onto the table. He sounded tired.

'So Anna wants you to keep quiet?'

'She wanted to find out what I knew.' Paz pulled a small golden thimble out of a pocket. He held it in the palm of his hand, letting it catch the light, looking down at it. 'She said she was going to meet you two at eleven o'clock and she wanted me to go too. She wanted me to tell you all what I know.'

'But you wouldn't.'

'It's dangerous. With that Grif person around.'

I remembered Paz at the Langtons' Open Garden. I had heard a scream of pain and then seen him standing with Grif. He was being threatened. 'He's trying to stop you talking.'

He said, 'Grif's watching Anna too. I didn't think she should be out on the street talking. I said she should bring you here. And then she should sneak away.'

Chess said, 'Are you going to tell us the truth then? That you did see Jacob that night?'

'No. I'm not going to tell you that.'

'Honestly,' groaned Chess. 'You're just playing with us. You cooked up a disappearing act just to confuse things.'

'No, not for that.'

There was a sad, knowing look in his eyes. The silence of the room was starting to get to me. That old feeling was coming back, that there was something happening just out of sight.

'It was a demonstration,' I guessed.

'What of?' said Chess.

I didn't know. 'Are you saying there was a space in Tim's room near the bookcase, behind a door or something? And Jacob hid there?'

Instead of answering Paz put the thimble on the forefinger of his right hand, closed his left hand over it, pulled it off, and then opened his left hand to show there was nothing in there.

'Wow,' I said very quietly. He flicked his eyes towards me with a tiny grin.

Chess snorted. 'It wasn't a demonstration! It's what I said the first time. You're just trying to confuse things. That's what you're up to, isn't it? Get Anna away from us and bring us here and bamboozle us again, just like last time. Because you don't want us to get at the real truth.

'But can't you see how stupid that is? If you're being threatened, then as soon as you tell the police what you know, you won't be threatened any more. There will be no need for Grif to chase you.'

Paz frowned at her. 'Anna said you were getting emotional.' He was still doing the lisping.

'Well, I have plenty to be emotional about, don't I?'

Paz smiled sympathetically.

'I'm sorry,' said Chess, in that hard way that means you're not sorry. 'Just let me clarify this, would you mind? Anna came to you to ask who had killed Tim Williams. So supposedly it wasn't her. And you told her … What?'

'I told her to go home and keep safe.'

'But you do know, don't you? You know who killed him.'

He didn't deny it.

Chess's voice went high and tight. 'Why can't you just tell us?'

'It's dangerous to know. There are people trying to stop you finding out.'

'But if we find out we can tell the police and stop it all.'

'If you find out, the person might want to kill you.'

'No. Paz. Who is telling you all this? Your father?'

'Knowledge is good but it kills everything. It makes everything flat.'

'Why do you carry on like this? Why can't anyone just give us a straight answer?' Chess's voice cracked.

Paz tried to smile but his mouth twisted.

I said, 'Maybe I can make it easier for you. There's a lot we already know. No one can have got into Tim's room before everyone left for the show. Almost anyone could have sneaked back to the house from the Town Hall, and almost anyone could have put poison in the flask without it being noticed. Including your father, because his alibi with Mrs Williams doesn't hold up.'

Paz was impressed and relieved. 'You guys are really into this, aren't you?'

'So who was it?' said Chess.

Paz started going pink. 'Dad doesn't want me mixed up in it.' Suddenly he did look like a young kid. 'He doesn't know I'm talking to you now. He said he'd try to talk you out of this whole thing.'

'He did try,' said Chess. 'It didn't work.'

'He's very — embittered. He's got problems. He doesn't like the police. He says there's a lot of corruption, and he said someone might come after me. He says it's best not to get involved.'

'That's a very selfish way of thinking.'

'Yeah. I know. Sorry. He just doesn't want anything bad to happen.'

'But bad things are already happening. Just not to you.'

Paz dropped his eyes and delicately rearranged the scarves on the table. 'It's not that I'm scared.'

'No, we know, Paz,' I said.

Chess had an idea. 'Anna disappearing like that. That was some kind of demonstration, wasn't it?' Paz didn't look up. 'Like the card trick. The Elsinore Vanish. You're giving us cryptic messages. Because you can't tell us, but you want us to find out for ourselves?'

'That's not the only reason. I also just like magic.' Paz opened his case again and pulled out a blue metallic cup. He put it face down on the table.

'OK.' Chess was getting interested now. 'So, the trick with Anna means ... that we never really know where people are? Is that it? Is it about Jacob? Is it about him sneaking out of the ball and no one realising?'

Paz shook his head.

Chess wiggled impatiently. 'Or are you saying the killer was never in Tim's room, that he stopped at some entrance place, or some hiding place and never got into the room. But we've been there. No one could've accessed the poison in that cupboard without going into the room. Are you saying he waited outside and you gave it to him?'

Paz had pulled out two more cups and lined them up on the table. 'I'll show you another trick if you like.'

'All right.' Suddenly Chess was taking the magic seriously.

In his hand Paz had a small red ball. He lifted the middle cup and put the ball underneath it. Then he started shuffling the cups around on the smooth cloth. Chess watched him. After a while he stopped and looked at her, asking her to find the red ball. Confidently, she pointed to the cup on the left. Paz lifted the cup. There was nothing underneath it. He lifted the middle cup to reveal the ball.

I thought of something. 'You taught Tim most of his magic.'

'Tim liked magic. He said it helped him escape a corrupt world.'

'And you like it too.'

'The thing about magic is, you get to see something impossible. And when that happens the whole world ...' He looked for a way to describe it. '... opens.'

'What?' said Chess impatiently.

'Magic makes you see that there's a whole universe of stuff that you don't know about. And that's something we should all remember. So we don't stop asking questions ... That's what magic is. It's an echo of the cosmos.'

I really liked listening to this kid. 'And is that what Tim thought?'

He shrugged. 'We talked about it a few times.'

'You and he were pretty good mates.'

'Yes. I liked him.' Paz glanced at Chess's face but looked immediately away. 'You don't have to believe that.'

He shuffled the cups around again, still with Chess watching closely. When he lifted his hands she reached for the middle cup and lifted it up herself. Nothing. Paz showed her the ball under the left hand cup.

He didn't look like a little kid any more. He looked strong, clever, like the picture on the cover of his Mephisto book. He looked happy, like Tim in his photo. He was looking at Chess, willing her to understand. He put the ball back under a cup and started moving them again. And something about the magic, the happiness it brought him, made him more co-operative.

'I'm going to tell everyone what I know. You're right. I thought I'd be safe if I'm not talking but I'm not.'

He stopped moving the cups. They sat there in a neat row, shining blue on his dull red cloth. Paz put his hands on the table behind them but this time Chess didn't pick one.

He went on. 'And other people are unsafe too. Especially now you two are here stirring it all up again. So I'm going to tell everyone who killed Tim. I'm going back to Elsinore to show them.'

'Back to —?'

'I'm going up to Langton House.'

'Thank goodness,' said Chess. 'Can we come?'

'No.'

I said, 'Is your father going to take you?'

'I told you, he doesn't want me involved. If you see him, don't tell him where I am. I'll walk. Don't tell him.' Now Paz did look scared. To cover that, he started moving the cups around again.

I said, 'We'll come.'

'No.'

'Just tell us what you know,' said Chess.

'Watch.' Paz shuffled the cups and then stopped. He looked Chess meaningfully in the eye. He lifted the cup on the left. There was nothing underneath it. He said, 'Magic is about the impossible. That's what makes it beautiful.'

Chess made an exasperated sound. 'Well I hope that's not what you're going to tell the Langtons. That you didn't see anyone that night. That it's a beautiful mystery. That the poison just flew out of a cupboard and into a flask half way across town.'

Paz lifted up the cup on the right. Nothing. He gave a strange little twisted smile. 'There's a lot to be learned from the impossible.'

Chess sneered. 'They won't believe it. No one believes in the impossible.'

She grabbed the last cup and lifted it. The red ball had disappeared.

Chapter 26

'All right.' Chess was battling to stop the frustration from tipping over into anger. She kept her voice very calm. 'All right. I'm not done with you yet. Tell me about Anna. At least we know how that trick was done. Anna was never in this room.' She held up a hand. 'We rushed in fast and we saw the door swinging …'

And suddenly she did see something. She hadn't even had to work it out. It was just something that came to her, all at once, in a kind of flash. Her hand stopped in the air and her face set into a stunned mask. She stayed like that for two seconds while the full meaning of what she had discovered sank in, and then she got a new expression. She darkened. Her eyes went glassy. Chess was horrified.

'What Chess?' I turned to Paz. 'What?'

Chess's eyes were out of focus. She took a step backwards and leaned against the wall, sunk in her own thoughts. Slowly she raised one hand to her forehead, partly covering one eye. The she raised the other. Then she sort of squeezed, as if her new thoughts were bashing around and they had to be held still.

And then she was moving. Without saying another word she launched herself off the wall and ran out the door.

'Chess! Wait!'

She had forgotten the brown van. We hadn't been inside very long. It was probably still out here, watching for us.

'Chess! We can't do this!' I grabbed at her arm. 'What? What's wrong with you?'

'Don't you see?' She could tell I had no idea. 'Matt!' she said angrily, trying to force me to realise something. She threw out an arm, back towards the hall. 'Anna didn't go into the room.' She stopped again.

I shook my head hopelessly.

But she was looking over my shoulder now. 'There she is!'

I whirled around. Chess was frantic. 'That's her! I see her!'

She was looking back down towards the shops and the post office, over a block away. There was a blonde girl among the people on the footpath but she was too small to be Anna.

But Chess was already running.

'Chess, that's not her!' All I could do was follow her again. 'Chess. It's NOT HER!'

She wouldn't stop until were over the side street and back at the shops. Then she stood, spinning around in a confused way. Now finally, after everything she'd been through and everything she'd held down, Chess was losing it. I'd never seen it before.

'Chess, what is it?' I said, as gently as I could. 'You don't think it was her, do you? You don't think Anna killed him?'

Chess gave a laugh at this. A bit wild and hysterical. 'Anna? Oh no! She's so pure and innocent. Anna?' She threw out the arm again, this time pointing at nothing. 'She's way too nice.' There were tears in her eyes. I hadn't seen that for a long time. 'Anna is like you. She draws. She's ... your friend.'

'Not really.'

'She's your ...' She made a sobbing noise.

This didn't make sense. It couldn't have been Anna who killed Tim. Anna was helping Paz.

And then I saw something, too. 'Not Anna,' I said. 'Paz.'

'We have to go.' Chess wasn't listening.

'Chess. Paz. Paz and Tim. They did it. What if Paz ...' I thought for a minute but really, it came to me all in a rush. 'Tim kept talking about Hamlet. And Hamlet wanted to kill himself because everything was so depressing. Tim kept saying he wanted to disappear. What if he did it himself? And Paz knows and is hiding it from everyone because it's so awful.

'Or what if Paz helped him? No wonder he feels so … That's what he's been trying to tell us. The world is horrible and magic is beautiful.'

Chess was glaring at me now, deeply angry, as if I'd betrayed her in some way. 'You —'

'No, no, no. Listen. It has to be it, Chess. And now Paz is going up to Langton House to confess.'

She hadn't heard me. Now, when I needed her, when I finally had a breakthrough of my own, Chess had just fallen to bits. It had been coming for a long time. Even when we got here, she'd been way too intense about this murder mystery. And then she got obsessed with Angus and his books, trying so hard to be just like him. And those little visits to me at night. The whole time we'd been here, Chess had been holding something down, refusing to feel it. Even when the van took her she tried to be hard and tough. She tried to get strength from the meeting with Angus, and by working on the puzzle, but in a way all that just made her more fragile. And when her father appeared the tough shell had really started to crack. Now she was desperate and kind of brittle.

I had seen all that happening and I hadn't done anything to stop it.

And I still didn't have time to deal with it. I had worked out who killed Tim. Paz had helped Tim with his final, deadly disappearing act. Paz was just a kid. And now he was going to Langton House to tell them. It was brave. I needed to help him.

We were standing in front of a butcher shop. Next to it there was an alley, too narrow for cars. 'Chess,' I said, 'come up here a sec.'

I didn't let her argue. I dragged her. After a few metres the alley opened out and there was a row of tiny shops. and some big steel garages. I found a small deserted yard surrounded by steel fences. There was muffled noise coming from somewhere, but no one around, just a blue rubbish hopper and a few mops and things. I sat Chess down on a milk crate. She put her elbows on her knees and leaned forwards, clenching her fists together, staring down at her bony wrists.

I said, 'I think Paz wants us to see it for ourselves, without actually telling us. He wants to explain why he helped Tim. There was some kind of message in the thing with the cups, wasn't there? And in all those other tricks he did. That first one he called the Elsinore Vanish. I think he was trying to explain it in his own way so that people will understand. He must feel horrible. He's very young. He must be starting to realise what he's done. You can see it, really. He's …' I thought of a word my Mum would use, '… troubled.'

Chess was off in her own little world. 'Things disappear. You make assumptions.' She looked up at me. She screwed up her face, in sudden pain. 'They put the lid back on.' But she couldn't explain any more. She looked down again.

'Is this something to do with Anna being my friend?' I said quietly. 'You still think it was Anna, don't you? But it definitely isn't.'

Chess wrapped her arms over her stomach and leaned forward. The yard went along the back of the shops. It had that sour doughy smell you get out the back of cafés.

I said, 'Chess?'

She rubbed at her eyes, smearing tears back towards her hair, then put her face in her hands.

'It wasn't Anna. Paz wouldn't have lied for her. He would have lied for Tim and he would have helped him. Tim killed himself and Paz helped him. It has to be that. You said it yourself. Anything else is impossible.'

She wasn't going to answer me. I don't think she could. She was trying to get her emotions under control again and this time it was a huge effort. She was holding herself so tight she could almost not speak at all. When she put her hands down her voice was caught up somewhere at the back of her throat. 'I need to see Angus.'

'Oh yes,' I said. 'Actually, I think you do.'

She was right. Angus kept Chess calm. She needed someone older, that she looked up to. She needed someone to lean on. She had always needed that and never allowed herself to have it. Until Angus. She got a lot of strength from him.

And Angus knew something. He had said that when she found an answer she should come to him. That fitted. It would be hard for him to tell people Tim had killed himself and that a little kid had helped him. Now he would help us tell people. We would all help Paz tell the story. I wished Angus was here now.

'All right. We finally agree on something. Let's go up to Langton House.'

Chess stood up and started walking towards the gateway. She was pale and her eyes were dark with something I couldn't recognise. At the entrance she turned around. 'We don't agree. It's …'

As she said that a beefy arm appeared from behind the steel fence, reached across one of her shoulders, over her chest and dragged her out of sight.

Chapter 27

What I should have done was start yelling. I don't know why I didn't. I think it took me a while to realise what had happened. I mean I saw the arm but it looked so ... stupid. In a way I felt as if Chess had just vanished. And that sort of thing stuns you.

I ran to the gateway and looked. The lane was blocked. By the brown van.

I still didn't shout. Because the van looked empty. I stood there staring at it. I could see daylight through the back window. I could see right through to the laneway on the other side. There was no one in the van.

Slowly I went up to it. And I was only a step away when I realised my mistake.

I couldn't see through the windows. They were reflective. It was a trick. Not even a good one. Not even a trick that anyone had meant to do. It was just my own useless panicky brain, not seeing things properly.

The side door rumbled open. Chess was in the back of the van, sitting on the ridged metal floor and the Russian-weight-lifter guy was in there with her. While I stood there gawping at them, the front door opened.

Grif was in the passenger seat. His hair was flat and sweaty-looking and his beanie was in his hands

I lost it. My nervous system had overdosed on fear and it just shut down and I started operating on a sort of auto-pilot override. I felt my mouth make a kind of smart grin and heard it say, 'Head a bit hot?'

Grif and I looked at each other for about five seconds and then I added, 'You want to try natural fibre. For that little sweat problem.'

He gave me another long tough-guy look and then spoke very quietly. 'We've got a message for you.'

Somewhere deep down my brain was grinding away, trying to make a plan. I had to get Chess out of there. I had to stall while I thought of something.

But my mouth wasn't connected to my brain. 'Let's have it then.' I looked Grif in the eye, waiting for my message. I made my eyes go hard and cold, like stones. My balls had done the same but he didn't know that.

Russia came to the door and edged out to stand behind me. Up close he didn't look quite so funny. He said, 'Gotta take you somewhere.'

'Na-a-ah.' I spoke pleasantly as if he was offering me a choice. 'Just tell me here.'

He didn't bother answering. He grabbed my arm and the back of my hair and shoved me through the side door. He slammed the door and went round to the driver's seat.

The back of the van smelled of petrol. The floor had two humps over the wheels and steel tool box. I scrabbled for a handle on the door, but nothing would move.

Chess was staring at me, wild eyed.

'We're going somewhere,' I breathed.

Russia hopped into the driver's seat and started the engine. There was a grate of wire between the back of the van and the seat but before I could get hold of it he accelerated away, sending us flying backwards. We hit the end of the lane with a big bump and then we were in the street, with Russia heavy-footing the accelerator and brake and swinging around corners. We weren't going fast enough to attract attention but it was enough to make Chess and me roll around like marbles in a jar. I tried a few times to sit up and say something but it was hopeless. After I went cracking into the corner of the tool box I decided it would be safer to just lie there.

From down on the floor I could look up through a corner of the back window. I couldn't see anything but sky and occasionally a tree. After a few minutes we slowed down.

'In there,' said Grif.

I got a grip on the wire grate and sat up and peered out the windscreen. We went around another corner, then bounced down a ramp into a builder's yard. There was a big red and white sign that said 'No Entry', but Russia just drove straight past it into a huge shed.

I didn't know where we were or what the shed was for. It had a concrete floor and bits of greasy old machinery around the walls. We drove through a pool of water, straight to the opposite corner and stopped.

Grif put his beanie back on which I thought was a bad sign. Russia opened our door. We climbed out by ourselves to avoid being dragged. I had to concentrate to do this, because my legs didn't want to move. I didn't like the empty shed idea. They had a lot of those on TV crime shows and nothing good ever happened in them.

Above us there was one long fluorescent tube and it was flickering with a sickly grey light. Around the top of the walls, open slits were letting wind in. The air tasted of stale oil.

To stop myself thinking I started talking. 'OK. We get the message. We're not stupid.'

'Shut up,' said Grif.

I couldn't. 'And yes, we have asked a few questions around the town about Tim Williams but we've totally failed to get anywhere.'

'Shut up,' said Russia.

'We've had enough anyway. So OK. Right? We agree. We drop it and leave town.'

I made a zooming motion with my hands which was supposed to represent Chess and me racing off home. I made a feeble attempt to move away from the van but Russia stepped calmly and heavily into my path. He pushed Chess and me back against the van.

'I know who sent you,' said Chess.

This actually completely ruined my story that we hadn't got anywhere but it probably didn't matter. They weren't listening.

'And I know who's paying you to scare us away.'

They didn't answer.

'You said you had a message for us,' I said.

Grif was looking down at his hands. Now he spoke quietly. 'Yeah. I got a message. For her.' He looked at Chess. As he finished speaking he casually swung an arm. It was a soft movement, as if he was flicking a fly away, but Chess's head snapped to the side and she almost fell over.

He lunged at her again but with a startled squeak she leapt away. Then she ran. I moved too, and maybe

I was going to help her and maybe I was going to run like hell. I'll never know because as soon as I moved Russia thumped me on the jaw.

I'd never been hit on the jaw before. We've all seen it a million times on movies and I've always thought it was fairly minor. Half the time guys just shake their heads and carry on. But this wasn't like that. I didn't feel it in my jaw at all. It was as if something had exploded behind my eyes, then my head swung sideways and slammed into the side of the van and the two blasts had my skull echoing like an empty bell.

Next I knew I was on the ground and Russia had a foot on my chest. There was a lot of weight. I wanted to tell him there was no need to worry because I wasn't going anywhere, but my bottom teeth were about six centimetres out of line with my top ones and my mouth wouldn't open.

Then he thought of something. 'Sorry mate. She's a friend of yours, isn't she?' His voice sounded bent and thin, as if it was an echo of something else. 'Wanna watch?'

He dragged me into a half-sitting position, up against a hot wheel, and put the foot back on my chest so I couldn't get any higher.

Grif had caught Chess. He dragged her back and pushed her up against the van. Then he let go and stood in front of her. He wasn't touching her but he had his arms and legs tensed, ready to go after her if she tried to get away.

'It doesn't matter who killed Tim Williams. It's none of your business.' He was talking quietly. 'We told you that last time but you forgot didn't you? Now we have to do something to help you remember.' He turned to his mate. 'What about pain Booney? I always remember things that hurt, don't you?'

He lurched forwards and as Chess tried to duck away he grabbed her by an arm. They stood there staring into each other's faces, then Grif held up the arm. Chess closed her eyes. In his meaty hands it looked like a little stick. He held it with his thumbs out towards each other as if he was about to break a piece of kindling. He made a little sharp noise with his mouth like a stick snapping.

Then he let go.

Chess opened her eyes. 'I'm not the only one who knows.' Her voice would hardly come out. 'The police will know soon.'

Before she finished talking she leapt sideways and pelted away from him. But Grif was fast and he was way bigger. He caught up and grabbed her, getting one shoulder and sending her into a spin. She went down on her back and he moved in.

I struggled. The foot came down harder. Chess was wriggling backwards and kicking to keep Grif away. Soon she was right up in a corner, between a pile of tyres and a rusty barrel. Her arm went into a metal tray. Grif went down on one knee. He grabbed her around the throat and dragged her into a sitting position, up against the wall.

'OK, Boons. You try convincing the boyfriend.'

Russia didn't have the style of Grif. There were no long scary pauses. No eye contact to psych me out. He just took his foot off my stomach and kicked me in the ribs.

My rib made a tiny little click. But the pain went everywhere. I felt it in my stomach and my throat and my spine. I felt it in my legs and my brain. My body vaporised. I was just a long skeleton of hot pain.

I closed my eyes. Suddenly it was all sound. The high roar of moving air, the hiss of the faulty fluorescent light, Chess screaming, 'Stop it! Stop it!'

And another sound. A light thudding pulse. Someone splashing through water. I opened my eyes. Booney was drawing his foot back for another go. From nowhere another figure came hurtling in. Tall, athletic, fast.

'Jacob!' I yelled that, but there was no sound at all.

Jacob leapt at Grif, one foot out, kicking him in the knee. Grif went down, Jacob leapt on him. I tried to slide away from Booney. My rib screamed in pain.

Jacob wasn't a fighter, but he was strong, and he hit Grif again before he got up. But now Booney had left me and gone up behind him. He got Jacob under both arms and held him around the shoulders. Slowly Grif got to his feet. He smiled and drew back an arm.

There was a flash of metal in the sickly light. Grif's head jerked sideways. He whirled around roaring. Chess was there, pale face streaked with grease, dark wet eyes fixed on Grif, holding the metal tray.

She had swung from the side and had got him around the front, over one side of his forehead. Blood was pouring down his face. He raised a hand to see what was in his eyes and brought it down red.

Chess stood with her feet apart, ready to swing it again. Booney and Jacob stood stunned. There was a second of silence that went for a year.

And then they ran for the van.

Dragging in air, holding my rib against the pain, I just managed to throw myself forward before the van started moving and then I lay on my stomach, arms over my head as it spun round me. There was a thumping roar, a cloud of heat and rubber and exhaust, and they were gone.

There was a clang as the tray hit the concrete. Chess sank slowly to the ground pressing two hands over her mouth.

'Chess!'

I tried to get over to her but I could hardly move. At first she just sat there, starting at a piece of rubber hose. Then, slowly she rolled over and got her hands on the floor. She started to push up but then stopped, on all fours, head hanging down.

My rib was on fire now and my stomach had been mashed by Booney's foot. Instead of feeling squashy it had gone hard. It felt as if there was a big metal plate across my ribcage.

Jacob was standing between me and Chess. He didn't know what to do. Chess's pony tail was half pulled out, the elastic tangled in a hank of hair lying on one shoulder.

I got onto my knees. The metal plate pushed up into my lungs, making me want to vomit. Chess stood up and took a step nowhere. She looked dazed. Her pants were covered in oil. She still hadn't said anything.

'Are you all right?' said Jacob.

She gave a kind of moan that ended in air. She moved to the barrel and got her hands on the rim. One hand landed on a sharp point but she didn't notice. There was a reaching sound but nothing came out except a dribble of spit.

I got to my feet and walked over to her. She stayed leaning over the smelly barrel, lips hanging forward, with a bubble stuck to them.

'Shit, Chess.' I put a hand on her arm. It felt stringy and hard.

'Matt,' she croaked.

'Chess? It's OK. You haven't hurt him.' I gave a high hysterical laugh at my stupid that comment.

'Matt …'

'What?'

She spat and swallowed and managed to speak.

'I need to see Angus.'

Chapter 28

Jacob wanted to take us to the Health Service but Chess wouldn't let him. She just kept repeating she needed to talk to Angus and Paz and it was urgent. So he drove us to Langton House. Nobody said anything.

Looking back it's hard to remember exactly what I was thinking. I had a stomach like a rock and I felt sick and every tiny movement gave me a pain like a knife in the ribs. I don't think I was thinking much at all. I still didn't think Jacob had killed Tim Williams. And he definitely hadn't hired Grif to scare us away. But if it was Paz — if Paz had helped Tim to kill himself, then now we were going up there to hear about it. It was going to be horrible and intense and sad. But if that was it, then where did Grif come in? It was possible Grif had attacked Paz because he hated him for helping Tim die, but why was he attacking us? It was just too hard. I wasn't capable of thinking about it any more.

But we were getting near the end. I knew that much. And Chess knew something I didn't know. So I suppose what I was expecting now was some kind of show down where Chess gathered all the possible suspects and told a long story, logically and clearly, finally revealing who the murderer was. She'd done something like that last time.

But looking at her in the car I didn't see how she was going to manage it. She'd already asked Jacob to pull over once so she could be sick in the gutter. If she was going to explain anything at all she was going to need help. And at least Angus seemed to know who killed Tim. He had said when Chess knew she should come and tell him. Hopefully now he would back her up, telling us the thing he thought he saw at the variety night.

Mrs Langton must have been watching for Jacob's car because as we pulled into the gravel space at the front of the house she came running out.

'Jacob. I'm so glad you're here. Where in this world have you been and why don't you answer your phone?' She was talking fast. 'That funny little boy is here.' She looked at Chess and me, climbing stiffly out of the car. 'Pass he calls himself. Heaven only knows what his real name is.' She turned back to Jacob. 'He wants to see you. I told him you were out and I didn't know when you'd be back but he's just *waiting*.' She stressed the word, as if waiting was some kind of deviant behaviour.

'Where is he?' said Chess urgently.

Paz appeared at the front door. Chess took a step towards the house.

'Chess, wait!' I tried to touch her but the movement sent a white hot pain down my left side. I bent sideways and grabbed a rib.

'Oh my goodness Matthew, are you hurt?' For the first time Mrs Langton noticed how dirty we both were, the blood on Chess's sleeve and the darkening bruise on her face. She looked at Jacob. 'What on earth have you been doing?'

Chess had stopped at my cry of pain. I managed to get a hand on her arm. I had to stop her running towards the house. I didn't know what she was intending to do but I knew she couldn't handle it by herself. That was how she got hurt last time. I made myself sound calm and reasonable. 'Wait. It's Angus you want to see. You need to talk to him first, don't you?'

The message sank in slowly. Chess was trying to think but she looked dazed.

'Matthew, what has happened to you?'

Jacob said, 'It's a broken rib, Mum.'

'Oh my good lord. How on earth did you do that? Did you fall?' She made some frantic movements with her hands. 'Help him, Jacob.'

Jacob came over and stood at my bad side, wondering what to do.

'What could possibly possess you to bring him all the way out here? He should have gone straight to outpatients.' For a minute it looked as though Mrs L was going to put us back in the car and drive us there herself.

This was not what Chess wanted. 'I have to see Angus.'

Mrs Langton looked at her, surprised at the rough tone. 'I'm sorry. He isn't here.'

'Paz then. I need to talk to Paz.'

Mrs L hesitated. She looked at Jacob. 'He's so peculiar. But as a matter of fact he said the same thing. He wants to see all of you.' She looked back at Paz, watching us from the doorway. 'He said he'd sent you to get them, Jake? Honestly it's all very crazy. He wants us all to listen to something he has to say. He wants me, and Anna and Dad. I told him Dad wasn't here.' She lowered her voice. 'And now he's just standing there.' She sent another nervous glance in Paz's direction. 'We'd better just go inside. I'll ring Doctor Winter.'

We started moving towards the house, me limping next to Jacob, who didn't know where to grab me without hurting me, and Chess and Mrs Langton following.

Inside, Mrs L steered Chess into what she called the powder room, which was a little bathroom near the front door. Seeing the way I moved, she didn't want to bother me with washing.

'Come this way.' She took us into the big room where we'd sat on the first afternoon, with the windows overlooking the lake. And she started talking as if I was unconscious. 'Put him on the couch, Jacob darling. Perhaps we can stretch him out. We really must get him in for X-rays. But maybe a drink first?'

On the coffee table there was a green bottle and five coloured glasses — two green, two blue, one pink. One green one and the pink one were full of juice, in front of empty chairs. Paz sat down in front of the pink one.

Mrs L started prattling again. 'It's sparkling apple juice. A family favourite. The green glass is Anna's. Lord knows where she's gone. You can all drink up. We have a whole crate in the pantry.'

The glasses were the Turkish-looking kind with swirly gold patterns around the rim. Mrs Langton lifted the bottle and moved a glass, about to pour me one. Then she stopped and looked up. 'Oh, here's Anna now. Hello darling.'

'Hello.'

We all watched in silence as Anna came in and sat down in front of the green glass. Then Mrs Langton looked at the open door.

'Where's Jessica?'

I looked around. Chess hadn't come out of the bathroom yet.

Mrs Langton said, 'Do you think she's all right?'

Of course, Chess wasn't all right. She never had been all right. It was what Dad had said — you can try as hard as you like, pretending you don't feel anything, but everything has to come out in the end. Even when we first got to Beechworth, she'd been too intense about this whole mystery, as if she had her whole life tied up in it. And she'd been getting more and more intense as the mystery got harder to solve. Even with Angus and his coaching and inspiration and encouragement, she hadn't been able to stay completely unemotional. And then something had happened at the youth centre. She'd seen something there that had really rattled her. And that had been before Grif had even got to her.

Grif had held Chess's arm in his hands like a twig and made a snapping sound. That had made me break into a cold sweat. What had it done to her?

Chess had swung a box at Grif's head. She'd felt it connect and seen the blood.

And now poor Paz had come to Langton House to tell everyone who had killed Tim. He might even been going to confess to it himself. But if that was it, then why was Grif trying to scare us off? Who was paying him?

Round and round.

Chess and I were supposed to be here to help Paz. But she'd finally reached some kind of limit. Her brain had just shut down. I'd seen that out on the driveway. And now she seemed to have got stuck in the powder room.

Later on she told me what happened.

After washing her hands and face she came out of the powder room and heard movement. Off to the right of the entrance hall there was a corridor. On the left it had rooms that faced the inner courtyard and along the right there were narrow windows, looking through bushes towards the driveway.

Half way up the corridor, moving away from her, was Angus. He turned to go into one of the rooms and as he did that he saw Chess.

'Jessica.' He sounded surprised and pleased.

Now, after insisting so many times that she had to see him, Chess couldn't speak. All the things she knew and all the things that had happened were spinning around in her head, tangling together. And over this, as she described it later, there was a kind of icy cloud. She felt weirdly separate from everything. She couldn't reach her own thoughts.

All she could say was, 'I know. I know …' Her lips and the ends of her fingers felt numb and tingly.

'Dad! There you are!' Mrs Langton had followed Chess back out. 'I didn't know you were home. I've been telling everyone you aren't here.'

Angus smiled in a vague way. 'Yes,' he said gently, still watching Chess. 'I am home now.'

Chess tried again. 'I don't … I didn't …' She was waving her hands towards her own head. She had a lot to explain to him but no words would come.

Mrs Langton put a hand on her shoulder to stop her trying to talk. To Angus she said, 'Jacob is back. And Jessica and Matthew are here. And Anna and that boy …'

'Paz,' said Chess harshly. 'Paz is here.'

Mrs Langton laughed in a panicky way. 'And Pass is wanting to see us all. In the lounge room. He seems to think there is something vitally important he must say.'

'No,' said Chess quickly. 'Not Paz. He won't tell it!'

Angus lifted his hands in a calming gesture. In one hand he was holding a pink glass with a gold pattern.

'Oh!' Mrs Langton gave Chess's shoulder a squeeze, trying to calm her down. 'You see. I told you we were all mad about that apple juice.' She had forgotten Chess wasn't there when she said that. 'Here is Dad, only home five minutes and he has tracked it down and now he's sneaking off to the study to drink some all by himself.'

Angus smiled humbly and waved his glass. 'As you see.'

'I have to talk to you!' Chess was almost shouting with frustration. 'I have to see you now. I know. *I do*.'

'I thought you would,' said Angus quietly. 'Yes. I see. I do see.' He gave her a meaningful look but he was trying to stop her from saying too much in front of Mrs Langton. 'But you must just wait for me now. Can you do that? Just one minute?'

Chess was about to argue. She started to take a step forward but Mrs Langton had her by the shoulders and didn't let go. Angus went into his study and shut the door.

'Come on, sweetie. Let's go and see how Matthew is getting on.'

As Chess turned away she thought she saw a movement in one of the windows, somewhere behind the bushes near the driveway.

So no, Chess wasn't all right. And because of that, the last scene of our little detective story was all wrong.

I don't know exactly what Chess had imagined when she started out on this little mystery. Ever since she had got to Beechworth — or actually, long before that — she had been building up this picture of herself as a rational, strong person in control of every situation, helping everyone else deal with things. And all along she had probably been hoping for something like the end of our last mystery, where everyone else was falling apart and she stayed calm and rational, explaining who the murderer was and how she had worked it out, giving lists of clues that no one else had spotted, explaining a clear reasoning process, step by step.

And maybe I'd been half expecting that too. She definitely knew now, who killed Tim Williams. But when she came back into the lounge room there was no way she would be explaining it calmly. You could see that in her face.

Mrs L was behind her, trying to get her towards a chair, but she just stood there. She had something to tell us but first she had to get control of herself, her fear, her confusion. Her anger. She wanted that control, wanted to be that person she imagined. She wanted it desperately. But she was losing the fight.

She stared at us, sweating, taking quick separate breaths, straining against all the thoughts that wouldn't line up into a neat order, mouth wobbling around words that wouldn't come out.

There was a silence. Jacob had been about to pour me a drink. He stopped with the bottle in his hand. Chess stared at it.

There were windows that looked out to the front of the house. In the corner of my eye I saw a movement out there. Someone had run across the parking space. But I turned too late to see who it was.

Paz had his back to the window. He picked up his glass, but when he saw Chess he stopped with it in the air. Chess stared at the glass. Pink, with little gold swirls that caught the light. And then, as he raised it, something seemed to catch Paz's eye. He bent down to the floor, grabbed it and held it up, frowning at it. It was a tiny zip-lock bag. Inside were glittery white crystals.

We heard a noise outside. Someone was calling, 'Paz! Paz!'

It was Calvin. He had run around from the front of the house and now he was at the side windows, the ones that looked over the lawn. He was shouting, screaming his son's name. He got to the glass doors, grabbing for a handle. They were locked. He started pulling at them, banging on the glass, screaming at Paz. 'No. No. Just go. Just get out of there!'

Slowly, still with the pink glass in his hand, Paz stood up. He lifted the glass.

And suddenly all Chess's control snapped. With a weird strangled cry of rage, she launched herself at Paz, knocking him sideways. He went crashing down, kicking the coffee table, Chess on top of him. The plastic bag went flying. The pink glass shot across the polished floor, leaving a trail of shiny juice.

Jacob and Anna leapt up. Mrs Langton gasped. Calvin stood stunned. Chess was already on her feet. Watching her, Paz stood up too.

Now everyone's eyes went to the window at the front of the house. In the gravel parking place, coming from the front door, was Angus. He was walking briskly to Jacob's car. Calvin saw where we were looking. He pushed away from the glass door and went running around to the front of the house.

And Chess ran too. She pushed past Mrs Langton and flew out the door. There was no time to stop her. We all stood watching.

Calvin was running from the side of the parking space towards Angus. He was yelling something. He was going to get to him before he reached the car. But Chess was closing the gap.

Angus seemed to have no idea what was going on. He just kept going towards the car. He had keys in his hand.

I took a step. I didn't even feel the rib. But it was too late for any of us to do anything. Mrs Langton didn't move. Jacob and Paz and Anna and I all moved to the window.

Angus had seen Calvin coming. He started running. Calvin slipped on the gravel, stumbled, but Angus was an old man and he was no runner. Suddenly Calvin was on him.

Chess was sprinting towards them.

Calvin grabbed Angus by an arm and whirled him around. But as he did it, Chess launched herself at them, high up, bringing both of them to the ground.

Jacob was moving now, and Anna and Paz, all running out, shouting things, with me following as quickly as I could. But we were too late. By the time we got there the struggle was over. Calvin was sitting on the ground. Angus was lying on his back, an old man, weakly flapping his arms, and Chess was kneeling over him, hands on his chest, holding him down.

She looked up at all the people around her. Her face was bruised and her eyes were hot and dark. And now I could see what that darkness was. It was rage.

'He wasn't helping me,' she said. 'He isn't my friend. Paz's story proves it has to be him. And then he had to get rid of Paz before people realised what it meant. I saw the pink glasses. Angus swapped the glasses. He left the powder on the floor beside Paz's chair.'

Suddenly she seemed to see what she was doing. She sat back on the gravel and looked at me. 'Get him up.' Her voice gave a wobble, then strengthened. 'And call the police. I'll tell them myself. Angus tried to kill Paz. Angus killed Tim Williams.'

Chapter 29

For a while nothing much happened. Angus stood up, looking stunned but all right. Calvin made a phone call. I just stood there staring at Chess.

Chess stood up too and she kept talking. She said Angus killed Tim Williams, that she knew it and Paz knew it and when the police tested everything they'd find cyanide in Paz's glass. She got all that out, standing there on the driveway while Calvin spoke to the police, and then she just sat down on the gravel, suddenly, like a puppet with the strings cut. I knelt next to her, keeping as much pressure off my rib as I could. I didn't know what to say. And Chess couldn't go on.

It looked like it was going to take a long time to sort this all out.

But then, amazingly, before we'd even gone inside, Angus confessed. He admitted killing Tim Williams and trying to kill Paz. I'll never know why he confessed. He just looked at Jacob's face, and Anna's and Mrs Langton's and he seemed to see something there.

I think I knew what he saw. They all believed her. When Chess said it was him, no one argued. No one said it was impossible. No one said anything. They all just looked at him and you could see it dawning on them. In Jacob's case there was no surprise at all. He had always known. And with Mrs Langton and Anna — they looked as if they had kind of half known it too. Known it without really wanting to admit it, even to themselves. It's hard to understand that, but however it works they now had no trouble believing it. No trouble at all.

Tim's death had been nothing to do with evil outsiders. It hadn't been Calvin or Grif or Anna or Jacob, and it hadn't been Paz. It hadn't been suicide and it hadn't been magic. It had been Angus.

Of course everyone knowing that wasn't enough to keep Chess out of trouble. She had knocked an old man to the ground. She had sent Paz flying across the room, knocking over furniture and smashing things. And who knows, it was quite likely that somewhere Grif would be turning up at a doctors' surgery to get his head stitched, saying he'd been belted by a skinny sixteen year old girl with a sharp metal weapon.

Chess was going to be asked a lot of questions and she didn't look as if she'd be able to answer them. Now that she'd finished her speech, she didn't look as if she had any answers left at all.

Mrs L looked really sad. She led Angus inside and we saw them turn right towards the bedrooms. Calvin took Paz and Chess and me into the kitchen.

Then at some point — I don't know how long it was — cars started arriving. Police cars, ambulances, vans. There were grim faces, huddled discussions, loud important phone calls. It was all weirdly familiar and at the same time strange.

I didn't let them take me to outpatients. I said I needed a parent with me before I went. I put a bit of emotion into it, trying to make it sound like a hospital phobia or something, but really I didn't want to be separated from Chess.

So I said I didn't want Mike called and I refused to go to hospital until my father arrived and I insisted Chess had to stay with me. And, like I said, I drove my message home with a hysterical act, which wasn't that hard given the way I was feeling. And, because we were minors, and our injuries weren't serious, I got away with it.

They found someone medical to look over us, so part of my big refusal to go to hospital involved downplaying the damage to my side. This was actually braver than anyone ever realised because it was *really* hurting. I was starting to imagine that one of my ribs had actually broken off and was sticking into my lungs. That's what it felt like. So maybe I get a few bravery points here, finally, after all the stuff ups.

It wasn't all bravery. As well as wanting to protect Chess there was another reason. I wanted to hear the full story.

I also wanted to talk to Paz. So as soon as the police agreed that Chess and I could wait at Langton House until Dad arrived, and probably pushing my luck here, I asked if Calvin could stay with us, as a sort of temporary guardian. Amazingly I got that too. And Paz stayed with Calvin.

Normally the police wouldn't do it this way. I'm pretty sure the rules say that as witnesses we should have been kept apart until we'd all been interviewed, to stop us comparing stories. But three of us were kids, dirty and bruised and smeared in blood, and, in completely different ways, Chess and I were both acting traumatised. Another thing I'd learned last time. The rules are different for minors and the police are actually a bit scared of getting it wrong. Maybe they were worried about being sued or something.

They wouldn't let us sit inside because that was a crime scene. And they wanted us supervised. So, while people prowled over the house and huddled and talked, and while the detectives dealt with the Langtons, they got a policewoman to lead us out to the front garden.

We must've made a strange picture. Out in the lawn, not far from the driveway, three wooden benches were arranged in a semi-circle facing a bird bath. Chess, covered in grime from the shed and brown dust from her tackle in the driveway, sat on the middle bench, huddled as far back as possible, with her arms wrapped around her. I sat next to her, turning a bit sideways, trying to find a position that didn't hurt. My feet were in Chess's space, pushing hers up against the leg of the bench, but she didn't notice. Calvin and Paz went to one of the other benches and sat in the middle of it, quite close to each other. And the policewoman was on the third.

People kept arriving in cars, talking in little groups and then going inside. One car load had already left. Someone taped off the front door. We sat and watched it all happen. We were all pretty stunned.

I had to get back to some normal way of thinking so I did what I always do. Grass, leaves. Light, edges, shapes. There were a lot of nice things to look at. The bird bath was made of a sandy coloured stone and it had some fairly realistic bronze wrens around the edges. The grass had long soft shadows across it and near the gate there was a mass of native bushes with oily leaves glinting in the late light.

Chess wasn't looking around. She sat staring straight ahead at the stalk of the bird bath. She was in some kind of mental shut down. It didn't look as if I was going to get much explanation out of her. But after a while I had a go.

'OK.' I looked around at Paz, Calvin and Chess and laughed weakly. 'What just happened?'

Nothing. Wrong approach. I spoke softly to Chess. 'This is Matty here. Could you please tell me what just happened?'

She didn't move. Didn't even seem to have heard me.

'You know? Maybe explain how you got where you got? Run through the clues?'

'There weren't any clues,' she said in a tiny voice. 'I just finally realised what Paz was telling us. And as soon as I got his message, I knew it was true.' She frowned. 'I just knew it was true, straight away, just like that. I didn't realise about the pink glass until it was nearly too late.'

And really, I had already kind of realised. I could see why it had to be Angus.

But I'm not like Chess. The more things bother me the more I want to talk about them. And I wanted to hear Paz's story. It didn't matter that the policewoman would hear. None of this was a secret. So I started talking.

'If something seems to have disappeared, then it was never there in the first place.' I looked at Chess.

She had lifted her eyes as far as the metal wrens, but she still didn't seem to be listening.

I tried Paz. 'That's what the tricks were all about. You were trying to show us.' Paz gave an anxious glance at the policewoman, laughed in an apologetic way and started tying a knot in the cord of his boardies.

So I turned to Calvin. 'Jacob pointed out a couple of things, too. The lid was still on the bottle. Not because the murderer put it back on, because the bottle was never touched.'

Calvin was watching Paz's fingers with a worried-parent expression. When he realised I was talking to him he turned towards me. He looked different. There was a new tightness at the corner of his mouth and instead of being closed off and guarded, his eyes looked deeply worried.

But he was listening to me, so I went on. 'And there was a bit of powder spilt on a table in Tim's room ...' I waited. I knew the significance of this, but I wanted someone else to talk with me. 'What's all that about?'

Calvin muttered, 'You have to see how the whole thing was done.'

So Calvin knew too. 'Well,' I said carefully. 'Could someone maybe run me through it? Starting at the beginning?'

Calvin gave one of his sad sighs, weaker than before. But he didn't mind talking. 'It started on the afternoon before the variety show. Angus heard Tim showing Jacob the poison. When they went out for the afternoon he went into Tim's room and found it. He emptied the bottle into a container of his own. He must have sprinkled some on the table then.'

'So he had it all planned out, right back in the afternoon, before everyone started getting dressed for the show. He'd already decided to do it?'

'It would appear so.' This wasn't the way Calvin normally talked. He had made those words clipped, kind of mocking. 'He wanted Jacob to be a lawyer just like him. I've heard bits of his background. Angus was one of those blokes ... His brother had been a successful barrister and Angus had never made it. I'd say he was too gentle. You have to be savage to be a barrister.

'And the brother's kids were lawyers too. There's a judge somewhere. And Angus had Helen. So he needed his grandson to prove something. You get that sometimes. So the pressure was on Jacob. Poor little kid. And when Jacob started mucking up, Angus was running around trying to keep him out of trouble.'

I said, 'Tim did some of Jacob's assignments. If anyone had found out he could've lost his ATAR score.'

'And Tim was threatening to tell everyone. Angus would've been pretty keen to stop him talking.' Calvin sighed again and seemed too tired to go on.

So I went on for him. 'And the plan was — what?' I looked into space, working it out as I went. 'He planned to slip some of the cyanide to Tim at the cabaret show.'

It fitted with Angus. Poisoning wasn't violent. All Angus had to do was pour some powder into a bottle. This murder was about being cold, rational, organised.

At the gate, the pine trees threw a deep shade that was grey and also green, and there must have been a breeze high up because the needles were making a faint electric hum.

'But he wanted to create the illusion that someone had come back during the night and taken the cyanide and then put the bottle back in the bookcase.

He deliberately spilled a tiny bit of the cyanide on a table. But it had to be on a crowded table, in a corner of the room so Tim wouldn't see it while he was getting dressed. And then, as it turned out, there were four young people in Tim's room that evening. None of them noticed the spilled powder. And there were four witnesses while Angus made his speech about being irresponsible and put the poison in the bookcase. What they didn't realise was that the jar was already empty.'

Paz had been listening. He didn't stop playing with his cord but his lispy voice said, 'It's all about stage setting.'

'It's pretty cold-blooded.'

Now Paz looked across at me. 'It's the way magicians do things.'

'I don't know how we didn't see it.'

'It's easier if you know conjuring.'

'No. I don't mean that. I should've seen it. Not the logic of it, or the way the disappearing trick worked. The personality thing.'

Calvin moved uncomfortably on the wooden bench and Paz looked down again.

I went on. 'The whole murder was so … emotionless. It was done in front of a lot of people. Right in front of Tim's family. The murderer hadn't cared how many people had to see it.' No one else seemed to appreciate what I was saying. Calvin was looking away pointedly, probably wishing I would stop talking. Chess was ignoring me and Paz looked embarrassed. But I had to talk.

'It was thought out carefully. The only thing that went wrong was the fact that Paz ended up sitting in front of that bookcase all night. Angus had no way of knowing that was going to happen. That was bad luck. But apart from that the plan was perfect. All along that's bothered me. Even if the murderer had gone back from the hall to Langton House for the poison, it was a complicated plan. There was a lot involved. It took quite a lot of little steps, and the person just kept going without changing their mind or chickening out at the last minute. It took someone steady and logical. Angus is the only person you could imagine doing it, really.'

Paz put down his cord and smoothed it along his knee.

'So your trick, Paz? In your flat that day, the Elsinore Vanish. Did you plan that out beforehand? Was the scene all set before we even got into the room?'

He looked at me solemnly. 'It's better if you never know how it was done.'

I laughed. 'For you maybe.'

'It's like I tried to tell you. Magic is …' He looked down, as if he was ashamed of something. '… beautiful.'

'Angus's trick wasn't beautiful.'

'That was a corruption. And also it's no longer a mystery. Once you know how a trick is done it becomes flat and dull and ordinary.'

'The banality of evil,' said Calvin.

'The what?'

'Never mind.'

So we drifted back into silence again. I was starting to feel sick now. Not sickened by the thought of Tim. That had come before, and it would come again. But at this point I was actually feeling physically sick.

A short distance away on the lawn there was a tree covered in young leaves of that pale clear green that the sun can shine right through. It would've been nice just to sit here and look at it. But my brain wouldn't turn off yet. I had another set of things I wanted to know about.

'And the police — they never worked out it had to have been Angus?'

Calvin said, 'Maybe they had it as a theory. But Angus was on stage at the cabaret all night. He would have gone to the loo a few times and that was about it. He made sure everyone could see him. And Mrs Langton and Jacob were around the whole night. He was confident they'd have good enough alibis as well. I think …' He glanced at our policewoman, who was pretending to be deaf. 'Look I know I like to say the police are gutless and corrupt. And that's what I would've said about this …' His mouth twisted in a wry smile. '… back in my radical youth. But really …' He looked thoughtfully at the big iron gate, the uniformed man there. 'They have to have evidence — good enough evidence to get a conviction in a criminal court. If they haven't got that they keep working. And they probably have to play their cards pretty close to their chest.'

'But there was Paz's evidence.'

He looked at me with lids lowered. 'What evidence was that?'

'That he was there all night in front of the bookcase and no one came in.'

'And how was that supposed to be enough?'

'He could've explained what it meant. That there was only one way the poison could have got out of the room.'

Calvin curled his lips, not angrily. He looked sad. 'The police don't need lessons in logic from a twelve year old boy. It's not Paz's job to show them how to think.'

'But it would've caught a killer.'

Calvin shrugged. 'It mightn't have been enough. The law isn't that simple.'

'And it wasn't like that,' said Paz.

'What do you mean?'

He looked warily at his father. 'Once it came out where I'd been sitting all night and Angus realised I was the one witness that could be used against him, he sent us a message. He sent Grif Griffiths.'

'Grif. Jeez. What did he do?'

'Grif doesn't have to do much. Dad and I aren't heroes. Just having him stare at you is enough.'

'So then you didn't —'

'I panicked and got confused.' Paz gave me a meaningful look, then swung his eyes towards the policewoman. I realised what he was trying to tell me — Grif had scared him into lying to the police. He couldn't admit that. He might get charged with … what is it? … Preventing the cause of justice. Something like that.

Paz said, 'It was pretty hard to remember exactly what happened that night. Especially when people kept asking things over and over. It was very late at night and I was pretty sleepy. I started to think I might've just stepped out of the room for a minute or two after all. I couldn't be completely certain. The police must have seen I was going to be a very unreliable witness.'

'But to us you said ...' I stopped myself. Paz had told us he definitely had never left the room. That was something else I couldn't say in front of the police.

'Yeah,' said Paz. There was thoughtful silence. Then he went on, 'But I still thought it was Angus. I just had no proof. I wanted someone else to come to the same conclusion. When you two turned up and started asking about it I thought you might get somewhere. So I tried to help.'

Calvin tipped his head back and spread his hands at the sky, complaining to God about his hopeless kid.

Paz said, 'Like I told you, Dad didn't want me to talk to you. For my sake and for your sake.' Calvin had his eyes shut now and he was shaking his head. Paz turned back to me. 'Dad thought you'd just give up. But I didn't want you to give up. And he never said I couldn't show you a card trick or lend you a book.'

Calvin made a hissing sound through his teeth, then he threw an arm over Paz's shoulders. 'Maybe it's you who should be the lawyer.' This wasn't a proud father saying how smart his kid was. It was obvious Calvin hated lawyers.

But Paz looked happy about the arm.

I said, 'You thought we'd realise how the trick was done. But then what? If we'd guessed it was Angus were you going to suddenly back us up? That wouldn't have made any difference. They would've just had three kids with a theory, instead of one.'

Paz blushed. 'The other aspect to my plan was just to keep you interested. I suppose I was hoping that if you kept asking questions, then that might worry Angus and force him into a mistake.'

'He was worried. He tried to warn us off at that first meeting. And Grif was in the garden being scary. Maybe Angus knew we were coming. Maybe he looked at Jacob's e-mails.'

'I wouldn't be surprised,' said Calvin.

'Grif was also there to threaten me,' said Paz.

'Yeah.' I remembered Paz that morning in the garden. He had made a cry of pain and Grif had been standing next to him with a heavy hand on his shoulder. 'So when we started asking people things, Angus sent Grif after us. And the whole time he pretended to help us, so that he could keep an eye on how we were going. He told Chess to come and see him when she made some progress.' I looked across at Chess. 'She would have, too. She thought he was fantastic.' Chess's face was still blank. I remembered how it had looked back in the Youth Centre when the truth dawned on her. She had said something about friends.

Paz said, 'And you did force Angus into a mistake. The mistake he made was trying to kill me.'

Calvin gave his shoulder a rough shake. 'I still can't believe you were going to drink something in that house.'

Paz said, 'I saw Chess had realised who the murderer was. So I came out to the Langtons'.' He looked at me. 'I was hoping you'd come and back me up. I thought we could force a confession. I couldn't do it by myself but I hoped that three of us would have more credibility. You have a proven record as detectives.' He turned to his father. 'Mrs Langton and Anna were quite unsettled to see me.'

'And you had a drink!' said his father. He rubbed an eyebrow hard with his fingers. 'Genius.'

'I thought Angus was out,' said Paz steadily. 'I saw him driving away as I arrived.'

Calvin sounded really tired. 'Angus knew Matt and Chess were getting close. You turning up at the house wasn't a good sign. Did that ever occur to you? Going there was too obvious. Did it ever occur to you that he would see you and come back on foot?'

'No Dad, it didn't.'

'The glass got this close to your mouth.' Calvin put some fingers up, a few centimetres apart. 'I was banging on the window.' He threw his head back again, spread his hands then slapped them on his knees. 'Chess saved your life. You realise that, don't you?' We all looked at Chess.

Finally Chess spoke. 'I saw Angus had one of the pink glasses out in the bedroom. While Paz and Mrs Langton were in the driveway talking to us, Angus had gone into the lounge room and swapped the glasses, and I caught him hurrying back to his room. I didn't put it together until Paz found the little packet of cyanide on the floor. Angus had planted it there. It was supposed to look as if Paz had killed himself. Fortunately it all came to me, just in time.'

There was a little silence. Calvin's voice became gentle. 'You left quite a trail of destruction. Paz, the furniture, then Angus and me.'

At the memory of Chess leaping on the two men, the sudden ridiculousness of it, my mouth twitched. It made a kind of snarly smile that started half way up the side of my nose. I looked down at my hands to hide it.

He lowered his voice. 'And I don't even want to know about that blood on your sleeve.'

'Grif,' I said.

Calvin eyes flicked over Chess's pale face, then to the policewoman, then to me. 'Tell me later.'

Now the sickness hit me again. A big wave this time, starting somehow in the pain in my rib. A picture had come. A rush of pictures. Grif's face with blood pouring down it. Him flicking his head. A red droplet flying. And the sound, that little breaking noise he had made, holding Chess's arm in both hands. That was somehow the worst thing that had happened all afternoon. At the thought of it the nausea flooded up into my head as dizziness. I shifted around to get straighter, gripping the seat with both hands.

At the foot of the bird bath there was a row of low bushes with disc-shaped leaves that shimmered on springy stems. I knew a lot about plants now. Not the names or anything scientific, but I knew a lot about shapes, the stiffness of twigs, the way leaves hang, colours, how there are a million different shades of green.

Chess would say that isn't accurate. She'd say that really there are an infinite number of greens, because whenever there are two greens you could still get another one in between them that is different … I dunno. Chess would be able to explain it but I don't want to. Sometimes Chess knows too much. She knows so much there's a lot she doesn't see.

Or maybe not. She might not be like that any more. I looked at her, sitting dazed while everyone else went through the solution to her mystery. Maybe this time Chess had finally found out just how much she didn't know. How much you couldn't know. The mystery of the human heart. The mysteries of the universe.

What had Paz said about magic? An echo of the cosmos. I smiled to myself, a real smile this time. I was going to have to drop that into a conversation one day.

And then, as if the nicer, normal thought had somehow made it possible, our faded Mazda appeared at the gate and Dad, seeing us there in our funny little group, just left it in the middle of the parking space for the policemen to deal with and came towards us across the lawn.

He was by himself. He must've managed to persuade Mum and Alec and Mike to stay away. I don't know what he said to Alec. Mum wouldn't have minded. She looks after everyone else in the world but when it comes to the family, Dad does the crises.

He was wearing his wonky straw hat and the black shirt with the bright wiggly lines — the one that makes him look like a screen saver. His face was fat and rosy from hurrying, which he never does, and the shirt was getting a bit tight over his gut. And as he came towards us he did his intellectually-challenged-gnome smile, and the sight of that made me want to jump up and throw myself into his big rubbery belly.

I didn't do it of course, partly because I still had some dignity, and partly because I couldn't move. But I was starting to think my hysterical behaviour hadn't been such an act after all, because my eyes were going hot and teary and I was starting to realise that what I had told the police about waiting for a parent was actually right. We had a lot of explaining to do. We'd been trying to handle everything ourselves. But now, with all the pain, and with everything so complicated, I did need … well not need him, exactly … but things were going to be easier now.

Lightning Source UK Ltd.
Milton Keynes UK
UKHW010735310521
384667UK00001B/85

9 781925 786682